BEHIND
THE MASK

A.J. RIVERS

PROLOGUE

3 years ago...

SOMETHING WAS WRONG. CHARITY STRUGGLED TO OPEN HER EYES and close her mouth. Her eyes finally fluttered open to slits, but something prevented her mouth from closing all the way. She couldn't sit up. Her arms were numb from the shoulders to her fingers, and her legs were painfully numb from hips to toes. How long had she been lying there?

Lying on her side, she flexed her hands and fought to pull them in front of her. The floor was cold and hard and unforgiving. The room was dark. Too dark to make out anything. And her vision was playing hell with her. It was like trying to look through grease-smudged glass for some reason. Probably the same reason her head thumped like she had the world's worst hangover even though she hadn't been drinking.

She concentrated on listening for movement of any kind that would suggest someone else was in the room with her, but heard none, so she started tensing her muscles and relaxing them to force the blood flow.

What was the place? Why was it so dark? And what was that high, keen smell of something that had been rotten for a long time? So long that it almost didn't smell bad anymore. Almost sweet.

Working the numbness out of her fingers and forearms, Charity grasped the thing that was preventing her from pulling her hands in front of her and kept her from sitting up. It was a cold metal beam. Her hands had been zip-tied behind her back and then that tie had been zip-tied to the pole.

If her arms weren't around the pole, there was a chance she could get loose before whoever had done it returned. The only sounds were her own panicked breathing and the steady trickle of water running close by her right side on the floor. From the sound of it, the water was going into a drain or ditch of some kind only a couple of feet in front of her.

She twisted her hands in opposite directions and the zip-tie bit deep into the tender flesh. She bit the fabric gag in her mouth, hoping it wasn't as nasty as it smelled and felt, and then twisted her hands violently in the opposite direction. She had read once that you could break the little locking mechanism with enough friction and force like that. Had even seen a petite woman break free of a large zip-tie around her wrists after a man bound her wrists in front of her. It had been a class demonstration given by an ex-FBI agent when Charity had been a freshman in high school.

She wrested her hands in opposite directions again, biting harder than ever on the gag to keep from screaming as the tie cut into her skin and drew blood. She scooted away from the pole as far as she could and jerked her hands toward her butt. There was a hollow thudding ring as the zip-tie around the pole held tight, but nothing gave. She was still bound.

Why was plastic so strong when it needed to break and so weak when it needed to be strong? Like the time she was five and her father had bought her a purple plastic shopping cart complete with little plastic groceries and cash register. She had climbed into that plastic shopping cart just because she had been five and it had looked like it might be fun to do. The thing broke, and Charity ended up with three cuts, two broken fingers, and more than a few bruises. A plastic shopping cart had been broken by the slight weight of a five-year-old, yet the two scrawny, insignificant bands of plastic holding her bound as an adult were apparently strong enough to withstand anything. She made a mental note to buy the biggest pack she could find at the local hardware store and keep them in her car. Who knew when she would need to tie a door back on or use one in place of a motor mount?

Thoughts tumbled and scrambled together leaving her confused and frustrated and deeper in panic by the second. Straining to regain control of her thoughts, she pressed her memory for the last clear thing she could remember.

She had gone to Sherrell's house. They were playing Marilyn Manson's cover of "This is Halloween" on repeat as they put on their Halloween costumes.

Tears leaked from her eyes. Her stomach churned. Where was Sherrell? Where were Steve and Tiny, their unofficial dates?

She yanked against the stubborn ties again. More blood. More searing pain. A muffled scream made it to the back of her mouth where it met the thick, choking fabric.

Sherrell had taken hours to perfect her zombie-fairy makeup and outfit. Charity had been jealous that her best friend had looked so much better than she had. In light of her situation, that jealousy sent a pang of sorrow through her heart. There was nothing wrong with going to a haunted house as a cute devil, was there?

As she inhaled the odors of things long dead and listened to her own ragged breathing, tasted her own tears, and felt her own blood running from her wrists, she no longer thought there was a damn thing wrong with it. It wasn't trite. It wasn't cliché as Tiny had said. There had been nothing to feel bad about, although Steve had suggested that Charity looked a bit too sexy and that it might draw unwanted attention.

Why hadn't she listened?

Because I wanted to be the prettiest one in the group for once. Because I wanted the attention instead of taking a backseat to Sherrell again, she thought.

It was amazing how unflinching and brutally truthful she could be when faced with such horrific realities as being tied to a metal pole in a darkened and unfamiliar room awaiting God knew what from God knew whom.

Her heart thudded harder as she strained against the ties again. Her shoulders cramped, and she squeezed her eyes shut just as they had begun adjusting to the darkness.

A loud pop followed by an electrical buzz drew her undivided attention. She opened her eyes and held her breath. A light had turned on somewhere in the distance. Not close enough for her to see, but close enough in the pitch dark that the ambient glow washed away some of the black at one edge of her room.

It was enough for her to work with.

She rolled her head from side to side, taking in the concrete floor, the room-length, foot-wide drain covered with metal grating, the skeletal remains of an overhead hoist system with some of the hooks and chains still intact.

Her stomach tried to curl into a tiny ball and disappear through her back. Her skin shrank two sizes.

It was Helton's Meat Processing Plant. The old abattoir where her father had worked until she was ten.

The scream was long and unbidden. Her convulsive thrashing was induced by pure soul-searing horror. She had been tied on her side to a pole in the center of the killing floor of the old, abandoned slaughterhouse.

The property was huge. There were no houses close by. No businesses. And acres upon acres of pens and chutes and buildings and loading docks for big trucks.

Helton's had been purposefully situated a little over a quarter mile off the main road to be out of sight. It had been purposefully placed in the middle of all those acres for much the same reason. Trees had been planted all around the property as a sort of blind and sound-damping technique.

Charity had gone there only once, when she was nine, and that had been more than enough to mentally scar her for life. Her father had given her strict instructions to remain in the truck, but being a curious and headstrong child, she hadn't listened. She had sneaked in only minutes behind him, right past the workers, and right into the killing room.

Meat had never been part of her diet again, and the experience had served as nightmare fuel forever after.

Even as she thrashed on the floor, those nightmares came back. Was she dreaming? Was it yet another nightmare?

The burning pain in her wrists and the cramps in her shoulders said it was not. The warmth of the blood running from her cut wrists smelled metallic. Would those vivid details be present in a nightmare? She knew they would not be.

A sharp whine cut through the building, echoing from the high ceilings and reverberating off the concrete walls to pierce her ears.

The icy fingers of dread traced her spine and gripped the base of her skull, effectively silencing her scream and paralyzing her efforts to break the plastic ties. She knew that sound. Even if she had never heard it before—though she had briefly that day when she was nine—she thought she would have known what it was.

A carcass saw.

Lucifer's Lounge.

That was where she had been going with Sherrell, Steve, and Tiny. It was a haunted house attraction that had moved to the edge of town the year before, but Charity had not gone, thinking it would be lame. After word got around about how awesome it was with all its gore and jump-scares and animatronics, and how the employees mostly turned a blind eye to the teens who were hitting on the devil's lettuce and sneaking booze, she thought she would give it a whirl.

Lucifer's Lounge.

Ironic that where she had been hogtied and gagged felt as if it were a more accurate representation of Lucifer's lounge, or his playground, or Lucifer's anything.

The saw turned off and so did the distant light.

Heavy boots tromped toward her in that darkness. Slow, methodical steps of a heavy man who meant to terrify her with his approach.

He didn't fail in his mission.

Male laughter echoed and bounced. Low, menacing, *evil*.

Was it the devil himself? Had Lucifer come topside to carry her off for poking fun at all things evil?

Childish, but her mind kept circling back to that thought. Maybe not childish but just hopeful because, deep down, she knew that would somehow be better than whatever a real flesh and blood man would have in store for her.

She had been separated from her small group at the haunted house when one of her stiletto heels got caught in some mesh over a doorway where a jump scare was supposed to happen. Her group went on ahead while she stayed behind to detangle her shoe with the help of a super-cute vamp boy. By the time she had freed her shoe and was ready to move on, the workers had let in a couple of late stragglers, and Charity had finished the tour with them.

What had happened after that?

She couldn't remember ever making it to the end of the tour or meeting back up with Sherrell, Steve, and Tiny.

Her head pounded, threatening to turn her eyeballs to mush and implode her skull. Her stomach crawled into her throat as the boots moved ever closer, and the laughter rolled again like distant thunder growling over the mountains, threatening to rain down destruction.

One of the stragglers? Both of them? Employees of Lucifer's Lounge?

A very tall shadowy figure stepped into view. He was broad at the shoulders, lean at the hips, bulky in a muscular way. He was slightly darker than the darkness around and behind him.

A bright blast of concentrated light made her gasp. If her hands had been free, she would have covered her eyes. Instead, she urinated on herself.

The figure leaned closer with the headlamp blinding her.

"You wanted attention so badly," the man said, pushing his voice to the limits of its bass capacity.

She strained her eyes against the brilliant circle of light, trying to see under or around it to get a hint of who the man was, but it was useless. "Who are you?"

"Everything you ever feared." He laughed and turned off the headlamp as he reached for her.

Charity screamed. She tried to evict her soul from her body with that scream. It was the loudest she'd ever screamed.

CHAPTER ONE

Dinner Finally

THE WEATHER HELD OUT NICELY. MOLLY, SHELLY, AND THE JAMESES enjoyed dinner outside on the back deck overlooking the peaceful backyard at Elizabeth and Hank James's house. Ava hadn't smiled so much in… well, she couldn't remember when. It had been a long time. Too long. And more than once, she wondered if she was being too happy, too joyous, and making a nuisance of herself.

Shelly tittered nervously randomly throughout the long meal and at things she wouldn't have found amusing years ago. Was she forcing her own appearance of happiness? Did she still hold against them what had happened to her daughter?

Could Ava blame her if she did?

The thought dampened her high spirits more than a little. No, she couldn't blame Shelly if she still held the Jameses at least somewhat responsible for Molly's situation. She also couldn't blame her if she couldn't find it in her heart to forgive them. Especially Ava. She was the one who ran away and left Molly with those awful men. Left her to a fate worse than death.

"Anyone want more wine?" Elizabeth asked, smiling broadly and holding the nearly empty bottle of red aloft.

Shelly covered her glass and shook her head. "No more for me, thank you."

Molly nodded. "You don't have to twist my arm." She held out her glass. The index finger of her right hand stuck out straight, unable to bend at any of the joints. It was, like so many of her scars, a stark and permanent reminder of what she had endured while being held prisoner for so many years.

Ava grimaced inwardly and made an effort not to flinch as Molly's shoulder caught and she had to set the wine flute down to prevent dropping it.

"Almost a whoopsie," Molly said, laughing as she picked up the delicate glass with her left hand and drained half the deep crimson liquid.

Shelly seemed embarrassed as she put a gentle hand on Molly's arm and leaned in close. "Molly, honey, you might want to slow down on that. You know you're not supposed to—"

"I know, I know, I know," Molly said, putting the glass down again. "It's not like I'm chugging shots of Jaeger, Mom. It's just a little red wine. Last glass. I promise." She smiled.

It took part of the bite out of her sharp retort, but Ava didn't like where the scene was headed. Her friend was changed in fundamental ways, and Shelly, along with the rest of the people who knew and loved Molly before she was kidnapped, were left wondering how the hell to deal with the new version of the sweet girl she had once been. Was that same version still in there anywhere? Perhaps buried deep in some dark corner, cowering, and still frightened. Or had she been eradicated with the years of violence and drugs and constant abuse?

"The doctors said *any* alcohol, honey. It's because of the medicines. It's—"

Molly jerked her head toward her mother and held up a hand in obvious irritation. "Mom, please. I think I can handle a little wine mixed with painkillers." She barked dry laughter and shook her head. "Like, it's definitely not the worst thing I've done in the last six months." One eyebrow shot up and her lips pursed into a thin line.

Shelly swallowed hard, glanced around at the others uncomfortably, and nodded. "I know. I'm sorry, honey." She patted Molly's arm and nodded again before turning her attention back to her plate. "Ava, you have outdone yourself with this meal. It's delicious."

"Thanks. Mom helped, or I would never have gotten it finished in time," Ava said, glad to help steer the conversation in a different direction.

"I helped, too," Hank added. "Don't I get any credit?"

Elizabeth scoffed and tossed a napkin at him. "For carrying in a few bags of groceries? Get out."

Everyone laughed.

Ava laughed, too, but she laughed mostly to hide that she was more worried about Molly than ever. The longer her friend was back in the *normal* world, the more *abnormal* she seemed to act. Was it the slow detox from the drugs the traffickers pumped through her system all the time? Was it the sudden and shocking change of environment from violent chaos to calm safety and little movement? To be able to help, Ava needed to understand the psychology behind the behaviors.

"Hey," Molly said a little too loudly and with a too-wide, too-loopy grin as she pointed at Ava. "You still taking me to do PT at the park tomorrow?"

"You bet. If you're up for it and still want me to."

"I'm counting on it."

The next day, Ava went to Molly's house half-expecting that her friend would cry off with a hangover. Instead, she was sitting on the front porch smoking a cigarette when Ava pulled up.

"Molly?" Ava pointed to the cigarette smoke curling upward.

"What?" Molly looked up as if she had no clue what Ava was pointing at.

"You're smoking," Ava said incredulously.

Molly nodded. "I can see why you're moving up in the Bureau so quickly. You're observant, quick, and you make astute judgments based on solid evidence." She chuckled as she took a long drag.

"Ha ha. Since when do you smoke, Mol?"

Molly shrugged and flipped the smoldering butt toward the road. It landed in the deadfall of autumn leaves, and Ava hurried to crush it out with her foot.

Molly held to the railing and limped down the steps. "See? You were cut out for your career. Always trying to save the world." She gave a thumbs-up and headed for the car.

"What about your wheelchair?"

"Leave it. I don't like it." She got in the car and shut the door.

Ava sighed and went to the front door of the house. She knocked before opening it slightly. "Ms. Peterson? It's Ava James. I just need Molly's wheelchair."

"It's in the front room," Shelly called from deeper within the house. "Good luck getting her to use the damn thing, though." She appeared in the hallway. "She's stubborn, and she hates that thing. Can't say I blame her, but it's hard to get her around without it some days. Maybe you'll have better luck."

Ava took the folded chair to the door. "I'll do my best. Have her home in a couple of hours."

Shelly nodded and turned away as Ava closed the door again.

With the chair loaded into the back, Ava got into the driver's seat and smiled at Molly. "All set?"

"I think I am, actually." Molly looked back at the house. "I've only been out to come to the dinner at your parents' place and go to doctor appointments a couple of times."

"We'll see what we can do about changing that."

Molly sat silent for several minutes as she flipped her cigarette pack over repeatedly against her left thigh. "What if I don't really want to change that?"

"Why wouldn't you? We used to love going to the park and just wandering around for hours."

"Yeah, when we were like fourteen and didn't have anything better to do." She kept her head turned so that she looked out her window and away from Ava.

"Next time, I'll take you to Fairhaven and we can do PT at my place and then order some Chinese food and watch black-and-white movies. Make a whole day of it. Sleepover, maybe."

Molly's face brightened, but it was short-lived. She shook her head. "No. You need to be ready to leave for your job at any time. I get that. No sleepovers. Besides, we're not teenagers. We're too old for slumber parties, don't you think?"

"If you say so. It was just a suggestion. I thought you might want to be out of the house for a while, you know? Just a change of scenery."

They arrived at the park, and Ava took the chair from the back. "Want to ride over to where we're going so you'll be fresh for the sesh?"

Molly snorted laughter and held up a hand. "God, don't ever do that again. You just sounded like the world's most almond mom ever. And, no, I most certainly do not want to ride. I'll walk using my own two damn legs, thank you very much. It'll be good exercise."

"Alrighty, then. As you wish. And maybe I am an almond mom." Ava held her head high, flipping her hair over one shoulder.

"Right. Not likely."

"Well, you're a dyed-in-the-wool smoker, so why can't I be an almond mom?"

"I have a damn good reason for my bad habit, and you're a childless twenty-six-year-old married to your job, so it doesn't work."

Ava gasped. "I am not married to my job!"

Molly leveled her with a look. "Call it friends with benefits, then." She was already puffing for breath as her hitching gait grew more erratic only a couple hundred feet from the car.

Ava kept her pace pushing the wheelchair beside Molly. "You need a lift yet?"

"Don't make me punch you."

"Better not try. From the sound of it, the exertion might just put you on the ground." Ava grinned but was only partially joking.

"Okay, fine. You win." Molly grabbed the handle of the wheelchair with her left hand and glared at Ava before making her way to sit in it. "Push until your little black heart is content."

"God, you're so salty over this thing. I don't understand. It's just to help you, Mol." Ava pushed slowly and steadily.

"You wouldn't understand, and I don't want to explain. Just get us there so I can get out of it, please."

Ava hadn't thought about the possibility that a wheelchair might have played a part in something the traffickers had done to her. Even knowing the injuries they had caused her, Ava had never even thought that they might have transported her in a wheelchair, and that could have been Molly's hang-up about the contraption.

As she pushed, her mind went down a twisted path with the wheelchair and the traffickers. Why had she not thought about all the things that could have been done to Molly in a wheelchair? Why had her anger and diversion not prompted more serious consideration on Ava's part? She walked faster with those thoughts and images running through her mind.

"We're here," Ava announced as they reached the wide flat area overlooking the pond and the field where people were free to have picnics, play frisbee, stroll at their leisure, or just recline on the grass to pass the time.

"Thank God." Molly pushed out of the chair before Ava could set the brake.

"Whoa," she exclaimed as the chair moved back violently and she put a foot under a wheel to stop it. "A little warning goes a long way there, Molly."

"Just testing those FBI reflexes. Gotta make sure you stay sharp." She turned and made finger guns to point at Ava. "Pow-pow."

Was she just making jokes to ease her own nerves? Was she being a little snarky because Ava got to go on with her life and become an agent while she was being trafficked around the world?

Ava's guts tightened and pulled toward her spine. She thought she knew the answer, but she didn't know how to address the situation, or even if she should. Not yet, anyway.

Molly sat on a low concrete wall that separated a small memorial garden from the rest of the park. "Let's get this show on the road, shall we?" She smiled and seemed genuine. "I thought sitting up here might make this part easier on your back."

Ava smiled. "Thanks. It will." She pulled off Molly's shoes, and her gaze was immediately drawn to the right ankle. Even through the compression sock, it was swollen to twice its natural size and looked *lumpy*. She pulled the left sock off first and then peeled the one off the right foot. The crosshatch design of the sock was embedded in the inflamed tissue.

Ava put a hand over the ankle and looked at Molly with all the pain in her heart surely showing in her eyes. She couldn't help it. She wanted to cry just seeing how badly that ankle was deformed.

"What? I washed my feet this morning." Molly laughed and looked out toward the pond. "If something stinks, it's the duck shit down the hill." Her voice had gone flat and her eyes vacant.

"Nothing stinks, Mol. I'm ready to start the massaging." She gripped Molly's right foot lightly. "Does it hurt you when it's massaged?"

"No."

Ava began the massaging process the way the nurse had shown her and Molly tensed. It wasn't much, but enough to notice. "Are you sure?"

"I'm sure."

Ava continued with her stomach riding high in her chest. When she had jumped at the opportunity to help Molly with her PT, she had not known how difficult it would be. No one had suggested to her that it would bother her mentally, or emotionally, and for some reason, she had not thought about it from that angle.

Just like with the wheelchair, she chided herself silently as she finished massaging the left ankle.

She helped Molly get her socks and shoes back on. "Ready for some of the exercises, or you need a break for a few minutes? We have plenty of time, but the nurse said not to give the muscles time to tighten back up between massaging and exercising. Your call."

"Can we start with the ones I do sitting down?" She pointed to the bench. "I'll sit there."

"Of course." Ava didn't force help on Molly, but she did stand by her with an arm outstretched just in case.

They did five sets of three on the exercises and were getting ready to start the walking when Ava's phone trilled.

"Is that your work?" Molly asked when Ava ignored the sound.

"It's a text."

"Aren't you going to check it?"

"Work will call me if they need me. Come on, let's get to the walking before your muscles start tightening up again."

"It might be Mom. Or your mom."

Ava took out her phone and opened the message. She read it a second time and then a third. "Nope. Not work. Not either of our moms, so we're not in trouble for anything." She grinned, stuffed the phone back into her pocket, and resumed stretching for the walk. "Now, come on," she urged Molly.

"Well, who was it?" Molly stretched a little. "If it was important, we can finish early so you can go."

Molly had just seemed to fall into a better mood. Ava didn't want to ruin it by telling her what was in the text, but she also didn't want Molly to think she was hiding something from her and risk putting her back into a foul mood.

"It was just an old friend. Nothing really. We can finish up. No rush."

"Ooh, an old friend? As in some guy? Hey, don't you dare let your cripple friend hold you up from some hot date. I will not be responsible for that." Molly sat on the bench and crossed her arms.

"Molly," Ava urged. "Come on. Let's go."

"Not until you tell me who he is. If he's an old enough friend, I might remember him. If I remember him, I might have an opinion about him." She leaned forward. "Or I might know some gossip on him."

They both laughed. Molly's gossip was at least eight years old.

"Seriously, tell me. Please? I'm not trying to be a pest, but I don't have any connections with anyone but Mom. If that's not pathetic, I don't know what is. I'm jonesing for some real interactions, even if they are just by proxy." She pointed at Ava and winked. "And you're my proxy, I guess."

"You remember Jamie Vos from high school? A little older than us? She's Jamie Hall now."

Molly nodded. "Brown hair, kind of plain jane in every way possible, and never drew attention to herself much. We were all sorta friends. I guess that's what you'd call it, anyway."

"Plain jane? A little harsh, isn't it? She was pretty, and she was super nice all through high school."

Molly laughed good-naturedly. "Pretty in a homely sort of way, and too nice, in my opinion. Hey, I liked her just fine, though. I'm not being mean. So, what did she want? I didn't know you two kept in touch over the years."

And she wasn't being mean. But she wasn't being the old Molly, either. Her ordeal had taken all her smooth edges and made them rough, like broken glass, and sometimes they cut by accident.

Ava shrugged. "Just checking in. We didn't keep in close touch. It's random mostly." She motioned for Molly to get up.

"Nope. I know that look and that body language. Some things the FBI just can't Bureau out of you, that's for sure. What did she want? And don't tell me it wasn't important because I can see that it was."

"It wasn't. She just texted to tell me that she thinks there's something hinky going on in her town." Ava flapped her hand in the air as if it was nothing.

"Something hinky, or something kinky?"

"Hinky," Ava said louder, remembering that Molly's hearing had been seriously diminished during her time with the traffickers. Guilt washed over her anew. So many things wrong with Molly that were permanent. So many things would never get better.

And Ava had left her there in Prague.

"Like murders? That had to be why she was texting you. Why else, right?"

Ava sighed and pressed her fingers to the center of her forehead. "Yeah, she thinks there's a serial killer loose in Woodsboro, Vermont, and that he only strikes on Halloween. I don't know where or how she got the idea, but it's so unlikely that I can't even consider it, okay?"

"No, it's not okay, Ava. You need to answer Jamie and go help her if you can. Get permission from Sally—"

"Sal," Ava corrected.

"Sal, if you need to, and go help. Halloween is just around the corner. What if Jamie is right? She wasn't some kook in school that made up stories for attention, or anything. Why would she do it now? She had to have a reason to say it, and an even better reason to tell you in your capacity as a federal agent, don't you think?"

"I don't know. There have been no bodies found, and she said it's happened over the last *three* years. Only on Halloween women go missing. *Missing.* How can it be a serial killer if there are no bodies?" Ava countered.

Molly shook her head and looked disappointed. Her eyes lost the light that had been in them. "Do you really want it on your conscience if she's right? What if, Ava?"

Ava looked over the pond and the field. Why couldn't life be as simple as that view every now and then? Nature doing its thing. Not questioning, not causing trouble, just doing what it was meant to do. Ducks quacking and paddling and waddling. Fish swimming and feeding. Birds singing and flying. So simple.

"But there are no bodies. The women are *just missing*. I don't see a serial killer in that scenario."

"Just because you can't see them, does it mean that germs and bacteria don't exist either?" She turned to face Ava. "Don't be willfully stupid. You know bodies can be hidden just as well as I do."

"But it's highly unlikely."

"When you start every sentence with *but*, I think it's time to start evaluating why, don't you?"

After dropping Molly back at her house, Ava drove back to Fairhaven and paced her living room with her cellphone in hand. Jamie's message took up the small screen, and Ava read over it several times.

Ava had doubts. Was it worth the trouble of the investigation? Three years. Six women. Missing—no proof of murder at all.

Bodies could be hidden. Ava had witnessed that several times on cases in the very recent past. Most killers, in fact, hid the bodies of their victims. Hiding was done for different reasons, and the degree of skill with which they were hidden depended on a lot of different factors, but most killers hid their victims. Serial killers were a mixed bag, though. Some would hide the bodies while others would display them for public consumption.

"That doesn't change the fact that Molly was right. Bodies can be hidden, and just because they aren't readily visible doesn't mean they aren't there," she muttered as she paced.

What if there was a serial killer with a Halloween fetish on the loose in rural Vermont?

CHAPTER TWO

What's going on in Woodsboro, Vermont?

AVA LET HER THUMB HOVER OVER THE DIAL BUTTON FOR SEVERAL seconds. Did she really want to make a voice call to Jamie for the first time in forever to talk about a possible serial killer? One that probably did not exist except in Jamie's overheated mind?

"Or in my suspicious one," she scoffed aloud, shaking her head.

She darkened the phone's screen and shoved the device into her back pocket. A strong cup of coffee sounded like a great way to get her head clear on the matter. So what if Jamie was right? Then there was a case to pursue for sure. But...

"What if she went batshit bonkers up there in lickspit rural Vermont, and she's seeing serial killers on every corner and ghosts in every shadow?" She thunked the carafe under the faucet and filled it to the halfway mark, thought about it, and finished filling it. It was a full pot kind of evening.

Jamie would not be the first person to move out into the sticks and lose her marbles after several years of being so far removed from society, and she surely wouldn't be the last. Isolation had a way of wreaking havoc on a person's senses and their perspectives; sometimes, it made them a little… *odd.*

But exactly how isolated was Jamie in Woodsboro?

Pulling up a topo map of Vermont on the laptop, Ava had a look around Woodsboro. Lots of forested areas. Lots of mid-size mountains. Lots of valleys where small pockets of houses formed tiny communities that seemed to range from five to ten houses. Dirt roads. Gravel roads. Old logging roads.

"Pretty dang isolated," she confirmed, pushing away from the table and the computer more undecided than before.

Woodsboro was expansive, but the residents were scattershot across that vast amount of land and probably had little contact with each other on a daily basis unless they lived in, or close to, town. And the town of Woodsboro was nothing impressive even from the street view on the map.

Ava paced as the coffeemaker gurgled the last drops of black gold into the carafe. Call Jamie, or no?

"If there is a chance she's right…"

Sighing, she poured coffee into the largest insulated cup she owned and went back to the laptop. It was hard to believe a killer was targeting women in such a rural place, but it wasn't impossible that it was true. No matter how hard she tried, she couldn't get that *what if* to go away.

Molly was right, and that was that.

She dialed Jamie's number and waited.

"Hello? Aviva? Is it you?" Jamie asked in a single breath.

"Hi, Jamie. Yes, it's Ava."

"You called because you believe me, right? About the missing girls and the serial killer. I know I'm right. I can feel it. Nothing else makes sense. Will you help us?"

"Jamie, I called to get more information. That's the first step here. I need enough information to decide whether there's even a case to pursue. Can you do that?" There was no need to worry about the conversation being awkward. Jamie was apparently ready to jump right to business no matter how long it had been since they had spoken over the phone.

"I can do whatever you need if it'll get us the help we need on this. You ask the questions, and I'll answer. I'll give all the details I have."

"Great." Ava pulled up a blank document in the Word program, put the phone on speaker, and laid it beside her cup of coffee. "I put you on speaker so I can take notes. Is that okay?"

"Are you at home, in the office? Where am I on speaker?" Jamie sounded suddenly uncomfortable.

"I'm at home alone. No one else can hear you."

"Speaker is fine as long as you aren't working with Sheriff Mills in some twisted plan to make me sound crazy and get me sent to the nut house." Her dry laugh held no humor.

"Absolutely not. Is that something we should address before we get into this, though?"

"No. Later. After you have the same information that I have so you can verify what I'm giving you. That way she can't make you think I'm crazy or acting irrational like I know she will try to do."

"Got it." Ava made a note at the top of the page about the matter and highlighted it. Was it something to consider? Was that a filter through which she would need to look at the evidence presented during the conversation? It wasn't like she hadn't thought of it herself. That very thought had almost caused her to put off calling Jamie altogether.

"If you think, at any point, I'm being irrational, please bring it to my attention without hesitation," Jamie said.

"I'll do just that, Jamie. But let's not get stuck on that right now, okay? I need you to tell me a little about Woodsboro. How big is it? What's the population? What do most of the residents do for a living? How far away are your neighbors in the rural areas? How close-knitted are the townies to the ones living out in the country? You know the drill, same as we used to talk about in high school. Give me the low-down on Woodsboro and its residents."

"Well, it's pretty large if you're only looking at the space it takes up on the map, almost a hundred square miles of mostly farmland and woods, but if you're looking at the population, it's not big at all. We're only thir-ty-five-hundred people. And that might be less by a few hundred since the last census. It's not exactly a boom town or anything.

"Lots of farmland is abandoned now, so there's even more desolate and empty places to hide if someone, like a serial killer, wanted to do so. We have the sheriff and her eight deputies, but that's not nearly enough people to search the area the way it needs to be searched, in my opin-ion. Most of the residents are farmers, or do something similar for a liv-ing. It's a quiet place to live, and by quiet, I mean *really* quiet. The only excitement around here is when the Women's Historical Society puts on a potluck dinner or the kids have a play at the school. That's how small the place is, Ava. We get excited to go see holiday plays at the school. So, you can kind of see how excited everyone gets about holidays. Especially the kids. Any holiday gets them over-the-moon excited. And all the fall festivals bring out townies and farmers alike. I think we're all ready to just mingle and have some company by the end of harvest season, to be honest. There aren't any real rivalries between the farming kids and the town kids because there's not that much difference between how they're raised."

Ava typed as fast as she could to keep up with the gush of information Jamie gave her. Jamie sounded completely logical and clear-minded. She gave the information as a resident who loved her town and had lived there a long enough time to know what she was talking about. Nothing irrational about it.

"That's great. Good information. Can you tell me how easy it is to get to the nearest interstate from Woodsboro?"

Jamie laughed. "Oh, dear. We're not close to an off-ramp or an on-ramp, if that's what you're asking. Honey, we are so far out in the sticks up here that we don't even have a Walmart or a Wendy's. We drive two hours south to get to either one of those. We are nowhere near being easily accessed by the highway."

"The nearest Walmart is two hours away?"

"I know, right? Sounds crazy, but it's true."

If there wasn't a Wendy's, Metford would grieve the entire time he had to spend there. Ava grinned at the thought. "Okay, now tell me all you can about the missing girls. Just the things you know are facts at this point. Not rumors or opinions. Just straight facts. I know it sounds cold, but I need to make lists that I can use."

"They're victims, but yes, I understand what you mean. Just so you know, I know some of them more personally than others. Or, rather, I *knew* some of them better than others, so there might be some personal insights sprinkled in that can't be helped."

"Okay. Tell me about the girls, then."

"Charity Beaumont was the first girl to go missing. That was three years ago on Halloween night. She was seventeen when she disappeared. Just to be honest, it was a tragedy, and everyone was upset that she had gone missing, but no one thought she had been murdered. You know, that sort of thing just doesn't happen here. Charity was a senior at Woodsboro High. She had strawberry blonde hair and light green eyes. She was slight. Maybe a hundred-ten, a hundred-twenty pounds, tops. And she was shorter than me, so I would say around five-five."

"And she disappeared before, during, or after the haunted house on Halloween night?"

"She went in with a group, but she never made it out the other side, and no one has seen her or heard from her since that night. Everyone in that group, all her friends and family, the workers at the haunt, and the owner of the land have all been questioned. Nothing for the last three years. Not a single trace."

"So… she disappeared during the tour of the haunted house while she was in the presence of other people doing the same thing, and nobody noticed?"

"Yes. The group of friends she'd come with said she fell behind a bit, but she told them she'd catch up with them. And that was corroborated by the other strangers she went through the rest of the house with. None of them recalled hearing her yell for help, call out in any way, or saw her in any sort of distress. I mean, it was a haunted house and all, but it didn't seem like anything actually real."

"And there's never been a body found that was suspected as hers?"

"Nothing. It was like she evaporated into thin air right out of the maze. We had a few people speculate that aliens beamed her up, and yet I'm the one being called a fanatic right now. That was three years ago. Two years ago—again, on Halloween—two girls went missing. Ashley Garland, age sixteen, light brown hair and light brown eyes. She was about five-seven from what I've read and what I've heard, and she weighed about the same as Charity. Ashley, however, wasn't with an anonymous group of people, she was with a friend, Laura Halvorsen, who had just turned eighteen the week before. They were at the tiny little movie theater we have here in town. Laura was five-four, weighed one-ten, light hair, blue eyes, but she was the epitome of a wild child. She worked at Sandy's Grab-N-Go here in town. She was always in some sort of trouble, and she never bothered to graduate high school. Of all the girls who have gone missing, she was the only one who was really troubled, I believe."

"Did you know Laura or Ashley?"

"Not really. I mean, I knew who Laura was, but then again, almost anyone in Woodsboro knew who she was. Like I said, she was always landing in trouble of some sort. Fighting, underage drinking, petty theft, breaking and entering. She was just…*troubled*. And she worked at Sandy's, so most everyone would have encountered her at least a few times a month, I would think. Sandy's is the cheapest convenience store around, and everyone on my end of the county frequents the place to keep from going on into town when we just need a loaf of bread or a soda."

Jamie was giving details about the girls as if she were reading them from a victim profile board. Did she have one of those? Was she that far into the serial killer idea?

"Anything else you want to tell me about?"

"Oh, my God, yes. There are still three more victims, Ava. The ones from just last year," she said with an incredulous tone.

"Oh, right," Ava said, slightly shocked that she had already filled several pages with details. It was unusual to get so many details about cases.

"I personally knew two of these girls. I'll start with them. Luna Bradford, nineteen. Blonde with the softest blue eyes you ever saw. Same height as me—five-seven. She was... how do I put this? She was... *different*. Maybe that's why I liked her so much. Her and her friend. Luna was a pagan, and she wasn't quiet about it."

"You mean she talked about it a lot to people?"

"No. Well, yes and no. She didn't go door to door trying to push it down people's throats like some people do with their religions or with trying to win political votes. She didn't even look at Paganism as if it were a religion, just a way of life, really. But if the conversation came around to it, she was passionate about her lifestyle and the positive changes Paganism had made in her life. Do you understand what I mean?"

"I think I have the gist of it."

"She used to come over regularly and buy vegetables and honey from me because they were organic. I laughed when she told me that because all the vegetables and honey around here are *organic*. She leaned in real close and grinned and told me that mine tasted the best, though. So, we saw quite a lot of each other for over a year. Luna was a sweet girl, and that I know of, she never hurt a person."

"What about her friend?"

"Tina Leeyung. She was twenty when she disappeared, but she looked way younger. I thought she was only about fifteen when I met her. She was tiny. Five-three, and a hundred pounds soaking wet. She kept her hair dyed to a light sandy brown color, but I think it was originally black or very dark brown because her roots showed sometimes. Her eyes were very light brown or amber color. I don't know if they were contacts or not, though. Sometimes, they looked darker than at other times, so I'm not sure. She was newly identifying as pagan. She and Luna had met online, and again at an in-person venue here in town at a pagan festival."

"Woodsboro has enough pagans to hold festivals in a venue?"

"Not really. Including Luna, there were a grand total of maybe five pagan residents. Tina moved here from New Hampshire only the year before she disappeared. The festivals are something planned online and the meetup places are designated each time. Sometimes that venue is the one in town, and sometimes in another town. I just know there are quite a few meetings here every year. Luna was always excited to tell me about them."

"Where did Luna and Tina disappear from and when?"

"They had arranged one of the little get-togethers and saw to the venue rental for Halloween evening. They were responsible for cleaning up and locking the venue afterward, so they stayed until everyone left, and the sheriff thinks it was probably after all the Halloween festivities were done in town that the girls disappeared. So it was at the venue hall sometime between eleven and midnight, but no one knows for sure. The attendees left at ten, and no one saw Luna or Tina again after that. No messages, calls, nothing. Just like with the others. They're just gone."

"What about the other girl?"

"The other girl?"

"You said there were three last year."

"Oh, yes, there were. Elise Abbot. She wasn't with them, though. She was in a totally different place. She was twenty with light brown hair and gray-blue eyes. She was a striking-looking young woman, and she had a strong personality. I didn't know her personally, but I had seen her around, and of course, I know the Abbot family. Who doesn't? Elise had been at a Halloween party with her boyfriend. They argued and she walked away mad. And alone. She told him she was going home and took off down the dirt and gravel road. She was only a ten-minute walk from her house. Maybe fifteen in the dark like that, but it was close."

"Did she fit the same description as the others?"

"Yes, she did. Five-five, one-twenty, light brown hair that some said was dark blonde with hazel eyes. All the girls were slim, young, fair-haired, had light eyes, and they were all knockouts when it came to looks. Not a homely one among the bunch. And they're so young, Ava. You have to agree that this would be the perfect playground for a serial killer, right? Especially one that only strikes once or twice a year. Halloween would offer the perfect cover with all the disguises and parties and such."

"I can't jump to those sorts of conclusions, Jamie. There's not been a single body found yet. Nothing that points to any of these girls being deceased at all. Murder wouldn't be the only reason for them being missing, you know. Some could be runaways. It's unpleasant to think about, but there's always human trafficking to consider. Or, some sick bastard could be keeping some of them locked up for his own twisted pleasure somewhere out in the willy-wags. It's been done before. There could even be a cult doing what we call hard-recruiting of women in the area.

At first, they kidnap the women. Eventually, they brainwash them. After that, the women agree to stay of their own free will. They actually see it as being in their best interest and can't understand why they fought against it in the beginning. There's a lot to consider besides a serial killer."

Jamie sighed. "I know you practically have to tell me that, but I'm still keeping my Bailey home this year. I'm not even allowing her to go trick-or-treating. His youngest victim was only sixteen, but I don't know that the killer wouldn't grab an eight-year-old who fit the profile if the opportunity presented itself. My little girl is pretty as a porcelain doll, she's small, has dark blonde hair, fair complexion, and hazel eyes that run on the lighter side. In a few years, she's going to fit that profile to a T, and I'm terrified he won't be caught unless the FBI gets involved—and the sheriff isn't keen on calling them for help. That's why I called you."

"How come you're so sure it's a serial killer, Jamie? No bodies equal no murders. If there are no murders, there are no killers, right?"

"Because none of them ever came back. Their families never heard from them again, and two of them would never have done that to their mothers. Never. Even that stupid Sheriff Mills knows that. At the last town meeting, I questioned the good sheriff about the status of the serial killer, and she blew a gasket. She ranted that there is no serial killer in her town and that I was just trying to cause trouble. She said there was no need to cause panic among the residents of such a quiet and peaceful town when the girls were simply missing and nothing more, and that all I was doing was scratching at wounds that weren't even healed yet to cause trouble and heartache for those families. She stands by the assumption that those girls left of their own free will to start fresh lives somewhere else, somewhere more exciting. She almost tossed me out after threatening me with a citation and a night in jail for disruption of a public meeting."

Was there something to Jamie's worries? She seemed completely level-headed and logical. She didn't go off on tangents about aliens and Bigfoot or ghosts in her closets or demons like some others in the past. She didn't seem delusional or violent, and she seemed reasonable. Except that she wouldn't let go of her idea about the girls being victims of a serial killer. It was something to consider.

Ava rubbed her temples. "Jamie, I promise I'll do what I can to help. Now, that's not a promise of anything. But there can't be any harm in looking into this for you. That I can promise. Maybe I can at least give you some peace of mind about it. I'll need to talk to my boss first, though."

"Thank you so much, Ava. That would be great. I owe you big time."

"I'll keep you updated as soon as I know something."

Ava read over the pages of information. Much of it stuck, but much of it rolled away as soon as her eyes were off the computer screen again. It was too much all at once.

Six girls. Three years.

"Three Halloween nights," she said, correcting herself.

CHAPTER THREE

The Death-Dealing Drug Smuggler

S AL WAS IN HER OFFICE EARLY. SHE HAD BEEN IN THERE EARLIER than usual for the last week because of a heavy caseload, and especially the current case. The attempted assassination attempt on Supreme Court Justice Stan Crother the previous week had caused a veritable shitstorm for everyone in the office since it had been in direct relation to one of their cases.

Ava knocked on the open door.

Sal glanced over the top of her glasses. "You don't have Evelyn Goldfield in cuffs, and you're not dragging her hogtied behind you, so I'm assuming this isn't about her?"

Ava shook her head and took a seat. "Not really."

"Not what I want to hear right now, but…" She sighed and dropped her glasses on the desk. "Did you at least bring coffee? Preferably super-charged."

Ava grimaced. "I did not. Truthfully, I didn't know if you'd be here this early. I did put some on to brew, though. Should be done in a few minutes if that's any consolation."

"An espresso IV drip would be great right about now, but I'll settle for the crap coffee in the breakroom, I guess." She grinned. "What's on your mind, Ava?"

"A possible case."

Sal blinked several times, the grin frozen on her face as if she couldn't believe what she was hearing, or perhaps she had heard wrong. "A case, or *the* case? Because we have plenty of cases." She let her hand thump onto the stack of files on her desk. "Plenty. But I need your focus on *the* case. You know, the one where we're supposed to be funneling all our efforts into finding Evelyn Goldfield so we can finish tying up this Ted Sanchez thing."

"I know, Sal. I know. Hey, at least she took out the hitman who tried to kill Crothers, right?" Ava smiled broadly in an attempt to be humorous.

Sal's left eyebrow shot upward and her grin evaporated. She shook her head. "Uh-uh. Don't do that. Don't even joke like that. Not in here. Not anywhere. We need her a week ago. We need her an hour before she pulled the damn trigger. That hitman should have gone to prison for what he tried to do; he should have served his sentence. Better yet, Mr. Ted Sanchez should have been so locked away that he never had a chance to contact the hitman, and then there would never have been an attempt on Crothers, and we wouldn't be in this political shitstorm right now."

"You're right. Sorry. I was just trying to lighten the mood."

Sal sighed again. "I know you were, but not right now, okay?"

Ava nodded.

"Okay, what is it about another case? Did you find something on one of the other cases I should know about?" She put on her glasses again and pulled the stack of files close.

Ava cleared her throat and sat forward. "Not one of those. It's another case. Maybe another case."

Sal stopped and looked over the rim of the glasses at her again in irritation.

"In Vermont," Ava added with a sheepish grin. "Woodsboro, to be exact."

Sal removed the glasses slowly and deliberately, placing them on top of the folders. "Woodsboro, Vermont?"

"Yes."

"What the hell is in Woodsboro, Vermont?" Her voice was too calm, too pleasant. Like it might be the precursor to an outburst Ava wanted nothing to do with.

"Well, from what I'm gathering, it could possibly be a serial killer."

Sal cocked the eyebrow again and laced her fingers tightly.

"Maybe a serial killer. But maybe not. I think it warrants looking into."

Sal considered it silently for a moment. "Enlighten me, please before I change my mind about listening, which I am very close to doing."

Ava rattled off the details as quickly as she could manage, emphasizing the most important ones like the similarities between victims, how all of them went missing on Halloween night each year, and how it was one girl the first year, two the second year, and three last year.

"What if it's four girls this year?" Ava asked.

"What about the bodies? Where are the autopsy reports? Have you looked at them yet? Is the method of killing the same or at least similar enough to warrant thinking this might be the same killer?"

Ava bit her lower lip and shifted her gaze to the floor. "I haven't seen the autopsy reports."

Sal was quiet for a moment and then leaned forward, resting her forearms on the desk. "Why?"

"Because there are none."

"There are no autopsy reports?"

"There are no bodies," Ava clarified stiffly, already dreading the skeptical look on Sal's face. It was probably the end of the discussion about the case unless she could come up with a viable reason to pursue it further. She launched into her deep discussion with Jamie, and the many reasons why she thought Jamie was not crazy or just seeking attention. When she had finished, she couldn't tell what Sal thought, and decided to sit quietly until her boss either tossed her out of the office or gave her the nod of approval.

In the end, she got neither result.

"Well, I will tell you that I think there might be something there to look into. Not because I want another case on the list, that's for sure. And certainly not because we need another one right now, but because I trust your judgment for one, and for two, I know some serial killers are cyclic in nature. Some only kill around certain dates like the full moon, the new moon, anniversaries that are important to them, and unfortunately, holidays, things like that. Some killers hide their victims while others don't bother, and yet others will display them for any and all to see. Six girls in three years isn't much to go on, and since there are no bodies to prove they're even dead, we don't have enough to step in on our own."

"But in a town that only has thirty-five-hundred people, six girls in three years seems like a lot, don't you think?"

"I do. In a place that small, everybody knows each other, or at least each other's families. They'd all have to be passing acquaintances, I would think. Like I said, there seems to be something going on there, but unless the sheriff asks us for help…" she shrugged and raised her hands. "There's simply nothing I can do, Ava. I'm sorry. Has he asked for help?"

Ava shook her head again. "*She*. And, no, she hasn't asked for help."

"Then I can't do anything. Maybe nothing will happen this year. Maybe it will turn out that those girls really were just runaways, and their families will find them living out in LA or up in New York. It happens all the time. You can't save them all, Ava. As harsh as that sounds, as bad as that sucks, you know it's the truth we have to live with."

But it wasn't the truth Ava wanted to hear. She had made a promise to Jamie, and she prided herself in keeping promises. She didn't make them lightly. And she hated to think that girls were being murdered or kidnapped, and no one was doing anything about it. So what if she went to investigate a serial killer and it turned out that those girls had been kidnapped and they were still alive? That would be even better. She could return them to their families damaged but still alive. She would count that as a win. A big win. But if she didn't get to investigate at all, those families might never know what happened to their daughters, and the daughters would never have justice. If they were alive, they might be suffering the same fate as Molly had suffered for the better part of a decade. No one should have to face that kind of torture.

"What if the sheriff had a change of heart and requested that I work the case? Would that make a difference? I mean, a real difference."

"Of course it would. That would work. But it needs to be an official request. She can't just call you up at home and say she'd like for you to come up to Vermont and spend the weekend at her place so you two can rumble through the files and see if there's a case there to pursue. It needs to be official and all above-board legit. That will give me something to work with, and I could get approval. Probably." She put her glasses on again and held up a hand. "But you can't take time away from the case we're working right now to chase that request from the sheriff, either. I need you on this too badly. I need your total attention on this Evelyn Goldfield and Ted Sanchez case. If I so much as suspect otherwise, you are in serious trouble. Got it?"

"I understand. I'm on this one hundred percent. I want this one closed just as much as you do. I'm tired of the political slap upside the head we get every time we walk through the office, too. None of us had a clue Goldfield would have the guts to even attempt killing Max because he turned on her longtime boyfriend."

"But we should have thought of that. We should have been watching for her. We should have had eyes on her. Lesson learned. Sanchez smuggled drugs long enough and made enough money that he and Evelyn were living in the lap of luxury. Maybe she couldn't stand the thought of being without her cash cow when he went to prison."

"And maybe she really loved him, after all. Who knows?"

Sal chuckled. "You always try to see the brighter side of things. Even people like Evelyn Goldfield. I bet her shriveled, greedy little heart is black as a lump of coal."

Ava smiled and stood. "And you know what coal turns into after being under pressure for a long time, don't you?" She went to the door with Sal's laughter following her. "Want me to bring you that coffee?"

"That would be a wonderful way to redeem this morning, if I do say so myself. And trust me, that woman's heart would never turn into a diamond. There's no bit of light in her, and I want my coffee as black as her and her husband's twisted hearts. Thanks." She scoffed and then chuckled again.

Ava knew people like Ted Sanchez and Evelyn Goldfield were mostly bad, but she didn't like to believe that they were beyond all hope. Logic told her they might be, but to keep her sanity, she had to believe that even the curs of society like those two harbored some kind of goodness inside, some sparkle of light within the cavernous blackness of their souls. If there was no good at all left in them, what good was the justice meted out to them? What good was any punishment? If they were completely evil and unredeemable, why waste the taxpayers' money to house them in concrete and steel cages for decades and to pay for their medical care and such? Punishments only worked if there was some shred of humanity left in the person being punished.

Otherwise, they were like rabid animals that didn't know anything but madness, distortion, agony, and violence as they blindly lashed out. In that case, there was only one suitable way to deal with them.

Ava shook her head to clear the thoughts before they could go any further.

That was the mental route she didn't want to go down. Not ever again. She had traveled that dark path before a few times after the Prague incident, and while searching for her mother. It wasn't pleasant by any stretch of the imagination, and it wouldn't take long for such an internal path to lead straight to the madhouse.

She took Sal her coffee with a smile on her face, hope in her heart, and the belief that Evelyn Goldfield did have a diamond fleck of humanity in her heart. It might have been buried under all the vile acts and the greed, but it was there.

She reserved her right to feel otherwise about people for those who truly deserved it—and if there was a serial killer in Vermont preying on young, innocent women… well, he would deserve it.

CHAPTER FOUR

There's No Stinking Serial Killer!

THE WOODSBORO WEEKLY HAD RUN STORIES ABOUT THE MISSING girls over the years, but had never run an article that even hinted that something sinister might have happened to any of them. Newspapers in neighboring towns had mentioned the girls when they had first gone missing, and all had reported each one as likely runaways, sprinkling the readers' imaginations with the possibility that the girls were most likely on their way to fame and fortune in Hollywood or New York City, or that they were stuck waitressing as a result of their choices. Either way, the girls left Woodsboro of their own volition, and they were fine out in the big wide world.

After the second night of research, and the second night of reading such stories about the six girls, Ava closed the laptop with anger burning in her core. Did no one give a single damn that those girls could be in a living hell? Was there not a single person in authority who thought they might actually be victims of a sadist, pedophile, sex offender, killer, or a thousand other kinds of creep? Why was no one trying to help the girls? The better question was why didn't the sheriff of Woodsboro try to help them? Why wasn't Sheriff Mills shouting for help and jumping mad about the disappearances?

The interviews with the parents were the most telling evidence that something sinister might have occurred to at least three of the girls, and possibly to all six of them. Ava printed all the interviews she found online and put them with her files on each of the missing young women.

If there was a killer who was going to strike, he might be trolling for victims while she was idly filing papers into folders and trying to figure out how best to approach the sheriff about the matter. He might have his next victims targeted already. Maybe he was up there in the wilds of Vermont preparing ways to torture and kill the women, or preparing the spots where he hid the bodies. Was he on the phone with traffickers making deals?

Halloween was just around the corner. She couldn't keep tiptoeing through the scant evidence and considering the sheriff's feelings on the subject. Sheriff Mills was a grown woman with a good head on her shoulders, surely. Likely, she was a bit stubborn. That was a hazard of the office she held, but that didn't mean she couldn't be persuaded to look at things from a slightly different angle.

Ava dialed the number for the Woodsboro Sheriff's Office and sat at the kitchen table with the folders spread out in front of her. She asked for the sheriff and was mildly surprised when she was put on hold. Then again, in a town of thirty-five-hundred people, the sheriff probably wasn't out on many calls very often.

"Sheriff Mills," a woman's gruff and grumpy voice trumpeted.

Pulling the phone away from her ear, Ava punched the speaker button even though she doubted it was necessary. "Sheriff Mills, hello," Ava said by way of greeting.

"Yah. We've established my name, now what's yours? What's your business?"

Ava grinned. The sheriff didn't seem rude, just extremely straightforward and all business. "I'm Special Agent Aviva James with the FBI. I wondered if I might have a few minutes of your time to discuss something of the utmost importance with you, Sheriff."

There was a dry, humorless chuckle. "This has Jamie Hall's signature brand of crazy scrawled all over it, Agent James. I'm sorry you've gone to all this trouble and wasted your time, but really, there is *no serial killer* running around Woodsboro. That's what all this is about, right? Jamie is adamant there is a killer, and she has hounded me, been a real thorn in my side for a year about it. She kept saying she was going to call the FBI if I didn't."

"Well, yes, that's what this is about, but I think there's enough evidence to warrant a discussion," Ava said.

Another humorless bark of laughter. "No, there isn't, Agent James. With all due respect, and all that jazz, there is nothing to discuss at all. There hasn't been a single body washed up on any riverbank, not one turned up anywhere, as a matter of fact. Do you understand? No bodies. The only deaths around here in the last fifteen years are from natural causes, car wrecks, farming accidents, suicides, and God bless her, Mrs. Jamison's allergic reaction to a hornet sting earlier this year. That's it. Jamie's not been… *right* since what happened to Scott, you know. If you want to help her, get her some professional help. She needs it, Agent. Those girls and young women are just *missing*. There's nothing to even hint otherwise."

That was okay. The initial reaction and rhetoric had been expected. "But what if she isn't completely wrong, Sheriff? What if something did happen to those girls? There seems to be a victim profile among the missing girls."

"What do you mean *completely wrong*? Either Jamie's right, and there's a killer on the loose, or she's wrong, and there's no killer. I've ticked the box by the latter choice because it's the only logical one. Those girls have gone missing over the span of three years. That's a long time. And the first year, it was only one girl missing."

"Maybe he was just getting started. Just getting a feel for it. She might have been his very first victim. The second year, there were two girls, right?"

"Yeah, the town wild child and her bestie, who wasn't much of a straight arrow herself, if you take my meaning."

"So, you're saying that because they got into some trouble and didn't keep their noses squeaky clean, they don't deserve justice if something nefarious happened to them? They don't deserve for people to even consider that something bad happened to them?"

"I never said that. Of course, we looked at every possibility. There was no evidence of any sort of foul play. Everything pointed to them just hoofin' it out of town. God knows, Laura Halvorsen had said she would put this town in her rearview enough times that it really came as no surprise when she disappeared. At least, not to a lot of people who knew her. And not to me, either. You are wasting your time and mine, Agent James. If there's nothing more on your agenda, tell Jamie I say hello and that I wish her well. And think about getting her that help, would you?"

"Jamie's not out of sorts, Sheriff. She's coherent and logical. She wasn't hysterical or babbling nonsense. She gave me straightforward facts in an organized and calm manner. Those are not the hallmarks of someone who needs psychiatric treatment."

"I'm sorry. I didn't realize you were licensed to make those assessments. How many face-to-face meetings have you had with her about this?"

The tone was smug and sarcastic. Ava's pulse ramped up and her palms grew clammy.

"None. We've spoken over the phone a few times. That's irrelevant—"

"No, that's the most relevant thing you've said so far. Goodbye, Agent. I have a ton of work to do before I can go home this evening. I really appreciate your concern, but there's no killer lurking in Woodsboro."

"Maybe he isn't there right now, but what if he comes to town during Halloween? That's when the women and girls go missing, isn't it? Maybe he doesn't stay in town. Maybe he lives on the outskirts; up in the mountains; out on a big, lonesome farm; in the next town over. What would it hurt if I came and had a look around? I could work with you, and we could peruse the files, put something together, just look at the separate cases as possibly being one big case and see what's there, or what isn't."

There was a short silence. "What exactly are you fishing for, Agent James?" Her voice had lowered to near a whisper and it was full of suspicion.

"I could come up there and do all the legwork, if you like. I would keep a low profile, and not ruffle anyone's feathers, if possible. All I need is for you to make an official request for me to do so."

"Oh," she said. She drew out the sound, making it four seconds long. "Now I get it. You're an FBI agent, so I don't think I need to draw it out in big, chunky crayon pictures for you. I don't need the FBI swarming the whole damn town and getting folks all riled up and panicked. The families of these girls are basically good, hardworking people, and they are trying to heal from this. You know, it might be easier for them if there was a murder involved because that means closure of some kind at least. But not knowin' what happened to your little girl? That's hell on earth, I would imagine. Don't tear the scab off this wound, Agent." She cleared her throat. "The fall festivals are a big damn deal around here." Her tone was hateful and accusatory. "I don't know if you are familiar with living out in the middle of nowhere, but we do. Very little comes our way that we get excited for, and I don't want a mob of feds descending on the place like locusts on the crops—that's the wrong kind of excitement."

"I know very well what it's like to live in a small town, Sheriff Mills, and you never need to draw anything out in big, chunky crayon for me or any of my coworkers, thank you very much. I just told you that it would be only me and that I wouldn't be ruffling any feathers unnecessarily, let alone ruining the fall festivals. I would be doing this for the families. Don't you understand that? Whatever happened to those young women, their families deserve the truth, not some sugar-coated lie. Do you really think the way you're handling it helps the families?"

"I'm not telling you how to do your job, and I'd sure as hell appreciate it if you didn't try to tell me how to do mine. I've been doing it for fifteen years, and from the sound of you, I'd say that's about how long you've been alive. Call back when you've got some years of experience and living under your belt. Goodbye, Agent James."

"Sheriff, don't hang up," Ava said, swallowing her pride and biting back on the rest of her argument.

"One good reason," Mills said.

"I'm sorry. I didn't mean to say all that. I'm just really passionate about helping women, especially young, innocent women, who land in any kind of trouble. It hits close to home; close to my heart. Again, I'm sorry. I was out of line."

There was a longer silence than the one earlier. "Apology accepted. Thank you."

"Thanks for listening to my thoughts, Sheriff. Goodbye."

"Bye, now."

Ava disconnected the call and glared at the phone. Swallowing her pride wasn't easy. Would she ever learn how to defend her position on anything without putting herself in a position where she might have to swallow her pride?

If there was anyone qualified to give her some advice on the matter of persuading Sheriff Mills, it was her mother. Elizabeth James was a great persuader, else she would have probably been sitting in prison for going rogue for a year when she had been tracking Molly.

The drive cleared her head a bit, and some of the irritation from the sheriff's condescending attitude wore off before she reached her mother's house.

"Aviva, I wasn't expecting you," Elizabeth said with a smile. "Come on in and have a glass of wine with me. Your father is gone to one of *those* meetings, and there's no telling when he'll get back."

"You know he won't be back before eleven. Those meetings always take forever," Ava said.

"I know, but he insists on staying at the restaurant until they practically throw him and his clients out by their collars. Says that's how you make and keep connections." Elizabeth rolled her eyes toward the ceiling and tittered. "And to think, I used to feel the very same way not so long ago."

Ava laughed lightly, but she knew it wasn't such a laughing matter. Elizabeth missed her job, and she missed having to attend *those* kinds of meetings and making *those* kinds of powerful connections.

"So, how was your day? It's kind of late for you to be out and about this far from home on a work night. Everything okay?" Elizabeth drank heavily from the glass and refilled it.

"It was good except for the sledgehammer hanging over our heads at work with this Sanchez and Goldfield case. Nothing out of the ordinary there, though. Everything is fine, but I did want to talk to you about something."

Concern or dread, or perhaps both emotions mingled, flashed through Elizabeth's eyes as she lifted the glass again. She sipped a bit more delicately and then nodded. "Of course, dear. What is it?"

Why did she seem insincere? Was it the over-brightness in her eyes? The smile that was about two inches too wide? Or was it the overt arch of her eyebrows over her too-wide and round eyes? Maybe she was sincere. She could have been in the wine before Ava arrived, and she was seeing the effects of a few glasses of wine instead of fake sincerity.

Ava told her about Jamie's text and their subsequent conversations about the missing girls and young women. Elizabeth seemed intrigued, but she also seemed relieved, which bothered Ava. What had Elizabeth been worried that Ava wanted to talk about so much that a possible serial killer case made her look and act *relieved*?

Ava only sipped at her own wine, but Elizabeth didn't hold back much. She didn't go at the bottle like a warrior, but she drank freely. More freely than ever before, in fact. It was her house, and she didn't have to worry about work the next day, so Ava kept her mouth shut about it. Her mother had earned the right to drink a little whenever she wanted to.

She told her mother about Sheriff Wanda Mills in great detail. Perhaps in too much detail, but she was still chapped by the woman's attitude.

"So, you need to get this rough and gruff county sheriff to put in an official request for help to the Bureau, and you just can't see how to do that."

Ava nodded. "Not just an official request for any help, though. I need her to specifically request *my* help on the case. Every time I try to get her to listen to me, she gets defensive and rude. I swear, she is so hateful a preacher would have a hard time dealing with her."

"Let alone a young female agent lacking patience," Elizabeth added with a small, knowing grin as she tipped her glass at Ava.

"What does being female have to do with it?" Ava asked, tipping her own glass in return. "Sexist," she muttered playfully.

They laughed.

"I can give you some advice on how to get the good sheriff to listen to you and maybe even come around to your way of thinking."

"Please do. I'm all ears. I've wracked my brain, and everything I come up with will certainly just end up in another near argument. She's so stubborn."

"God, it's a good thing I don't know anyone else like that," Elizabeth said.

"I know, right?" Ava said. "Dad's a real handful when he gets a stubborn streak going."

Elizabeth snorted laughter and pointed at Ava. "I wasn't talking about your father, and you dang well know it."

"I wasn't being stubborn with the sheriff, Mom. She just wouldn't listen to reason no matter how hard I tried to get her to."

Elizabeth let out a sigh. "Really?"

"Yes, really. She just got angrier and angrier every time I tried to get her to see the case for what it might be and that Jamie might not be wrong. Or, she might not be *completely* wrong, anyway."

Elizabeth held up a hand to stop Ava. "Okay. It's really simple, dear. If you want the sheriff to listen to you, and I mean really listen to you, simply take Jamie completely out of the equation. No more Jamie. Don't mention her at all. And, if the sheriff mentions her, steer the conversation away from Jamie and back to the case. Jamie just taints the sheriff's perspective of the situation. Bald facts only. Strip it all down to bald facts on paper if you need to. Give this Sheriff Mills a reason to trust you. Give her a reason to listen and believe that young women in her town might be in danger this Halloween. And give her a reason to believe that you can do something to keep them safe, if she only requests your help." Elizabeth drained her glass and set it down gently. She looked at Ava pointedly. "After all, honey, Halloween is only ten days away."

"I know."

CHAPTER FIVE

Nine Days before Halloween

AFTER THE MORNING BRIEFING, AVA HEADED TOWARD HER OFFICE but didn't make it inside. Metford and Dane caught up to her first.

"So?" Metford asked. His face was bright and his expression expectant.

"What?" she asked as she looked from him to Dane suspiciously.

"Did Sal say we could go with you?" Dane urged quietly as she glanced toward the boss's office.

"We're all looking for Evelyn Goldfield until she's found. If we need to team up, we will, but for now, I think it's best if I work alone, and each of you follow separate leads until backup is needed. Just like I said in the meeting."

"She has her hard hat on," Metford said directly to Dane.

"What are you talking about, Metford?" Ava asked, starting to get irritated. "I need to get on the phone with these people ASAP. Get to the point. We need to find Goldfield, and the sooner the better."

Metford nodded emphatically. "So you can get to that case in Vermont. We know. That's what we're talking about."

"Yeah, did the boss say we could go with you?" Dane repeated.

"A Halloween serial killer to chase down doesn't seem like a solo case to me. Who better to go with you than us?" Metford asked, grinning ear to ear and trying to keep his voice down.

"You two are really chomping at the bit on this one, aren't you?"

"Yes," they answered in unison.

Santos joined them. "Well, I'm not. I'm perfectly happy to stay right where I am. Or go chase down one of the other cases we have piling up—just like you two should be thinking about." She pointed to Dane and Metford in turn with a stern expression. "Those cases ain't gonna solve themselves, and they have been hanging around longer than this Vermont Halloween case."

"This one is time-sensitive. Halloween is days away," Metford countered.

"And this one might be a whole bunch of absolutely nothing but pissed-off and bored young women who decided to leave their old lives behind," Ava said, being realistic. It wasn't beyond the realm of possibility. That didn't mean she had to like it. Good thing, too, because she didn't. It was just necessary to squash the conversation and move on with the current case as quickly and painlessly as possible.

"That sounds like it might just definitely be somewhere I want to be then. If that happens every Halloween in increasing numbers..." He shrugged and grinned even wider. "Who knows what might happen?"

"Well, I doubt if any of those women could ever get bored enough to run off with you," Santos said.

Metford laughed and walked away. "You never know, Santos," he said as he rounded the corner to the breakroom.

"No, but I can make an educated guess," she said to Dane and Ava.

"What about Ashton?" Dane asked. "You think he'd want to go?"

"I seriously doubt it," Santos said. "Probably have to use the Jaws of Life to pry his hands off those presentations he's been prepping and giving ever since we were in San Fran."

"That's right," Ava said. "He's been hounding the Bureau for the upgraded tech like they had out there. I almost forgot about that. It would be nice to get some of that approved, though."

"Is that why he hasn't been around much?" Dane asked.

Santos nodded. "Every spare minute, he's working on presentations, making calls, gathering more information, you name it. He's on a mission, for sure. I've never seen him like this."

"So who *has* Sal approved to go with you, Ava?" Dane asked as they all headed for the breakroom.

"No one. I'm not even approved to go yet."

"Why?"

"The sheriff hasn't put in a request for help yet, and until she does, we can't step in."

Santos' phone rang, and she walked away to answer it.

"Keep me and Metford in mind if and when that sheriff does put in the request, please," Dane said.

"I don't know that she will. Like I said earlier, there may be nothing there." Ava grabbed a donut and poured a cup of coffee.

"But you think there is, right?"

"Maybe. I don't know." She didn't want to give any false hope or any false ideas about the case despite her deep-seated belief that there was, indeed, something going on more than runaways.

"Your gut is telling you there's a killer up there, isn't it?" she whispered.

Ava shook her head and bit the donut.

"I'll take that as a yes. At least, a hard maybe." Dane poured a cup of coffee. "I've got five leads for this morning. I'm heading out. If you need me, you know how to get hold of me." She smirked and walked away.

Was it a curse that her internal feelings were so easily detected by others? Was it something in her eyes, or her expression? Her body language?

Making a mental note to never play poker with any of her coworkers, Ava went to her office and started her day.

Walking to her car that evening, Ava dialed Jamie's number again. She couldn't wait to get home to make the call. It had been eating at her all day. There were questions she needed to ask about the girls, things she needed to hear directly from Jamie, and things she needed to talk to Jamie about before she could make up her mind entirely. Time was running out. She needed to move quick.

"Jamie, it's Ava. How are you?"

"I saw the name on my phone, Ava. I'm okay. What's up?"

"I'm just off work, and I wanted to ask you some things about the girls, if you don't mind and you have time."

"I always have time. If not, I'll make time. This needs to get done. The sheriff told me that she talked to you. She was less than thrilled that I had called you, but I told her there was nothing she could do since you and I were old friends and that we had stayed in contact over the years. It's not like I was trying to stir up any trouble. I simply voiced my concern to you."

"She let me know that she wasn't too happy about it, too, but that's okay. About the girls, I'm assuming that all of them were residents at the time they went missing."

"Yes. Lifelong with the exception of Tina Leeyung as I told you before. She had only been here a year, but she was living here when she went missing. All of them had jobs in Woodsboro, too. Even Tina."

"And they all went missing from different locations?"

"Ashley Garland and Laura Halvorsen went missing on the road between the outdoor Halloween festival and Laura's apartment. Then Tina and Luna went missing from the same location: the rented venue. It's called The Great Hall."

"The Great Hall?" Ava asked.

"Yes. I have the address, if you want it."

"No, no. I'm driving. Just text it over so I can put it in my notes later. I just wanted to be sure about the name of the place. Some of the newspaper reports I read were a little hazy on the exact time the girls were reported missing—"

"I've seen the reports. All of them were reported by family and friends as missing the day after Halloween, but some were thought to have actually been missing since Halloween Eve. That's probably where the haziness came from in the articles. But the reports at the sheriff's office were each recorded the day after Halloween."

"That first girl—Charity—went missing in the corn maze. She had gone with friends. Did she drive there?" Ava asked.

"No, she rode there with her friends."

"What about Laura and Ashley? Were they driving?"

"On foot. They walked from the festival, and no one ever saw or heard from them again."

"You already said one of the girls from last year got into an argument with her boyfriend at a Halloween party and walked off toward her house because it was pretty close," Ava said.

"Yeah. That was Elise Abbot. She only lived about a ten-minute walk away from where the party was. Again, she walked away, and no one ever saw her again."

"Did any of these girls drive on a regular basis? Did they have their licenses? Do you know?"

"Yeah, they all drove. Charity hadn't been driving long, but I remember her dad being really shredded about the fact that he had just bought her a cheap first car, and that he had tried to get her to drive that night because she'd had her license for several months. He thought she would be safer driving herself than riding around with a bunch of people who might have been drinking or smoking pot. He really beat himself up over that. That interview was on the local news after she disappeared."

"But none of them were driving on the nights when they went missing," Ava said thoughtfully.

"Luna and Tina Leeyung drove their cars to The Great Hall. Their cars were still in the parking lot on the first of November, but I think they were taken the night before Halloween."

"Why do you think that?"

"Because they were at a pagan festival. Tina and Luna had formed a little pagan club, and they were so proud and excited. They told me about the celebrations they planned to do throughout the year, and they sounded fun. Like something I might like to look into sometime. But that All Hallows' Eve celebration was special. It was their first festival with the few members they had acquired. Thing is, no one talked to them on Halloween Day, but their cars were in the parking lot all day. I even remember seeing the cars there when I took Bailey to the school Halloween party, but I didn't think much of it. I knew they were going to have that celebration, but it didn't register to me that it had been the night before."

"And you are positive that Tina and Luna wouldn't have spontaneously decided to leave Woodsboro with, say, one of the members of their club? Maybe to go on some grand adventure, or something?"

"Absolutely not. They had worked so hard to get that club started and to get some slight recognition here. Why would they have left so abruptly after their very first festival? It just doesn't make sense. They had put their roots down here. Those women were not flighty. Some people thought they were a little flaky because of their beliefs, but they weren't. They were sweet, and they saw the good in everything and everyone. They were gentle influences everywhere they went."

"Where were the members of the pagan group from?"

"Woodsboro," Jamie said without hesitation. "I don't know who all of them were, but Luna would have written their names down somewhere like a minutes of the meeting type of thing, I'm sure. She was just so excited and wanted to have a record of everything to look back on. She might have even taken pictures that night, but we will never know unless she's found."

"What about Elise's boyfriend? Is he still around?"

"He is as far as I know. He could up and leave tomorrow, but I saw him just last week at the grocery store."

Ava made a mental note to speak with all the members of the pagan group and Elise's boyfriend as soon as possible.

"Thanks, Jamie. That helps a lot with the case. So, how are you doing since Scott's accident? I've been meaning to ask you, but with this case and all…"

"Oh, no worries. I've been good. Some days, at least. It's been three years, and I still expect to see him riding that stupid tractor home at dusk some evenings when I'm fixing supper and happen to glance out the window over the sink."

"I'm sure it's hard. I'm sorry you've had to go through that. You and Bailey both. How are you doing financially? Not to pry, but you don't work a traditional job, do you?"

"No, I don't. Haven't since we moved up here. Scott wouldn't hear of it." She chortled. "He was such a traditionalist. Always wanted to take care of me, and when Bailey came along, he really hit his stride with that notion. He was a good provider, too. I got bored of just being a housewife pretty quick, though, and I started raising chickens, keeping honeybees, and keeping vegetable gardens on the land here at the house. It was my little hobby to sell eggs, honey, and vegetables at the farmers' market."

"That actually sounds really nice," Ava said, comparing that laid-back-sounding lifestyle to her own chaotic and super-dangerous one. Maybe one day she would slow down and be able to try her hand at a slower-paced life.

"Good thing I did it, too, because I've had to sell off hundreds of acres of our farmland to pay off all our debts and our house and this few acres so that Bailey and I have a place that's not mortgaged. We have some money in the bank from the sales, and I make a good chunk selling my wares. It could be worse, but it could be oh, so much better if Scott were still with us. Some days I feel like an untethered kite being pushed and pulled at the whim of the wind. Then I look at Bailey, and everything is alright again. It has to be. For her."

"It sounds like you've been stronger than I could ever hope to be under the same circumstances. Bailey is a very lucky little girl to have such a great mom. Keep being strong, Jamie. I'm going to get off here and see what I can do about this case again. I'll talk to you again soon. Thanks again for the information."

"Anytime. Good luck with the sheriff."

They hung up, and Ava parked her car at the house. The sheriff had said Jamie was unstable and had even gone so far as to heavily insinuate the woman was crazy. She was anything but crazy. Scott's death had changed her, had hurt her in ways Ava couldn't possibly imagine, but it had not broken her mind.

CHAPTER SIX

Eight Days before Halloween

Ava met with Metford at Mandy's Burger Shack. It was one of the all-season local food joints that overlooked the beach but wasn't dependent on the tourists to stay in business. The burgers and fries reminded Ava of the little place on the river where she and her father used to go when she was younger, and she always suggested it when Metford wanted to meet for lunch and mentioned Wendy's. A woman could only take so many Wendy's burgers, after all.

"Any of your leads pan out this morning?" Ava asked.

"Nope, but Dane got a hit, or she thought it might be one. That's why she didn't come with me."

"How long ago? She didn't tell me."

"About an hour-and-a-half ago now. She said she'd text or call when she checked it out."

"Santos and Ashton didn't get anything from theirs this morning, and Santos is getting edgy about it. She thinks Goldfield might have left the US already, but I don't think she would."

Metford shook his head and shrugged as he finished off his burger. "I don't think she'd leave behind all the money she's making here. It's illegal, but it's still funding her lifestyle. Although, she might be planning on leaving. Especially if she thinks she might get into any trouble for the hit on Crothers."

"Sanchez ordered it, but someone had to move the money around and keep him updated on Crothers' movements."

"And I would just bet that someone was female, five-eight, bottle-black hair, spray tan, and walking around in designer clothes that I couldn't even put a down payment on."

Ava made a face. "If I gambled, that's where I would put my money, too."

"Heard anything else about the Vermont case yet?"

"You just asked me yesterday, Metford. And again this morning. I've not heard anything else. I promise, I'll let you know when I do." She dropped the paper napkin onto her plate and pushed away from the table. She slid a ten under the edge of her plate before taking the table ticket to the register to pay.

"You still do that? With *cash?*"

"I do. She deserves her tips at the end of her shift. If they're paid by card, she'll have to wait until payday to get them. Call it a personal preference."

He grinned and shook his head in disbelief. "Always thinking of everybody else."

She paid for her meal and walked out the door to wait for Metford. Her phone rang.

"Hey, Dane," she said. "We're at Mandy's Burger Shack if you want to meet us here. We'll wait."

"No, I'm following Evelyn right now. Silver Escalade. She's headed toward the other end of the beach, to the boat docks. Two of her thugs are in the car with her, and she had three bags packed into the back. She's planning on skipping out."

"You're sure she's heading to the docks?"

"Yes. We'll be there in five minutes."

"We're on our way. Do not try to apprehend her alone, Dane. We are on our way. I'll call Santos and Ashton. Do not approach her alone. Do you understand?"

"You're breaking up."

"Don't you pull that shit on me, Dane!" Ava yelled into the phone as she rushed toward her vehicle. "Hold back until we get there, and I mean it."

Metford came out and ran to catch up with her. "What happened?"

"She found her. Heading to the docks. ETA five minutes. I'm calling Santos and Ashton. Let's go." She jumped in and started the engine.

The drive to the docks was a blur, and if anyone had asked her for details of the drive, Ava would have been hard-pressed to give them. By the time the docks were in view, the adrenaline was already high.

Dane was parked off the shoulder of the road in the grass. Ava pulled up beside her but stayed on the pavement. She rolled down the window.

"They're out of sight. I couldn't see where they went," Dane said.

"Okay, get in. Santos and Ashton are on their way. Metford is behind us. We'll roll by and see what's going on. If we can grab her, we will."

They rolled toward the boat slips looking for the silver SUV.

"There!" Dane yelled, pointing to a speeding silver vehicle. "They're heading straight for us."

"Hold on," Ava yelled, putting her vehicle in the center of the road and hitting the lights and sirens.

"They're not stopping!" Dane shouted, gripping the bar over the passenger window.

The silver vehicle sped up. Ava held her foot on the brake and reached for her gun. Before she could draw it, the other car swerved to avoid a head-on collision. Metal squealed, and Ava recoiled as the side mirror exploded into shards. She made brief eye contact with the driver. Short, slicked-back brown hair, dark tan, well-groomed beard and mustache, deep scar from left temple that disappeared under the beard. He bared his teeth in what could have been a snarl, an intimidation tactic, a smug grin, or a bastardized version of all three.

A shot rang out from behind them, and Ava's gaze jerked to the rearview. Metford had taken aim at the grill of the silver car. There was immediate return fire from the car, and Dane jumped out, gun drawn, to run toward Metford. Ava threw her door open, but the silver SUV fishtailed as the driver accelerated away.

Metford waved out the driver's side window at them. "I'm fine. Follow them. Let's go," he barked.

Ava didn't need to be reassured. She was in the vehicle and speeding after Evelyn Goldfield in a matter of seconds.

"Goldfield was in the back of that SUV," Dane said.

"I saw her. Got a good look at the driver, too. Get hold of Ashton and let him know what's going on."

"What about Santos?"

"She's driving them." Ava gripped the wheel and clenched her teeth as they neared an intersection and Goldfield's car didn't even slow down. Cars hit their horns as they hard-braked and slid around as if on ice.

Taking a sharp right into a small suburb, Ava glanced at the dashboard clock. Two in the afternoon. Not time for the kids to be out of school yet, but close. The car didn't slow down at all as it zipped through the streets, swerved to miss a car backing out onto the road, and passed a slow-moving minivan.

"He's going to kill someone," Dane said.

No sooner than it was out of her mouth, a car backed out of a driveway, and the Escalade slammed into it at the rear tire. The impact sent the small two-door sedan spinning sideways and into a tree. The SUV wobbled and slowed momentarily, but ultimately kept going.

"Call it in," Ava said.

They exited the neighborhood and headed toward the water again. The driver slammed through a chain-link fence barrier at the end of the parking area, and the front of the vehicle came to rest on a loamy bank above the walkway to the boat slips. Three of the doors flew open. Two men and Evelyn Goldfield hit the ground running.

Ava skidded to a stop and jumped out to pursue them. If they made it to a boat, they would be gone. Possibly forever.

"Evelyn Goldfield, FBI! Stop!" she yelled as she ran toward them. She had to slow down and go along the fencing to the gate. Their vehicle had the hole in the chain link plugged tight.

The trio didn't look back, and they didn't slow down.

The sound of running feet behind let Ava know that Metford and Dane were hot on her heels. She focused on Goldfield's long black hair flipping wildly, and she concentrated on breathing deep, pumping her legs, pushing faster. She had to catch her.

The two men outran Evelyn. One jumped into a speedboat and fumbled with the ignition for a moment. The second yelled to Evelyn that she was going the wrong way. He motioned wildly and then movement caught his attention behind Ava, and he turned to run toward the boat.

Metford cut in front of Ava and headed for the dock at full speed. Ava didn't take her eyes off Goldfield, who was flailing as she navigated her way along a rough patch of bank above the walkway farther away.

The boat's engine turned over, and the man whooped. "Goldfield!" he bellowed. He pointed in the opposite direction of the dock.

Immediately, their quarry turned and ran in that direction. The route was less convoluted, and within ten steps, she was on the boards. Twenty more, and she turned left. The boat puttered toward the end of that dock as Evelyn ran for the end.

Ava closed the distance between them quickly, but Evelyn was infuriatingly fast, and she leaped into the water fifteen steps ahead of Ava. Ava dropped off her vest and went in after her without hesitation. She caught up to Evelyn effortlessly in the water, and as she closed the distance, the man in the boat shook his head and accelerated away.

Evelyn struggled, still trying to swim after the boat. "Gunther, you bastard!" she screamed.

"Stop fighting," Ava said as she wrapped her hand in the woman's shirt. "Your friend left you, and you're not going anywhere."

"Gunther!" she screamed so hard that her voice cracked. She stopped fighting and let Ava drag her backward for several feet before turning to face her with a burning glare. "Screw you. I should fucking drown you, bitch."

"I wouldn't suggest trying that, Miss Goldfield. It's been known to be detrimental to one's health to try killing federal agents." Ava fought to keep her breathing deep and even and her one-armed strokes through the water even and strong.

Metford, Dane, Santos, and Ashton pulled them out of the water. Dane cuffed Goldfield and placed her in the back of the SUV.

"You okay?" Metford asked Ava as he steadied her.

Ashton brought her an emergency blanket. "Use this to dry off."

"Thanks. Yeah, I'm okay. What about the other guy?"

"I got him," Metford said. "He's in my car."

"They hit someone back in that neighborhood," she said, struggling to calm the shaking in her muscles.

"EMS was just reporting there were only minor injuries. It was a mom going to pick up her kids at school," Dane said.

"Thank God the kids weren't in that car," Ava said. "Did anyone call in about good ol' Gunther in the boat?"

"I did," Ashton said. "Coast Guard is on it. I gave them the boat info, so it shouldn't take long."

"Good. Let's get these dirtbags in a cell where they belong and mark this case off the board."

"Want me to drive?" Dane asked. "Pretty long trip back to the office."

"Why not?" Ava said.

"Well, you clean up nicely," Sal observed with a chuckle as Ava walked in. "But I think you got a little seaweed there in your hair."

"Ha-ha. Is the case closed yet?"

"You better believe it. And I'm glad, too. Maybe the politicians will go back to their respective corners now."

"Wouldn't that be something," Ava cracked as she took a seat. "Have you heard anything about the Vermont case yet? Did they approve me to go check it out?"

Sal's smile faded. "No, they didn't, Ava. They said there isn't a case."

"Seriously? With all the evidence, and with all the experience we have dealing with serial killers, they still think there's nothing there?" Ava scoffed and ran a hand through her hair.

"Maybe your friend is just scared since her husband died. He died three years ago, right?"

Ava nodded.

"That's the year the first *victim* went missing, isn't it?"

Ava looked up sharply. "Yes. Charity Beaumont."

Sal pursed her lips and laced her fingers on the desktop. "It's natural for women to feel insecure, scared even, after their husbands are gone. Especially if their husbands die in some totally unexpected way like a car accident. Jamie moved up to Vermont with him when she was barely out of high school. Moved away from her family and friends, everything thing she knew and was familiar with. Then he was just suddenly gone. And sometimes, it takes women a very long time to move on and feel safe again. They don't stop seeing monsters behind every bad thing that happens or connections between unconnected incidents for years and years. Sometimes never. It doesn't make them crazy. I'm sure your friend is as sane as anyone. But maybe she's just scared."

Ava shook her head. "No. That's not what's going on here, Sal. If it was, I'd know it. If she was scared, she wouldn't still be there. She would move back to be closer to her family. She could sell her home and land, and be back here in no time. She has money in the bank. She works for herself. She still operates a small portion of the farmland, raises chickens, keeps honeybees, grows vegetable gardens. Does that sound like she's scared? Like she's seeing monsters?"

"I'm just saying that there isn't enough there. There isn't a case in the eyes of the Bureau, and they won't budge on it."

Ava held up her hands. "Right, right. I understand that much. Thank you for trying. I really appreciate it." She rubbed her palms against her thighs. "I'm not getting clearance." She looked at Sal hard. "But there is a case there. I don't know that it's a serial killer, but something bad is happening to those girls."

Sal unlaced her fingers and crossed her arms. She looked thoughtfully at Ava for a few moments. "Ava, you can't do what you did with Memphis, either."

Ava shook her head but said nothing.

"Nope. That's not cutting it. I want to hear you say that you are not going to do that. I want to hear the words come out of your mouth while you make eye contact with me." She sat forward and held Ava's gaze intently.

"I'm not going to do that," Ava said. That could mean anything. Usually, technicalities weren't her loophole, but if it came down to it, she would totally use them on this case. Someone had to help those girls— or at least their families, because it was probably too late for the girls. As distasteful a thought as that was, Ava had enough experience to know it was probably true.

"Ava, I mean it. I won't back your play with this. I'm with the Bureau on this one. There is no case here. I've been over the information you submitted several times with an unbiased eye, and I'm seeing nothing. You're already stretching yourself thin with Molly and your mother. I know you're helping them both in every way you can. You're not running to Vermont every time you can hop a plane to chase down some phantom serial… serial *what*? Killer? Kidnapper? You don't even know if there's anything going on, and I can't afford to let you off work like before. That was your *mom*. I worked with you, and I would do it again. But not this time. Now, let me hear you swear to it."

Ava sighed and cringed inwardly. There was no fenagling around it after that little speech. "I swear that I won't do with this case like I did with Mom's case. I swear I won't hop a plane to Vermont like I did to Memphis. You have my word, Sal."

Crestfallen wasn't even close to how disappointed she was when she left Sal's office. But what choice did she have? She couldn't go against Sal on it. Sal had gone out on a limb for her during Elizabeth and Molly's case. Sal and Ava could have both gotten into a lot of trouble for what Ava did. There was nothing to do but respect Sal's authority and her friendship with the Vermont case.

How was she supposed to tell Jamie that she couldn't help her after she had promised that she would?

As she left the parking lot, Ava rang Jamie again.

"Ava?"

"Jamie, I have news."

"Oh. I can tell by your voice, it's not good." Jamie sighed, and it sounded as if every hope she had in the world had just been crushed. "What happened? Was it Sheriff Mills?"

"No, no. It was the Bureau. They looked over the evidence I presented, and they just didn't see it the way I do. They said there's not enough there to prove there's a case to pursue at all. I can't get the clearance. I'm really sorry."

"I understand. It's not your fault. You have bosses to answer to, and I never want to get you into hot water with them. Sheriff Mills, on the other hand, is a damn fool. She can't be so stupidly blind that she doesn't see there's something going on. She just doesn't want to admit it. It would somehow reflect badly on her if there's a serial killer running around killing young women while she's sheriff, I guess. She just needs to get her head out of her ass for five minutes."

"Listen, I am sorry. Will you keep in touch and let me know if anything else happens? If it does, maybe I can get clearance. Maybe the pattern will be clearer for the Bureau."

"God, that sounds so horrible. Why do more girls have to get hurt, go missing, get killed, or whatever before anyone will believe me?"

"I know it's awful, but right now, it's the best I can do."

"Of course, I'll keep in touch. If anything happens, you'll be the first person I call."

Ava cut the call short partly because she was mentally and physically exhausted, and she wanted a little time to herself in which there wasn't a constant bombardment of worldly horrors being flung at her that she needed to process. And she needed an hour before going to Molly's to carve pumpkins for the last-minute neighborhood competition.

She cut it short mostly because she felt like the world's biggest horse's ass for having to go back on her promise to Jamie, though.

CHAPTER SEVEN

Eight Days before Halloween: Early Evening

MOLLY LAUGHED AS SHE PLACED THE CAP BACK ON THE JACK-O-lantern. "He's the least scary jack I've ever seen."

Ava chuckled as she eyed the lopsided, snaggled grin and rectangle eyes. Molly's hand had slipped while carving the second eye, and the knife went in all the way to the handle. It broke out a chunk and turned the triangle into a rectangle. Molly thought it was funny, and restructured the other eye so it was a rectangle, too.

"It's okay. I guess he looks a little wonky, but he's definitely unique," Ava said.

"Unique enough to win Mrs. Benson's impromptu neighborhood competition?" Molly made a face as she pulled half-dried pumpkin guts off her shirt. "Because if I don't win that collection of cheesy Stephen King movies after all this, you know I'm going to be upset."

"You can have the movies. I want that five-pound bag of candy corn and the black cat doorstop she made." Ava handed Molly a wet cloth.

"I know what you're doing, you know."

"Helping you get cleaned up? You look like a cartoon crime scene."

"Pushing me to get back into the community in every way possible." She wiped her shirt with the cloth and then tossed it onto the table. "I appreciate it. I do. But—"

"But, schmut. Leave it alone, Molly. I just thought it would be something fun. Not everything I do is therapy."

"You are possibly one of the worst liars I have ever met. It's okay. I don't mind. If you weren't here pushing me, I'd just sit in my room with the lights off and the blinds shut."

"Good because next month there's a Sadie Hawkins dance down at the senior center, and Mrs. Benson is going to invite us to that as well. She said Mr. Bowman has had his heart set on one of us asking him to dance ever since she mentioned it to him."

"Oh, my God, he's like ninety, Ava. I'm not asking him to dance." Molly laughed and shook her head in disbelief.

"I was just mentioning it because I thought you might want to start out slow and work your way up to busting a move at the club."

Molly scooped up a handful of the pumpkin seeds and threw them at Ava. "You are unbelievable," she said through her laughter. "A horrible liar, but mischievous as hell. How did they ever let you into the Bureau?"

Ava took it like a champ. She much preferred that side of Molly to the sad, withdrawn, brooding side that trusted no one and only wanted to be left alone. It was a good day for her, and that put her day in perspective. It put her life in perspective, actually.

Ava's phone rang, and their laughter died as if someone had turned the volume down on a radio suddenly. She looked at her phone, saw that it was Jamie, took a deep breath, and looked back at Molly. She shook her head and shrugged.

"I'll call her back later. Let's do another jack." She moved to get another pumpkin.

"No, c'mon. Answer the phone. It's okay. I'm fine. Mom will take me to the competition. It's just at the end of the block. Answer your phone."

Two rings later, Ava answered the call. After listening for only a moment, she interrupted Jamie. "Jamie, you're going to have to slow down. I can't understand anything you're telling me."

"I'm sorry," Jamie said. She took a deep breath. "The town is in a panic. It's all to do with the haunted house that was set up last year. Well, I think that's part of it, anyway. But the missing girls are the catalyst that started it all. I am sure of that much."

"Started what? Take your time and tell me what's going on."

"Okay, did I tell you about the haunted house at the edge of town? The new one?"

"I don't think so. But it's close to Halloween, so there are going to be haunted attractions setting up all over the place, I would think. There are tons of them around here."

"No, no. This is the one that went up for the first time right when the girls started going missing. It's called Lucifer's Lounge."

"Okay, but what does it have to do with the missing women? None of them were actually taken from the haunted house. They weren't anywhere near it, were they?"

"No, but apparently the youth group from Saint Mary's Catholic Church thinks the haunted house workers have something to do with all the missing women. The Youth for Salvation are protesting the haunted attraction right now, and they promise to do so until it shuts down. For good. They believe the workers there are kidnapping and killing the women as sacrifices to Satan. It could turn into an ugly scene rather quickly. I don't think Sheriff Mills realizes how bad it could get, or how quickly it could get out of hand."

"I totally agree with you, but we've been over this. There's nothing I can do unless she puts in that official request for me to help with the case. Besides, protests on a small scale aren't something we normally step in on. That's up to the sheriff to take care of. She can call in help from neighboring counties to get the protestors under control, if she needs it."

"That's not the only protest going on. There's another group from another church protesting all forms of festivities in town for the holiday. They are stating that the women are going missing as punishment for the town celebrating the devil's holiday. The townspeople know it's wrong to celebrate the devil or anything of his, but they're doing it every year, like it's a ritual. They know it's wrong, and they're doing it anyway."

"Woodsboro is so small, it can't be all that many people in these two groups. It sounds like two rival churches trying to outdo each other and perhaps win over some parishioners. Maybe it will calm down in a day or two, Jamie. I wouldn't worry myself sick over it."

Of course, any kind of protest in a town that small would be a reason for worry and excitement. Nothing ever happened in Woodsboro that wasn't planned. Except the protests. Jamie probably wasn't the only resident who was on the phone with someone about it.

"Two big Halloween displays in the middle of town for the little kids have already been burned down, and two of the businesses have had their display windows spray-painted to block their Halloween displays for kids. This is going to come to a head and turn dangerous. It won't take much to push these mobs over the edge, Ava. We're going to have full-blown riots on our hands. The Baptists are preaching in the streets that we shouldn't be indoctrinating our children by dressing them up as demons and ghouls to honor Satan because it's the same thing as devil worship. We're no better than the ancients who sacrificed their children, threw them into fires for their pagan gods. It's in their eyes, Ava. They really believe what they're saying."

"I understand what you're saying, but there's still nothing I can do. I have already been warned that I can't take time off work, and I can't come up there to work the case without prior approval, which I don't have. Why don't you and Bailey take a trip? Go somewhere for Halloween and stay with a friend or family member this year. Just get out of it and try to have fun and relax for once."

"I don't have anyone to take care of the animals, or to look after things for me here. I can't."

"Not even for three days? That should give this enough time to blow over."

"No, not even that long."

"Surely, someone close by could stop in a couple times a day and feed the chickens and the cats. It's not like you'd be asking them to plow fields."

Jamie was silent.

"You still there?" Ava asked.

"Yeah, I'm here." Her tone had changed somehow.

"What is it? Did I say something to upset you?"

"No. It's just…" She blew out a breath. "No one really *wants* to help me out right now."

Ava snorted. "Of course they do. That's what people in small towns do, isn't it? Help each other out in bad times."

"Yeah, unless they think you're the cause of the bad time."

It was Ava's turn to be silent. "Jamie, you're *not* the cause of what's going on in Woodsboro right now. Why would you even say that?"

"Not everyone thinks that, but a lot of people do. I was at the town meeting bringing up the missing girls and the serial killer, and now everyone has been thinking about that theory, I guess. They've somehow linked the serial killer theory to the Halloween ideology, and this is where it ended up. Who knows? Maybe I did cause it in a roundabout way. I wanted someone to give it some serious thought, but I didn't want them to go crazy with it."

"It's not your fault. This is just a couple of religious groups having a go at Halloween. It's never been a popular holiday with Christian religions. It'll pass after Halloween."

"It's not just the church groups, though. The town is in an uproar from all sides of the situation. There are those who really believe the Christian aspect of the argument, those who think it's just a harmless kids' candy holiday, and those who believe it's just a tradition passed down from ancestors to celebrate the last harvest of the season and it's totally harmless and there's no religious aspect to it at all. It seems like everybody fits into one of the groups, and they all have an agenda they're going to push using this as their platform. Sheriff Mills just needs to open her eyes and realize this could go sideways fast, and it will derail more than just our fall festivities when it does. But she can't get over being pissed at me long enough to focus on what's important here."

Ava motioned to Molly that she was sorry, and Molly flapped her hands that it was fine, no worries.

Ava paced the small yard and talked with Jamie for another twenty minutes as she continued to reassure Jamie as much as she could. Once Jamie calmed down a bit, Ava got off the phone and returned to Molly.

"That sounded kinda intense," Molly said.

"Yeah, it was. It still is up there, but there's nothing I can do."

"Let me in on it. What's going on?"

"You think that's a good idea?" Ava asked as she began carving at the smaller pumpkin's mouth.

"I'm bored, Ava. Yes, it's a good idea. Just tell me."

Giving in, Ava explained the situation in Woodsboro to Molly. It helped to talk it through with someone. That someone was Sal not so long ago, and then Metford when they were on duty, but with Molly, it was different. She didn't want to give Metford the idea that they were going to get approval to go up there and help, and she didn't want Sal to think she was trying to con her way into going without that approval.

At seven, Ava and Molly put the jack-o-lanterns in the car and headed to the competition.

"It sounds to me like the townspeople are panicky even without the feds being there, or *swarming* as the sheriff put it, so what would it hurt for you to talk to Sal again? Ask her what it would take on your part to get that approval, and maybe she can give you some advice," Molly said.

"I will call her. Right after this." Ava smiled as she parked at the curb and killed the engine. "Right now, this is more important."

The competition lasted for an hour, and Molly's oddball, unique jack came away with an honorable mention, a bag of mixed candies, and a caramel apple. Not a bad haul.

Ava dropped Molly at home and then dialed Sal.

"I don't really know what to tell you, Ava. They denied you working that case, and you know that. I can't do anything about it, and you can't be distracted with that case while you're working. This is your job, your career. You are responsible for people's lives when you're in the field."

"I know, Sal. I take that very seriously, too. I was just wondering if there was anything I could do to get the approval I need. Do you have any advice?"

"Get that request. That's the only thing that will change their minds. Work on getting Mills to put in the request. And if she is pissed at you and your friend Jamie, she might request that someone else work the case instead of you. If that happens, you still won't be going."

"That's fine. I just want it looked into. I just want to know that someone is trying to make sure those women get justice no matter what happened to them, or what might still be happening to them."

"If they are victims at all," Sal said with a warning tone.

"Right. If."

But there was no *if*, she was convinced of it. Ava knew they were victims. Her gut told her they were victims. Would there really be riots in Woodsboro if the women were only missing and missing of their own free will?

CHAPTER EIGHT

Protests and Runaways

Aᴍ ʜᴀɴɢɪɴɢ ᴜᴘ ᴡɪᴛʜ Sᴀʟ, Aᴠᴀ ʟᴀɪᴅ ᴛʜᴇ ᴘʜᴏɴᴇ ɪɴ ᴛʜᴇ ᴘᴀꜱ-
senger seat until she got home. Calling Sheriff Mills might not be a
good idea so late at night.

"But then again, it might be perfect," she mused as she opened the
front door and went into the house.

Catching Mills after a rough day in the office might be the best time
to convince her that she did indeed need outside help to get things
under control.

It only took another ten minutes to convince herself that she
was right.

The phone rang three times, and Ava began mentally preparing a short message to leave on voicemail. One that Mills was sure not to answer.

"Mills here," the sheriff said into the phone.

"Sheriff Mills, it's Agent James again. How are you this evening?"

"Don't play with me, Agent. I don't have the time or the want-to this evening. I saw your number on the screen. I'm not senile, you know. What do you want? I'm a little busy here."

It was much easier to believe her that time when she said she was busy. "I didn't think you were senile. I was just calling to check on things up there in Woodsboro. I heard that—"

"Yeah, I bet you did hear. I bet you heard about what's going on in great, painstaking detail, didn't you? That's what Jamie does. She finds something to obsess over, and then she ropes someone else into sharing her obsession, and before you know it, there's a little group of obsessed people right up the crack of your—"

"Sheriff Mills," Ava said a little louder than she meant to. "With all due respect, that's not what's going on here. She came to me with a legitimate concern, and I looked into what she was saying. From my own unbiased findings, and based on my experience with such cases, I decided to call you."

"That was the first time. I'm talking about tonight. You know about the protests, and she told you. That's why you called, isn't it?"

"Well, I'm not going to lie to you—"

"Well, I'll be sure to put a gold star by your name on my little chart. Could we cut to the chase and get to why you called? In case your friend didn't tell you, I've got Catholics protesting at one end of town, Baptists vandalizing businesses in town and preaching end times on the streets, and traditionalists protesting the Catholics' and the Baptists' protests, and then we have some rogue group just out to tear shit up who decided it would be fun to burn down some Halloween displays meant for the tykes in town. Expensive displays, too. So, if you have a point, make it, please."

"Fair enough. Do you need my help, Sheriff Mills? I would be more than happy to come up and help you out. I could be there tomorrow."

For the first time, there was silence on the other end of the line. Mills let out a heavy breath and then inhaled sharply. "To investigate runaways? No way. To bust up a couple of religious kids' groups whooping and hollering? I think I got it, Agent, but thanks for your continued concern for my little town."

"Alright. Again, fair enough, but I think my presence might settle some nerves."

Mills laughed. It was a big ol' belly laugh, as if Ava had told a real knee slapper. "Your presence would settle some nerves, huh? That's really what you believe?"

Mills was looking for someone to burn down. She was riled and up in the air because her town was in chaos. It wasn't the first time Ava had seen it, and it wouldn't be the last. "Sheriff, I'm not pressuring you, and I'm not trying to overstep my bounds. I'll give you some time to think about my offer to help you. It's a standing offer, just so you know. You don't have to be overwhelmed with all this."

Mills fell silent again. She cleared her throat after a few seconds. "I appreciate that."

"You're welcome."

"Could you do me one favor?"

"Name it, and if it's within my power, I'll give it my best shot."

"Jamie Hall. Could you talk to her about keeping quiet about the serial killer crap? The crazy talk is getting out of hand."

"Jamie isn't crazy, sheriff."

Mills scoffed. "Jury's still out on that verdict."

"I'm not saying that because she's my friend, either. I've talked to her, and yes, as an agent, I do have a certain amount of training that allows me to detect when someone is possibly having a break with reality or if another mental disorder is at play. She's not crazy, she's just seriously worried for the safety of the young women in Woodsboro."

"She is worried for nothing, Agent."

"I think she might have a good reason, actually. I have been on a good many cases involving serial killers. I've also worked kidnapping cases, trafficking cases, and straight-up homicides, and what you have in Woodsboro seems like some of those cases. It doesn't seem like a bunch of girls and young women who just got tired of their lives and decided to walk away. They didn't take any of their personal things other than what was on them. They wouldn't do that. They were *young women*, and you should know how attached to their personal things young women are. Cell phones, clothes, makeup, jewelry, shoes, cute hats and hair accessories, their *cars* even."

"Mmm," Mills grunted, obviously displeased that she didn't have a suitable rebuttal. "Maybe, but there's no evidence that anything else happened either. Young women are among the most temperamental creatures on Earth. You should know that. They get angry, and they do things they often regret."

"Yes, they do, but then they rectify those things with a phone call or an apology. They reach out to someone. Those girls did none of that. No one has heard from them at all since they disappeared. Either they have been killed, or someone took them and they are being held against their will. Either way, it seems as if someone needs to be looking a little deeper."

"You're pretty damn persuasive for a fed, Agent James. Or is it Special Agent James? I'm never sure about the fed titles."

"Ava is fine. Ava or Agent James or Hey You."

"Doesn't matter what I call you as long as I call you?" Mills laughed again. "I'll give your offer some thought, but don't be surprised if you don't hear from me. Like I said, I think I got this under control. I'll think about the girls' case, but I don't think I'll find any reason to pursue it further."

"I'm not pressuring you at all. I'll call you back at a later time to see if you've changed your mind. It's still a standing offer. Just remember, it seems like the town is pretty riled up even without the feds being there. So, in the end, what would it matter if there was one there looking into that case?"

"I think maybe you were an insurance salesman in a past life. I'll talk to you later, Agent James."

"You got it," Ava said.

She didn't necessarily pat herself on the back for a job well done, but she did feel pretty darn good that she had put a dent in Sheriff Mills' thick armor over the phone. She was one step closer to getting her to put in that elusive request.

Ava dialed Jamie's number with a smile on her face. It would be nice to deliver some good news to her friend for once.

"Ava?" Jamie answered the phone sounding worried.

"It's me, Jamie. I just got off the phone with Sheriff Mills."

"Did she agree to put in the request? I knew you could get her to see logic."

"I wouldn't go that far, but I did get her to at least listen to me, which is a big step in the right direction, I feel. We talked for a good while, and she was actually being quite civil to me for the last quarter of the conversation."

"What? You mean no passive-aggressive cutdowns? No outright jabs that went to your core? I think you might have been talking to the wrong person. Mills is never completely civil to anyone. I'm sure it probably happened to someone at some point, but not in the last forty years, surely. That woman is *sour*."

"It was Sheriff Mills. The town being in such an uproar has her upset. I think she's on the brink of being overwhelmed. I told her she didn't have to be overwhelmed, and she didn't have to feel as if she were alone. I'm here to help if she will just ask for it in an official capacity. I also told her it was a standing offer and that I wasn't pressuring her."

"Wow, you're good. Probably because you don't have to deal with her on a daily basis, and you talk to her over the phone. If you had to see the condescending and scathing looks on her face when you're trying to speak to her about something serious, you might punch her in the throat. God knows I feel like doing that sometimes."

"Mom, who punched somebody in the throat?" Bailey's voice called from far in the background.

"Oh, no one, honey. Mommy was just telling a joke to a friend. You go back up and get in bed. I'll be up to tuck you in soon. Go on, now."

"That's not a very nice joke, Mom," Bailey said, her voice fading as she presumably retreated toward her bedroom.

"Well, I guess I'll be trying to explain that to an eight-year-old tonight." Jamie snickered. "Kids, right?"

Not having a clue, Ava agreed. "I won't keep you. Sounds like you've got a busy night ahead of you."

"What, trying to explain to the little warden why I was telling a *joke* that ended with someone being punched in the throat… and that I felt like doing that sometimes? Pshaw! That's nothing. You should be here when I have to explain the really fun stuff like where babies come from and why I have breasts and she doesn't, and the random double innu-endo she heard some guy spout at the waitress at the diner earlier in the day. Those are the really fun days."

"Oof. No thanks. I'll leave that to you, but if I ever need pointers, I know who to call," Ava said, grinning and fighting a laugh.

"You ever going to have a rugrat of your own, or are you too focused on your career?"

"Eh, who knows what the future holds?" That was not a conversation she was willing to have with anyone. She didn't even allow her own mother to broach that subject.

"Well, let me tell you, the deck is stacked. If you don't want kids, you better take precautions. And I did say precautions. Plural. More than one method."

"Right. Back to Mills and the case before we hang up, though. I think we need to double-tap Mills. I'll call her again tomorrow. I think it might be a good idea if you go to the station and talk to her, too. Something along the same lines. Not rude, not pushy, not loud, just consistent. Let her know it's not going away, and that you have legitimate concerns. Let her know you have this vast collection of knowledge about each of the women. You might have it collected in a way that she doesn't, and it might make a difference in how she sees this situation."

"I can do that. If she sees me coming, though, she might go out the back door before I get in the front. She doesn't really like me all that much, and she does all she can to avoid me. On the rare occasion when she can't, she turns nasty in a hurry. Usually makes me sorry that I ever tried to approach her."

"Try the softer approach. Do you have any of your information printed out anywhere, or written down?"

"I do. I have it all printed out and in a huge file. I've been adding to it since the second year. That's when I really started to think something bad was going on. By last year, I didn't have to think anymore—I knew."

"Good. Is there any way you can print the highlights to take with you tomorrow?"

"Definitely."

"Don't take everything. We don't want it to look like you're a fanatic."

"Too late, I'm afraid. You've talked to her. You should know how she feels about me by now."

"We're going to try to change that, though. Put the basic information about a girl on the front of a page with a small picture of her. On the back, list a few personal bullet points about her that you know are factual. You don't want anything there that will upset the family. Can you do that by tomorrow?"

"I have all night. I'll get it done in plenty of time and go to the sheriff's office in the morning after Bailey is off to school."

"You need to sleep sometime. Again, you don't want to walk in there looking wild-eyed and frazzled. You need to be calm, put-together, organized."

"That's not happening. I haven't slept more than four hours in a single night since I had Bailey, and maybe three in a single night since Scott died. I won't look any less presentable than normal. Besides, if I go in there looking like a Stepford Wife, she'll know something is off before I even open my mouth."

"Okay. You do your part from that side of things, and I'll do my part from this side. We'll see what we can accomplish."

"We're just asking a stubborn sheriff to ask for help that she thinks she doesn't need on a case that she believes doesn't exist. How hard could it be, Ava?"

Exactly. How hard could it be? It had already been much more difficult than Ava had ever dared think. Then again, she'd had run-ins with small-town sheriffs before, and none of them exactly rolled out the red carpet for the FBI, and especially not for her.

CHAPTER NINE

Seven Days before Halloween

Sheriff Mills sat at her desk with a large black coffee and the beginnings of a tension headache. It was only nine in the morning, and she had already been out on calls since before seven. Those damn rogue kids had been out vandalizing more Halloween decorations and setups all over town and in people's front yards all night. Her town was going to hell in a handbasket, and she couldn't quite pinpoint the exact cause of it all.

Why was this Halloween so damn different than any of the others in the past fifteen years she had been sheriff? Or in the five she had been a deputy before that? Or the twenty she had been a resident before that?

"The damn cell phones, that's what's different," she grumbled as she flipped the plastic cap off the aspirin bottle and tipped it over her open mouth.

The directions said to take two, but two would just piss off this monster of a headache. She dropped four in her mouth and set the bottle down without replacing the cap. She'd need them again soon enough if things kept on the way they were going.

She chewed the aspirin. The bitter taste flooded her mouth and caused her gut to roil unpleasantly. She chased the acidy mush down with several gulps of hot black coffee.

"Sheriff, we might have trouble coming this way," Deputy Marsh said from the doorway.

"What now? Christ Almighty," she said, pushing away from the desk angrily.

"Whole group of people headed across the parking lot. They look upset."

Mills hurried to the front of the building, took one look at the mob, and felt like she might throw up. "What is this, the apocalypse? The whole town is losing their ever-loving minds this year."

Deputy Marsh shook his head. "Want me to call for backup?"

"Backup? You nitwit, you *are* the backup. Marty and Latham are in the field. You're with me, and the others are sleeping right now so they can come in for the overnight. We have Ginny, if bad gets worse, ain't that right, Ginny?"

"Sure thing, Sheriff," Ginny said.

Mills didn't like the tremor in the woman's voice, but she knew Ginny would take orders without question or hesitation.

She recognized Shannon Beaumont at the front of the crowd, and a few of the Beaumonts with her. Brad and Pamela Garland were right behind her with Ivory and Deliah Halvorsen. She didn't need to look closer at the others in the crowd. It was the families of the missing girls.

"Christ Almighty," she said in a low voice. "I swear on Mamaw's grave that if Jamie Hall is behind this, I'll arrest her on sight."

"Jamie isn't in the crowd, I don't think," Marsh said, craning his neck to see.

"No, but that crowd is mostly made up of all the missing girls' families, and if I don't miss my guess—"

The door flew open and Shannon stepped inside. Her eyes flared wildly. "Sheriff Mills, we need to speak with you."

"Well, Shannon, I'm right here. What's going on now? More lawn decorations get destroyed? Somebody's car get egged?? She was hopeful that it was something so mundane and easily rectified.

"We don't care about any of that," Brad Garland said. "We care about our missing daughters. In one week, Pam and I haven't heard from or seen Ashley in a year."

"And I haven't seen or heard from Charity in three," Shannon said.

Deliah Halvorsen pushed between them and held out a picture of her daughter. "Laura has also been gone for two years this Halloween, Sheriff. She wouldn't have just up and left like that without a word." Her husband, Ivory stepped up beside her.

They were normally a quiet couple. Kept their heads down, worked hard, kept to themselves, paid their bills, and went about life in a fashion that was nothing resembling the way their daughter had done.

Mills cleared her throat. "Mr. and Mrs. Halvorsen, Laura was *troubled*. We all know it, and I'm not being hateful when I say that. Maybe she just got it in her head that the grass was greener somewhere else. Maybe she thought there were more opportunities for someone with so much *ambition* and *gusto* for life. I'm real sorry that she left, but there's no evidence that anything else happened."

Ivory shook his head. "Hell, if nothing else, she would have called me and her Mama by now asking for money or to come back home because she screwed up and she knew it. We ain't saying she was an angel. We're not stupid, Sheriff, but we know our daughter better than you. Better than anybody, and she wouldn't have kept radio silence all this time. She would not have left that night without a word, without coming back home first, and without some of her things."

"We want you to open the cases back up, Sheriff Mills," Pamela Garland said. "Ashley is our only child. Just like the Halvorsens, we know she wouldn't have kept away all this time without a word. And she wouldn't have taken off without coming back home for her things. She was in costume. Who runs away in their Halloween outfit? It doesn't even make sense."

A rumble of outraged agreement ran through the crowd. The din grew loud enough that Mills felt it rumbling through her midsection like the bass in a car radio. She held up her hands and yelled over it.

"That's enough, now. This is getting us nowhere. Settle down and we can talk this through civilly, or I can disperse you without further discussion. We're not having a riot at the station. There's enough going on right now."

April and Summer Bradford stood to the side clutching pictures of their younger sister, Luna. Mills spotted the matching tattoos on their wrists. The full moon with quarter moons on either side. They had gotten the tattoos in honor of their sister.

"April, Summer, I see you, and I feel your pain. I do," Mills said.

"How could you? Did you lose your baby sister with no explanation? Did your father commit suicide six months later? Is your mother dying in the hospital? Did you know that her one wish is to know what happened to her baby before she dies?" Tears wetted Summer's face.

"I've suffered my fair share of losses, Miss Bradford, and again, I'm sorry for your pain and your losses. I know you're both going through a tough time. I'm sorry Luna's gone, but maybe she and Tina went somewhere they thought their religion would be accepted better."

Summer's face contorted to a mask of rage, and she stepped forward. April snagged her sister's arm and pulled her back. She shook her head and held up her tattooed wrist. Summer calmed.

A young man came forward and the crowd quieted again. "Sheriff Mills, you don't know me. I am Chris Tam. Tina Leeyung was my cousin. We grew up together. You give all these reasons why these other women might have left suddenly, but Tina didn't do things like that. Ever. My family has sent me to find out what really happened to her."

"Mr. Tam, glad to make your acquaintance. You say Tina wouldn't have left suddenly, but did she not leave your family to come here just a year before she went missing from here?"

"She did, but it was only with the family's permission. She held to a lot of the old traditions, and she didn't want to do anything that would upset our grandparents."

"Stop trying to explain it all away, Sheriff," a man yelled from the back.

"Yeah, we want you to open the cases back up and look again," a woman in the middle said.

Charity's mother stepped forward and handed Mills a folder. "You are the sheriff of Woodsboro. It's your duty to protect and serve. You didn't protect these girls, so the least you can do is find out what really happened."

"And stop telling us our girls ran away when we know better," Carl Abbot said. "Elise had an established life here. She worked at the hospital, for Pete's sake. She'd been at that job for two years and had only missed two days. Does that sound like a woman who just suddenly decides she's going to leave?"

"And leave her apartment, her car, her cat, her cash, her clothes, and even her laptop?" Jenna Abbot pressed. "She left everything, Sheriff. You know she didn't run away, and don't hand me that line about arguing with her boyfriend and being all hysterical and irrational again either. Everyone knew she argued with Bobby at least once a week. It wasn't anything unusual, and she was never irrational enough to *walk* away from everything she had and knew."

"And I'm right here," Bobby said. "I can vouch for that. We only argued because I wanted to stay longer than we agreed. She had to work the next day and didn't want to risk oversleeping and being late for her shift. Mitzy was pregnant and only supposed to be working half-shifts. Elise was going in to relieve her that next morning."

"And her apartment building was a ten-minute walk from the party," Carl reminded everyone.

"On a dark, wooded road," Mills countered.

"Ten minutes," Carl said loudly. "Something happened during that ten-minute walk. Someone took her, and we want to know who it was, and what he did with her."

"For all we know, these girls could all still be alive somewhere out there being held against their will," April Bradford said.

"Excuse me," Jamie Hall said loudly as she made her way through the door. "Excuse. I need to speak with the sheriff."

"Well, join the rest of us," a woman said.

Jamie held her file aloft. "Sheriff Mills, please? Just a moment of your time."

"Hell's bells," Mills said under her breath to Marsh.

"Want me to take her to an interview room so you can, uh, do that thing you were talking about earlier?" Marsh asked.

"Sheriff Mills, I have some information put together here about all the girls. It's in one file, and I think if you look over it, you'll be able to see that something happened *to* them."

"Jamie, did you do all this?" Mills asked, nodding toward the crowd as Jamie made her way to the front.

"What do you mean?" She looked over her shoulder at the people.

Mills saw the proverbial lightbulb go on over Jamie's head as she realized who the people were.

"No. I haven't talked to anyone, Sheriff. Just you. Just now." She smiled and looked over her shoulder again.

"This really isn't the time. Why don't you follow Deputy Marsh to an interview room, and I'll speak with you after I've finished here with these good people?"

"How about no? How about we all talk about it together?" Jamie turned to face the crowd. "You're here about your daughters, no?"

Everyone agreed that's why they were there.

Jamie turned back to Mills. "Are you still telling them that their daughters just up and ran away for no apparent reason?" She held out the folder with a smile.

Mills glared at her and then at the folder. She didn't take it. Didn't want it. The crazy might be contagious. Agent James was convinced that Jamie wasn't crazy, but she hadn't witnessed what Jamie was capable of in person.

"I know your theory, Jamie, and I'm warning you only once." Mills kept her voice low and her eye contact solid.

"I'm not here to start a riot, Sheriff. I'm just here to try and talk some logic to you. Halloween is only seven days away, and that's when more of our young women, our *girls* will go missing. Do you know how many this year?"

A rumble of discontent went through the crowd. Mills only glanced up at them. She wanted to throw Jamie in a cell. A padded one would be great, but she didn't have one of those.

"It will be four this year. That is if the killer holds true to his pattern, and I think he will. They are slaves to their patterns most of the time. It's a psychological thing. A mental thing, you know. And I think it's his way of escalating the killings, getting away with it for years until you figure it out, and then he can laugh because he was so much smarter than you."

"A serial killer?" Chris Tam asked with wide eyes. "You really have evidence it's a serial killer?"

"She has no such evidence because no such evidence exists," Mills said as Chris moved toward Jamie with his hand out toward the file. Mills stepped forward and took it before he could.

"If it's not a serial killer then it's a trafficker. Someone is trafficking women who fit a very similar profile," Jamie said.

Jenna Abbot put her hand on Jamie's shoulder. "You're right. All the girls looked a lot like my Elise."

"Very similar," Pamela Garland added.

"Did you even realize how much the girls all looked alike, Sheriff?" Ivory Halvorsen asked. "Because, just to be honest, until just now, I didn't."

"Me neither," Summer Bradford admitted.

April shook her head and looked shocked at the realization.

"Even Tina looked similar to the others, Chris," Jamie said. "She kept her hair dyed lighter, and her eyes were light. She had a fair complexion, and she had a slight build."

Chris nodded and looked at the floor as he cleared his throat.

"Did you consider a serial killer, Sheriff?" Jenna Abbot asked.

"I would have if there had been any evidence." She gripped the folder so tight that her fingertips burned.

"That would explain why the girls went missing so suddenly and inexplicably," Brad Garland said.

"There were never any bodies found, Brad," Mills said, trying to reason with him and the others.

Jamie pointed to the file in Mills' hands. "I took the liberty of putting some notes in there about how some serial killers will hide the bodies of their victims and why. There are lots of reasons. Don't worry, I cited the sources, and they are all reputable. I even double- and triple-checked the facts."

The tension headache flared into a full-blown migraine as the crowd ignited into a firestorm of demands and heated requests that Mills reopen the cases and look at them from a different angle. The worst part of the whole thing was that she couldn't deny crazy Jamie might be onto something. Was it because she had been harping into one of Mills' ears on the serial killer theory at every turn for so long? Because she had the FBI agent involved, and she was talking about the same theory in the other ear every other day? Or because the town was crying out about it en masse?

Ava's phone rang as she was opening the file on the next case in her office.

"Jamie, I'm at work," she said instead of the normal greeting. If Sal knew she was getting calls from Jamie about the Vermont case on work time, she would be pissed.

"I know. I'm sorry, but it's too much to text, I didn't know when you'd get to check your email, and it's too important to wait."

Ava pushed her door shut and returned to her desk. "Okay, I'm listening, but be quick."

Jamie told her about the commotion at the sheriff's office earlier.

"I'm just saying that it might be a good time to call Mills again. This just might be the day she decides she could use some help," Jamie said, unable to disguise the glee in her voice.

"How long has the crowd been cleared out of the station?"

"Maybe an hour."

"I'll give the sheriff another hour or two to go over the files you gave her and then call her. That'll give me time to get out of the office here, too. I'm not supposed to be doing this while I'm on the clock."

"Got it. I'll let you go. Let me know what happens," Jamie said with that same gleeful tone.

Ava couldn't blame her for being happy about it. After so long of being ignored and threatened and even called crazy, Jamie was finally being heard. The townspeople seemingly had accepted her and her wild theory about the serial killer.

"Either she's extremely good at convincing people of crazy ideas, or there's something to it," Ava said under her breath as she put away her phone.

It was notoriously difficult to get even a small band of people to stand behind a single idea with loads of hard evidence. If they were giving credence to Jamie's idea with only circumstantial evidence, surely there was a chance the woman was right.

Someone had done something to those girls, and Ava was convinced it was the same person perpetrating the crime year after year. She was also convinced that same person would strike again in seven days, and this time he would take four young women.

Why? Because that's what serial killers and serial kidnappers and traffickers did. They followed patterns.

CHAPTER TEN

Seven Days before Halloween: Phoning Mills

A N HOUR LATER, AVA CALLED SHERIFF MILLS. "SHERIFF MILLS, it's—"

"Agent James, yeah," Mills grunted. "Figured I'd be hearing from you soon enough."

"So, have you had time to think about my offer?" She avoided asking what was really pressing at her thoughts. The less Mills knew of her and Jamie's communications, the better.

"Actually, I haven't even had time to wipe my nose with all the hell coming down around here. I don't suppose you know anything about how the commotion at the station got started this morning, do you?"

"No, I don't know how it started. Jamie said there was quite the scene when she got there, though."

"Jamie Hall is going to be the death of me, I swear it. Chaos follows that woman. It trails along, clinging to her like the train of a wedding dress."

"The way I understood her to say it, the chaos was in full swing by the time she arrived."

"That was only this morning. Only once. And I'm sure she had a hand in getting the people riled up behind the scenes somehow before they reached the station. Who knows how long she's been whispering her theories in their ears and making them crazy with this stuff? All I know is that right now, I do not need this extracurricular shitstorm of nonsense. I have enough to deal with right now."

"Then why didn't you arrest her? Or give her a citation for disturbing the peace? Or hold her in a cell and charge her for inciting—"

"Because," Mills bellowed indignantly.

Ava nodded on the other end of the phone. She thought she knew exactly why. Mills was stubborn, but she wasn't blind. She had Jamie's file, and if Ava didn't miss her guess, that file was meticulous and thorough, and it would be hard to look past the fact that something had happened to those girls.

"Because why, Sheriff?" Ava pushed.

"Because she gave me a damn file, and for better or worse, I looked through it."

"A file changed your mind?"

"No. Not really. If I had arrested her, I would have had to arrest the other twenty-odd people standing in the station. Same if I had cited her. What would that have accomplished? They were the families of the missing girls. They're hurting and scared, and now because of Jamie, they're worried to death that their little girls were killed by some maniac who's still running around loose in town. Besides, I don't have enough cells to hold all of 'em," she ended sounding defensive and almost petulant.

"And since you looked through that file, you're not so sure Jamie is wrong, are you?"

"God's teeth," she grumbled. "No, I'm not sure. Do you have any idea how bad that sucks? To doubt yourself like that? If those girls were…" she let the rest of the sentence go unsaid.

"I understand better than you give me credit for, I think. And if those girls were victims of a serial killer, you aren't to blame. No one is but the killer."

"I won't sleep a wink wondering if it's my fault that more of them are missing and possibly *dead*. I have to take care of the protests that are slowly turning into riots that'll eventually turn neighbors against each other. Who knows how soon before violence breaks out? I know they're church groups mostly, but that doesn't automatically rule out violence. The groups are mostly made up of teens and young people in their early to mid-twenties. Is there a more volatile age group in the universe?"

"Toddlers," Ava offered.

Mills gave a dry bark of laughter that hurt Ava's ear. "Yeah, those little ankle biters can be pretty ruthless. I've got this file of Jamie's stuck in my head while I'm trying to figure out which of the teenagers in town have turned into little vandals, and how I'm going to handle it when I catch them. And then there's Jamie. Always Jamie on my mind and in my face. Showing up at the worst possible times to wreak more havoc. And now? I have to bite the bullet a little because she has made her point. When she figures that out, she will torment the life out of me about this, I'm sure of it."

"Are you ready to ask me to help you with this, Sheriff Mills? I could come in and just work on the down-low, fly under the radar, and put the serial killer theory to bed for you. One thing off your list of worries. I could keep Jamie at bay for you, too. Then, I could help you calm their worries and help with the protests, if you want."

"Real Jack of all Trades, eh?" She chuckled lightly.

"You could say that. What do you say? Ready to put in that request?"

"It'd just be you? Not the entire damn Bureau?"

"If that's what you want, it would just be me." Ava smiled.

"I think I can handle just one of you. That might actually help me out instead of wreaking havoc in my town and scaring folks worse than they already are."

"You're making the right decision, Sheriff. You just need to put in an official request." Ava spent another ten minutes on the phone with Mills, talking her through what would happen over the next day or so. "As soon as they let me know something, I'll let you know."

"Appreciate it. Christ, I hope I don't regret this."

"You won't."

Ava hung up with triumph building in her chest and a bullet-point list of things she needed to do when she got to Woodsboro forming in her mind.

She continued to work her current case, got lunch by herself, and had an afternoon briefing with Metford and Santos before appearing as a witness in court for another case, and through it all, Ava avoided saying anything about Mills putting in the request. What if she had changed her mind? What if Mills had only said she wanted the help to get Ava to leave her alone?

After court, Ava headed back to the office as always, mentally drained and doubting that some people possessed a molecule of human decency. The serial rapist had gone to prison, but Ava was left wondering just how much of his sentence he would serve. Prisons were overcrowded, underfunded, and understaffed. Like it or not, bad people were released back onto the streets to free up space for worse offenders, and sometimes just to take some of the burden off the struggling prison system.

Metford met her in the bullpen. "You look beat. Another catch and release?"

"No, he went to prison," Ava said as she pulled off her jacket and draped it over her arm.

"For how long is the question, right?" Santos asked as she headed out the door and toward Sal's office.

Ava pointed at her. "Bingo."

"How much longer you going to be here this evening?" Metford asked.

"Depends on what's on my desk when I get there." She walked over to Ashton's desk and looked over the files stacked there. "Is Ashton still here?"

"He's working a lead on another case in the field. He probably won't be back today unless he forgot a thumb drive. He almost drove me nuts with that tech talk today. I'm pretty sure he speaks Greek when he gets all wound up about it because I don't understand a thing he says. But I've learned to nod and smile a lot. Otherwise, he tries to break it down and in-depth explain it, and that's just too painful to go through more than once."

Ava grinned. "I'm glad he knows so much about the tech. You know he's a certified genius, right?"

"Certifiable, you mean." He laughed. "I think Sal was in your office earlier with some files. I saw her go in there when I came out of the breakroom."

"Where's Dane?"

"With Ashton." Metford looked up sheepishly at her and raised a hand. "Hey, I just couldn't do it today. He was in overdrive, and I needed to get this paperwork finished." He flipped a stack of papers.

"If you wouldn't let it build up for days, it wouldn't take you forever to get through."

"I need a secretary, but you know the Bureau, always saying they don't have the budget for the necessities and that we need to be more efficient." He scoffed, feigning indignation.

"Right." She patted his shoulder as she passed by. "You're a real trooper, Metford. Never seen a man so dedicated to suffering through so much just to do his job. I want to be just like you when I grow up."

He laughed as she walked out and headed for her office. It was a quarter past five when she hung her jacket on the wall hook. Almost time to call it a day, and no word about Mills' request. If anything had been said in the office, Metford would have told her as soon as she walked through the door. Maybe Mills had second thoughts. Maybe the protests turned into riots quicker than she anticipated, and she hadn't had time to make the call.

Nothing to do but check the files for the next case on the list. Ashton and Dane were working a smaller one, and they would probably have it closed by the next day. That was good. Ava liked marking cases off the board and knowing her team was making a difference in the world, making it a safer place one bad guy at a time.

She opened the file on top and took a deep breath as the picture of a murdered woman came into sharp view.

There was a knock at the door, and Ava looked up.

"Hey," Sal said as she walked in and shut the door.

"Hi. What's up?" Ava sat back in her chair. Shutting the door usually meant something was up and it was not good. Had Mills called in a complaint instead of a request? Sweat oozed from her palms.

"It's about the Vermont case. Mills contacted the Bureau late this morning."

Ava shifted in her seat and swallowed the lump in her throat. "I told her that she needed to put in the request if she wanted my help. I didn't know if she would or not for sure, though."

"She did."

"And? Did they approve it?"

"They did. They said you are to go to Woodsboro tomorrow morning. Get there as soon as possible and put the serial killer theory to bed."

"I can definitely do that. I'll pack tonight. Thank you."

"I like how you played that, by the way. Getting the okay to investigate a serial killer case that might not even exist. That was pretty smart, Ava."

"What do you mean?"

"You didn't get approved to go investigate this because the Bureau thinks there's a serial killer on the loose. They approved it because Mills wants you to prove to the families that there is *no* serial killer on the loose, and then she needs you to help get the protests under control. She thinks the killer on the loose theory is what sparked all the uproar."

Ava glanced down at the picture of the murdered woman lying face down in tall weeds near a stream in a forested area and then back to Sal. "It is. One group thinks the women were sacrifices to Satan. Another group thinks they were taken because the townspeople are celebrating Satan's holiday. Yet another group thinks the other two are wrong and that Halloween is just a harmless tradition passed down through the generations celebrating the last harvest of the season, and they're mad at the others for trying to get it outlawed in Woodsboro."

Sal nodded. "And then there are your opportunistic teens using the situation to be destructive, Mills said. Sounds like she might have needed more than just you to help out. Has she reached out to neighboring counties?"

"Not that I know of, but I will revisit that subject when I get up there tomorrow if things are as bad as she is saying."

"You're going to be on your own for this. The Bureau expects you to go up there and find nothing to support the serial killer idea, put it to bed, shut down a few protests, and be done. You won't even have backup. Just you, Mills, and whoever she has."

"That's fine. I can handle it, Sal."

"You'll have remote support from the team anytime you need it, and you have all my numbers. Don't get in over your head up there in the sticks, and risk getting hurt, or worse. You hear me?"

Smiling, Ava nodded. "I won't. Thank you."

"I'll leave it up to you to tell the team you're going to Vermont. I know Metford and Dane wanted to go with you. They're not going to be too happy."

"I got this. I'll explain it to them." That was a conversation she was not looking forward to having.

At six-thirty, Ava headed home from the bar. Metford and Dane assured her that they were okay-ish with staying behind. The final decision hadn't been hers, after all.

As soon as she made it home, she called Jamie to announce her arrival the next morning.

Her next call was to Sheriff Mills.

"I was expecting you to call a lot earlier than this," Mills said.

"I only got the news just before I left work. Is there a hotel or motel in town where I can stay and be close to where the last three girls went missing? I want to work the newest cases and work my way backward."

"I can arrange something a bit more private for you. It's a small house between The Great Hall and where the Abbots live. Not much, but it beats the fifteen square feet you get in the motel rooms, and you don't have to leave to get something to eat unless you just want to."

"Thanks. I appreciate that. How soon can you have it arranged? I'll be there by morning."

"I can have it arranged within the next ten minutes, Agent. All I need to do is make a call and get a code for the lockbox that holds the key."

"I can catch the early flight at four in the morning."

"You'll be coming in from Burlington International. You should be here in time for breakfast. I'll see you then. Come to the station and see me as soon as you get here."

"I'll see you then, Sheriff."

Ava finished packing and then proceeded to toss and turn in bed until after one. When her alarm sounded, she sat bolt upright and wide awake as if she had not slept at all.

CHAPTER ELEVEN

Six Days before Halloween

To say Woodsboro was small was an understatement. As Ava passed under the red light at the beginning of town, she could see all the way to the end of Main Street, or at least where Main Street split in two directions.

A large shopping plaza on the left held a dozen or more small shops, and in the same parking lot at the far end was a large feed, seed, and hardware combination store. There was a large sign announcing farm equipment sales and repairs behind that building.

Across the street from the shopping plaza, a strip mall had been started but never finished. There was a doctor's office, a rent-to-own place, a gym, and two or three empty spaces that sported For Lease signage. It looked like an unfinished idea pulled from someone's head and plopped down on pavement. Only three cars sat in the parking lot and they were parked in front of the old Victorian Era house that had a sign out front stating that it was the Women's Historical Society of Greater Woodsboro, Vermont. Est. 1959.

"Greater Woodsboro?" Ava asked as she idled by the place.

At the end of the block and separated from the unfinished strip mall by small concrete curbs sat the post office, and beside it was the court-house—both larger than necessary, she was sure.

According to the signs, the sheriff's office was behind the post office and down the hill a bit.

Ava signaled to turn even though there were no other cars in sight on the road. She turned at the intersection, mildly surprised to see that the road stretched farther than she had thought. There were a few more businesses and restaurants down that way.

She pulled into a slot in front of the sheriff's office. If twenty-five people had crowded into the front lobby of that station, it would have been a claustrophobic experience for everyone involved. It was probably one of the smallest stations she had ever seen.

"Thirty-five hundred residents," she reminded herself as she looked around the lot.

Walking into the station, she was greeted by a stocky woman with a mountain of mousy brown hair pinned up on her head.

"Hi, how can I help you, ma'am?"

"Special Agent Aviva James here to see Sheriff Wanda Mills," Ava said.

The woman's eyes went wide for a second and she nodded. "Hold on. I'll call her, honey, uh, I mean, Special Agent James." The woman's cheeks reddened as she fumbled with the desk phone.

A few moments later, a tall, solidly built woman in her mid-fifties rounded the corner from the hallway.

"Agent James, I take it," she said, thrusting out her hand.

Ava returned the gesture. "And you must be Sheriff Mills."

"I am. Good to finally meet you in person. I must say, you're a lot skinnier than I thought you'd be, but I guess you'll have to do. Can't throw you back now, can I?"

"No, I'm afraid this isn't a fishing trip, Sheriff. And don't let my size fool you." Ava tried to hold her temper in check. Mills wasn't outright being offensive, it was just so much a part of who she was that she didn't even realize she had said something offensive. Small towns sometimes bred and fed that kind of behavior. Which causes outsiders to feel ostra-cized and offended. Ava was becoming accustomed to being the outsider, and less and less offended by the way she was spoken to.

Mills laughed and clapped her on the back. That hand was big and hard. It was a good ol' boy's gesture that Ava had not been expecting, and she had to shuffle her right foot outward to keep her balance.

"Come on into the office and let's have a chinwag for a minute before we get this day started."

Ava followed the sheriff four steps down a hallway and into the office. There were no pictures of Mills holding her kids or playing with her dogs. No pictures of her looking tenderly at her husband and vice versa. No construction paper jack-o-lanterns and ghosts made for grandma by the grandbabies, either. Mills' ring finger didn't have a ring or an indentation or even a white line to indicate that a ring had been there in the last few years. Had she ever been married? Did she have kids? What about parents? There were no pictures of people at all in her office space. It was a cold space. Cinderblock, tiles, metal, glass, calendars—and not the foofy kind with cute little pictures, but the big boxy kind with big open squares to write stuff in—a computer, a couple of guest chairs, and boxes filled with files. That was it. No personalization beyond the Humane Society coffee cup on her desk with pens and pencils jutting out of it.

Mills handed Ava a business card. "I put the code on the back underneath my personal number. Don't lose that. You never know when you might need it. Deputy Marsh's number is on there, too. If for some reason you can't get me, Marsh will help you. I've already given him the low-down on what's happening. I'd let you meet him, but it's his turn to pick up donuts for the office. He won't be in until eight."

"That's fine. I'm sure I'll meet him soon enough. Do you have the files on the missing girls? All of them?"

"I do. The digital files are online, too. I have a couple that comes in every quarter and makes sure everything is digitized and filed correctly. I never learned how to use this damn thing for all the stuff they want me to use it for. I'm old school to the bone." She bent to the side far enough that Ava was sure the wheels on the chair would just skeet to the side and send the sheriff crashing to the floor. There was a thick thudding sound and then Mills hauled a brown file box from the floor. "Here it is, but I really don't know what good it'll do you. Seems like a mighty waste of time to me."

"As I said, I want to go over all the files just to cover my own backside. I have to double-check everything as part of the assignment," Ava fibbed without the slightest hesitation. There was no way she was going to go through the trouble and worry of getting on the case just to breeze through it and say there was nothing there without making sure. If she was wrong, fine. If she was right, she would investigate it just like any other case, and she had full confidence that the Bureau would back her play.

Mills huffed out a weary sigh and shrugged. "All I can say at this point is if it gets this business cleared up about the serial killer, knock yourself out. Just please, don't go ripping through town and questioning the families unnecessarily so they get any more upset than they already are. I don't want people turning on each other. I don't want any more trouble than we've got right now."

"You've got my word. I'm here to help, not hurt. And I'll fly under the radar as much as I possibly can. Now, is there somewhere I can get a good breakfast?"

"Get back up to the intersection and turn left on Main. There's a little diner two blocks up on your left wedged in between a smoke shop and a coffee shop. It's called Bluebird Pancakes and More. They specialize in breakfasts of all kinds, too, not just pancakes. The coffee shop next door is the best coffee and pastries in town, too. They're open seven days a week, seven to seven."

"I didn't realize Main Street went that far up. I thought I was at the beginning of town where I came in."

Mills chuckled. "It don't go much farther. It's only a little over a mile long and has only three red lights. No need for them in this town. You won't need much time to get the layout, and you don't need to worry about getting lost in town, either. It's farther out where you might run into a little trouble. GPS isn't so spot-on out in the willywags sometimes."

"Oh?" Ava had planned on using GPS to find her way around the county so she didn't need to have Jamie, Mills, or a deputy escorting her everywhere.

Mills nodded. "Guess that happens when you get so far out from bigger cities. We don't have the best internet speeds up here, either. Like I said, though, if you need anything call me or Marsh."

"Thank you, Sheriff." Ava took the box of files and headed back to her car.

At Bluebird Pancakes and More, she reached for Charity Beaumont's file and then thought better of it. Taking it into the small diner would attract attention, and anyone who glimpsed it would likely recognize the name. Being a new face, Ava would attract enough attention as it was. She left the file and replaced the worn lid on the box. At least the thing didn't look as if it had been put on a shelf and left untouched. Mills had obviously put all the files for each girl into the box at some point, and she had revisited the box often. Why had she done that if she was convinced the girls were just runaways?

Ava spent the rest of the day after breakfast in the small house on Pine Street going through the box of files and getting to know as much as she could about the missing women and their lives.

Time and again, it hit her hard how young Charity was. She was a high school senior with a 3.7 GPA, and everyone said she was a good student, a great friend, and a reliable, trustworthy person in general. The picture of her showed a slight girl with fair skin, light green eyes, and long strawberry blonde hair who probably melted hearts with a smile. She looked like the kind of sweet girl who had Mom, Dad, Grandma, and Grandpa wrapped around her pinky by the time she was an hour old.

And Ashley Garland was even younger. She was only sixteen, and though not as sweetly pretty as Charity, she was still a beautiful young lady with her whole life ahead of her. She struggled in school, and there were notes about her truancies in the file. She seemed to have come from a more difficult position than Charity in the popularity forum as well, but in Ava's opinion, she was just like a million other sixteen-year-old girls. No worse at all, and no worse off.

By the time she had read through the files, it was dinnertime, and her stomach wasn't shy about letting her know it was unhappy with meals being put on the back burner yet again.

Back on Main Street, she went to the large shopping plaza she had seen on her way into town and parked in front of The Grill. What grill with such a creative name served bad food, after all?

A cheeseburger and plate of fries later, she once again headed out the door. She followed Main Street to the forks in the road and followed the straighter one. It took her to a large Catholic church. Saint Mary's. She recognized the name. The youth group protesting the haunted house was part of Saint Mary's Catholic Church. She had a location to put with the group when she met them. And she would inevitably meet them. Turning around in the parking area, she went back and took the other fork.

The utility company was at the end of the first block, and after that, there were only residential houses on large lots lining both sides of the street. She drove for two miles, and the houses became sparser and the road less pristine until finally, she was on a gravel and pavement mix road that didn't even have white lines on the sides. There was only the ghost of a double-yellow line down the center. She drove for another fifteen minutes without seeing another house at all. Only scrub and fields and a couple of small areas with trees that looked to have been small orchards once upon a time.

The sun descended in the west, and Ava turned to head back to the house on Pine Street. As she neared her destination, she looked for The Great Hall, but didn't see it.

Mills had been right about not getting lost in town, and about not needing long to get the layout memorized. It was simple as long as she was only traveling the grid of streets in town, but the businesses were crammed together, stacked on top of each other, and laid out so that she was going to need someone to point out where the girls had spent their time. They all worked and lived and hung out in Woodsboro. She needed to be able to go to those places and walk the same paths the girls would have walked, see the same things they would have seen, feel the same ambiance of the town that they had felt—or as close to it as possible.

She called Jamie once she settled on the sofa.

"Are you here? Where are you staying? If you don't have anywhere yet, you can stay with me. I mean, Bailey's here, too, but she won't bother you. Are you in town or at the airport?"

"Jamie," Ava said.

"Sorry. Yes?"

"I've been here since before breakfast this morning. I told you last night that I would be here early this morning, remember?"

"Yes, but I hadn't heard from you, and I just thought that maybe your flight was delayed, or something came up at work. I'm just excited that you're here, and I want to help in any way that I can."

"I appreciate that, and that's actually why I'm calling you. I need your help."

"Whatever you need me to do. Wait, if it's something tonight, I'll have to call a sitter. It might take me a while. The Banners live way out—"

"No, not tonight. I was thinking tomorrow."

"It's Saturday tomorrow. I'll still need to get a sitter, but that will give me enough time to call the Banners tonight and see if Julie is free. If she's not, I can get the agency to send someone over. They're really good about that."

Ava hadn't thought about the next day being Saturday and Jamie needing a sitter for Bailey. "Maybe this isn't a good idea. I wasn't thinking. You have Bailey."

"No, I want to do this. I want to do this for Bailey as much as I do for the missing girls and their families. This is our home. It's Bailey's home. We love it in Woodsboro." She went quiet. "And it's the only place Bailey remembers her dad. The last place I have memories of him, too. I want to feel safe here again, and I want to know it's safe for Bailey as she gets older. Can you understand that?"

"I can." She didn't have to have kids of her own to feel that on a soul-deep level. Everyone deserved to feel safe in their own hometown.

"I can meet you, or you can come here about ten. Does that work for you?"

Ava cringed. "Sure. That sounds just fine." It was better than asking Mills or one of the deputies to show her around. At least Jamie had a personality that was people-friendly. Ava imagined riding around with Mills would be akin to riding around with a grizzly bear. One that had access to a firearm and an arsenal of sarcastic insults at the ready.

"Great. Thank you. Now, you want to come here since you've never been? It's easy to find, I promise."

"I'll take your word for it," Ava said.

"Ooh, famous last words of valiant adventurers the world over." She tittered nervously. "I'm just kidding. It is easy to find. If you can remember a couple of turns, you'll have no problem."

"I'll also have no problem calling you to come get me if your directions get me lost, either," Ava joked half-heartedly.

"Oh, cells don't work all the time out this far."

"Seriously?" Ava's heart sank. What had she gotten herself into?

"Yeah. I hate to tell you, but… kidding again. Mine works fine most of the time. It's farther out where they give you trouble. I better stop, or you'll be thinking I live a hundred miles from nowhere."

Almost too late for that. If town was any indication, the rural areas would be just that. Ava noted the turns from Main Street and read them back to Jamie.

"You got it. You won't have any problems. I'll see you at ten?"

"I'll be there."

They got off the phone, and Ava wondered if she had signed up for a day of chaotic nervous joking from Jamie that would hinder her progress on the case rather than help. She wasn't used to working with someone as chatty and energetic as Jamie seemed to be.

She went back to the files and fell asleep amid the fanned-out pages detailing the last sightings of six young women who should have been enjoying the coming holiday with their friends and families.

Her dreams were splattered with blood and scattered with bones that cried out for help as she made her way over them in complete blackness.

CHAPTER TWELVE

Five Days before Halloween

IT ONLY TOOK THIRTY MINUTES TO GET TO JAMIE'S HOUSE THE NEXT morning. The only traffic was a few pickup trucks and two tractors once she got out of town.

Jamie's property was far enough removed from town that it certainly felt as if she lived a hundred miles from nowhere. There were fields and trees as far as Ava could see in all directions. The few structures out in the distance were barns. Isolation seemed to be the word of the day.

The house was a large, white farmhouse from about the sixties that had either been maintained very well or updated very well. The land was flat around the house and two very big vegetable gardens were laid out to the left. The only things growing were pumpkins. She couldn't tell what the green sprouts in the rows beyond were, or if they were anything at all.

The smaller garden that Ava imagined was Jamie's personal garden had been laid out closer to the back of the house.

"Ava," Jamie said as she rushed out the side door.

"Jamie, hi."

Jamie had not changed much since high school except that she looked older. That was true of everyone nearly a decade after graduation, though. Her hair was the same shade of soft brown, and her smile was just as measured as it had been in school.

She came in for a quick hug, catching Ava off guard. Before she could reconcile the hug with even an awkward pat on the back, Jamie had pulled away.

"Come on in. Bailey is just putting on her shoes and getting her whiffle ball out from under her bed."

Ava looked around, confused. "Is the sitter already here?"

Jamie stopped walking. "Shoot, yeah, about that. Would you care if we dropped her off at the preschool? That's where Julie Banner is for the day. She is running a daycare out of the building on Saturdays now, and I didn't even know it. Haven't had to use her in a hot minute." She shrugged and grinned sheepishly and she motioned around the place. "No need, you know?"

"Oh, well, yeah. That's fine, I guess." A child in her car? While she was driving? And it wasn't even her child? Yeah, she could do that. No sweat. No big deal to be responsible for someone else's kid at all.

"If you don't want to, that's fine. I'll just take her in my car and meet you there."

Why had Jamie not called to let her know about the new development before she drove all the way out to her house? "No, it's fine. If you trust my driving that much, who am I to question it?"

Jamie laughed and motioned for her to follow her inside.

Bailey was a carbon copy of her mother except for her lighter shade of brown hair. Jamie had called it dark blonde, but Ava would have called it light brown. It was instantly obvious why Jamie worried that Bailey would fit the killer's profile in a few short years. She was only eight, and she looked all of eleven.

"Gosh, you're tall for your age," Ava said.

"Daddy was tall, too. Mama says I get it from him." Bailey smiled as she clutched the whiffle ball between her hands. Jamie's description of her looking like a porcelain doll had been very accurate.

"Come on, Bailey. We need to go so we don't make Ava late for her work."

"Are you going to catch the mean man who did something bad to all those girls?" Bailey asked, taking Ava's hand as they went out the door.

Ava lifted her hand, trying to gently pull it away from the little girl, but she held tight. "Uhm, well, I'm here on a case, Bailey. I'm not allowed to discuss the details with anyone. Especially little girls who should be thinking about all the fun they're going to have with Julie and the other kids at the preschool today."

Bailey's eyes lit up and her mouth formed a little O. "Julie always gets us ice cream in the summer, if we're good. It's almost Halloween, so she'll give us candy. Maybe even caramel apples. Yum!"

"I heard that, little lady," Jamie said as she opened the back door of Ava's rental car. "And no, you won't get caramel apples because there will be little kids there today and that wouldn't be fair to them." She motioned for Bailey to get in.

"Aw, Mom," she whined. "Not the *babies*. I hate it when they're there. They're always crying and running around tearing down our Lego towers. Why didn't you tell me they'd be there?"

Jamie shut the door and got in her seat. "Because then you would have argued about going at all. Macy and Hannah will be there to play ball with. Be happy with that, little lady."

"Fine, but can we get a caramel apple after?"

"We'll see. You have to be really good to get one of those."

"Yes, ma'am."

Bailey quickly bounded out of the car the instant they parked at the preschool.

"For all the fussing and pouting, you'd never know she was unhappy about staying today, would you?" Jamie asked as she got back in the car.

Bailey ran and whooped with a group of girls that looked to be her age. They laughed and tossed the ball back and forth as they went.

"Not at all."

"You want to start with where Charity lived? It's pretty close, and so is her friend's house where she was getting ready for the corn maze and party afterward. Then I can show you where the corn maze was. The field is empty this year. There's never been another corn maze in it since then."

"Where is Cool Scoops, the ice cream shop where she worked after school?"

Jamie pointed toward the back of the shopping plaza buildings. "Just around there. Like almost everything else, it's on Main Street."

Ava drove there first. The shop was, like the others in the plaza, very small. Ten customers might have fit comfortably inside at once. Any more than that, and it would have been crowded.

"It's not somewhere people typically go for a sit-down unless they're waiting for a movie to start, or they're just wasting twenty minutes," Jamie explained. "That's why they only have those three little booths along the far wall."

"Do the same people own the place as when Charity worked here?"

"They do as far as I know. Charity worked about sixteen hours a week, and most of those hours were over the weekends. She only worked a couple of hours after school three days a week. Monday, Wednesday, and Friday afternoon. I know, because Bailey insisted we come every day after school. She came in long enough that the other girl could take a break and stock things up in the back, put away the truck orders, just things like that. The weekends are when they're busiest. I guess for you, though, it wouldn't be very busy. I bet things in DC are crazy compared to here, aren't they?"

Ava chuckled. "Most of the time. I live in Fairhaven, Maryland now, though. It's not as fast-paced and crowded. I have my own little house with a little yard. I get to look out over the Chesapeake Bay. Nothing like what you have, and I do have neighbors. Everywhere. But it's nice. And it's quiet for where it is. I like it."

"That's good. I'm happy for you. Got a Mr. James hanging around waiting for you to get back home?" Jamie smirked and it was the same mischievous look from all those years ago in school.

"Nope. Just me."

"A dog?"

Ava shook her head. "I'm away from home too much. A dog wouldn't survive me, I'm afraid."

"Get a cat, then. They're like having a cactus, you practically can't kill them by being absent or not putting out food for them every day. They will eat the rodents and be glad you're not around annoying them with attention."

"Wow, and I thought you were a real animal lover."

"I am, but I'm also a realist. We have five cats at my house."

"I didn't see any."

"Exactly. They aren't social at all with outsiders and only come around during the middle of the day to be petted and noticed for a while. They demand food, take naps, and then they're off again until it suits them to come back."

Ava shook her head. "I wouldn't want a cat wandering my neighborhood while I'm at work. Too much traffic." They got back into the car. "Point me to Charity's house."

Ava followed directions and listened to Jamie's flood of information about the girl. It was amazing how much she knew about Charity Beaumont. How did she remember it all? Perhaps she had known the girl better than Ava at first thought. Passing acquaintance in Woodsboro, Vermont might mean something a bit different than it did in Maryland or DC.

Jamie proceeded to show Ava where the friend's house was located, the corn maze. She took Ava to Laura Halvorsen's apartment building, pointed out the unit, and gushed a bunch of personal things about her that made it seem as if she had been buddies with the young woman who'd been labeled the town's wild child. She did the same with Ashley Garland and Elise Abbot, even taking Ava along the road where she believed Elise was snatched from that night.

Even in a town of only thirty-five hundred people, Jamie shouldn't know everyone as if they were family members, and that was almost how well she could give details about some of the girls and their families. She just rattled off small details as if she had been around to witness them firsthand.

"That was a lot, huh?" Jamie asked as they pulled onto Main again.

"It was. It really was. Are you up for a late lunch, or do you need to get back to Bailey? I don't know what time you need to pick her up."

"Oh, not for a few hours yet. Sure, I'd love lunch. Want to go to The Grill back at the shopping plaza? I love their crispy chicken sandwiches. I know they're deep-fried and horrible for me, but I can't help it. Sometimes, I have to indulge."

"If I hear your arteries start chugging and slugging, I'll make you put down the sandwich."

Jamie laughed. "You won't. I'm in good health. I know it'll catch up to me if I don't keep my bad habits in check. That's why it's rare that I do indulge."

Ava had to hand it to Jamie, the crispy chicken sandwiches were great. And absolutely slathered in delicious grease.

"Scott loved these things." Jamie indicated the sandwich. "We used to come to town a few nights a week and eat out. No matter where we went, if we had time, he always came by and got two of these to take home. He'd take them for his lunch the next day."

"Did you two have a lot of different crops and land to keep up with?"

"Yeah. Eight hundred acres of just fields." She blew air between her lips. "It was a time, let me tell you. We really made the money. It was great. But we spent a lot, too. Just the upkeep and prep for the next planting season took a lot of money, but we still had plenty. We farmed pinto beans, soybeans, sunflowers, corn, and peas. I started keeping the bees and the vegetable gardens. Did you see them? I have two one-acre vegetable gardens just past the house, and the one smaller garden at the back that we use for our own cooking and canning."

"Yeah, I saw them. It looks like a lot of work to me." Ava grinned.

Jamie shook her head. "Not really. It's all I've got. It's all I know, really. I sold all the planting fields except for fifty that I plant in soybeans. I can't keep up with the other stuff. Soybeans are simplest to manage and the lowest maintenance I could find. I sell enough honey, eggs, and vegetables to make my bills and groceries every month. Everything else is profit."

It sounded like a hard life, but who was Ava to question what made someone happy? It seemed to make Jamie happy, and Bailey certainly didn't seem to be suffering from the lifestyle.

"It was in July, the height of summer when Scott was killed," Jamie said absently as she pushed fries around with her finger. "Bailey was only five, and I was so devastated and terrified. I had a five-year-old and eight hundred acres of fields that were contracted out for the next season, workers depending on those fields for their paychecks. I didn't know what to do." She sighed and dropped the fry. "That seems like a hundred years ago. Or another lifetime altogether."

"It's getting easier to cope with now, though, isn't it?" Three years ago. Height of summer. July. The first girl went missing three months later.

"Yeah. What is it they say about time?"

"It heals all wounds?"

"Yeah, that. Well, it's bullshit, but that's what they say. Ain't healed a thing for me, but it has made it easier for me to get out of bed and face the day without my husband by my side where he should be. It has made it possible for me to see our little girl growing more every day, and seeing how much she looks like her father without breaking down into tears and wanting to hide in my bed for days."

"I think she's a carbon copy of her mother."

Jamie shook her head. "I see Scott in her perfect little nose, in the slightly mischievous uptilt at the corners of her mouth, in the length of her face, the height of her forehead, the dip in her left eyebrow, and her mannerisms."

"Must be things that only parents can see."

"When you have one of your own, you'll totally get it."

Ava just arched her eyebrows.

"Ha, I can see it on your face. That's a mighty big *if*. Right?"

She nodded. "How long after Scott's death did you sell all that land? I'd imagine that would take a while, right?"

"No, not at all. There are some big farmers that a lot of people don't necessarily like always willing to snatch up prime farmland—especially if it's in a good location. Five hundred acres of ours were in such locations. I hated to see it sold, but I didn't have a choice. It was gone by the second week of October."

Scott died in July. And on Halloween night, Charity Beaumont went missing from a corn maze. How far away was that maze from any of the land Jamie had to sell?

"I can't even imagine what eight hundred acres looks like. It's like having millions of dollars. I can only imagine it's numbers on a page."

"Oh, I could show you where a lot of it was. Some of it was close, some of it was here in Woodsboro County, and the rest was located counties away. If I could have managed it, I would have kept more than fifty acres in Woodsboro, I'll tell you that much."

"That'd be great. I would love to see some of the land while I'm here. I have an affinity for agriculture and animals."

"Yeah, I remember. Me, too."

They had shared the love of animals through school, and Ava had an interest in agriculture, which Jamie had been passionate about even back then.

July, she lost her husband, and her entire life changed drastically. October, her property holdings dwindled to practically nothing. October, Charity was gone.

Did it mean anything? Was there a connection? Surely not. Just coincidence. But could she be certain?

Would she need to investigate her old high school friend?

CHAPTER THIRTEEN

Four Days before Halloween

WOODSBORO WAS MORE THAN MAIN STREET AS AVA HAD FIRST seen. There were small shops of the mom-and-pop variety down every side street, and the place had a homey feel to it with all the banners hanging across the streets announcing the festivals and the decorations strung between the lampposts along the sidewalks.

Walking through the town gave her some insight that she could not get from the driver's seat of a car. For instance, it was half past nine on Sunday morning. There was hardly any traffic out, and it seemed that businesses were open as usual. Driving along the street, she would not have noticed that the lights were on in a lot of the establishments, but there were Closed signs on the doors. The hours of operation underneath uniformly had the closed businesses opening at one in the afternoon and closing again at five. Had she ever lived or even visited a town in which businesses operated around Sunday church service hours?

She recalled her grandmother talking about stores being closed on Sundays when she was a little girl. Not that Ava had ever given it much thought over the years, but had it been because everyone in town attended church services? Or was it a religious observance not to work on Sundays? Or to shop, perhaps? She made a mental note to question her mother about it when she got back home.

Remnants of the protests clung to the town like soot from a wildfire. Shredded decorations here, spraypainted storefront windows there, leaflets flapping against the curb that preached against celebrating the vulgar, unholy holiday.

A couple of store owners had gotten creative with their painted windows and used them as backgrounds for Halloween paintings of their own that announced pre-holiday spook-tacular sales on candy and costumes and decorations.

As for the protests, it seemed that they had quieted, and no real violence had broken out. Ava was glad of that much, and Mills had to be happy about it. A small group of teens came out of a shop and headed up the sidewalk toward Ava. An unhappy storeowner stood behind them, shaking a flyer and telling them to go home and play video games and leave him alone.

Ava kept walking. The group must be from one of the protesting churches, but which one?

One of the girls smiled sweetly and held out a flyer. "Do you know Jesus, ma'am?"

Ava didn't reach for the paper. "No thanks. Are you from Saint Mary's, by any chance?"

The girl looked horrified and shook her head vehemently. "You're not *Catholic*, are you?"

She said the word as if it were a dirty word. Ava shook her head. "I'm not. I was just asking. Are you from First Street Baptist, then?"

The girl's face relaxed, and she nodded. "Yes, we all are. We're out trying to get people to accept Christ as their savior so their souls will be saved, and they can go to heaven and live in paradise forever. This isn't the only life, you know."

"But shouldn't we all try to be good to each other and respect each other's rights and property while we're here anyway? This life matters, too, right?" Ava countered.

The girl blinked twice, and a mutter wafted through the small group. Several pairs of confused eyes blinked at her as if entranced.

"We do try to get along with everyone, respect their rights, and we do respect everyone's property," the girl said, thrusting the paper toward her again. "Just take this and read it. It might give you some comfort during hard times."

Ava looked down at it and shook her head. She pointed to a painted window a few yards away and the destroyed decorations across the road that had been set up in a kids' park. "That's respecting people's rights and property?"

Several sets of eyes dipped toward the pavement and then couldn't quite find their way back to Ava. The girl's face was one of five that went completely crimson. "That's different. They're celebrating evil and indoctrinating the little children so that they grow up thinking it's okay to worship Satan in all his vile forms." She shoved the paper toward Ava angrily. "You should take this, lady. You need Jesus as bad as they do if you think all this is okay. Lucifer's Lounge? Dancing Devil Productions? Do they sound like moral establishments to you?" She motioned for the group to follow her, and they all walked away quickly, casting smug looks at Ava as they went.

Ava folded the paper and stuck it in her pocket. They were kids. Granted, most of them were old enough to know better than to follow along blindly, and the girl was plenty old enough to know what she was doing by leading them, but they seemed to believe their convictions wholly. They didn't come up with their ideas on their own, either. They had been taught by their elders. Parents and grandparents and their community leaders. It was hard to change generations of belief, and that wasn't her job in Woodsboro. It wasn't anyone's job.

Ava had not made it to Lucifer's Lounge. She had been more interested in getting a good look at everyday life for the girls in Woodsboro. Continuing her meandering walk, it didn't take the skills of a super-detective like Sherlock Holmes to see that there wasn't a lot to do in Woodsboro. Not for girls or boys. Or women or men, for that matter. Ava walked around until church services were over and the town livened up a little to get a look at family interactions. She did a lot of sitting on benches and standing in stores so she could see the few customers, moving around only enough to keep from drawing unwanted attention.

Woodsboro seemed very traditional in its values and societal roles for men and women. Men did the wood chopping, and women did the cooking. Men mowed the lawn, and women washed the laundry. Men were the mechanics and worked on the cars to keep them running while women raised the kids and kept the house neat and presentable—that sort of ideology.

Not the ideal setting for modern girls coming of age in the twenty-first century, surely. They would feel claustrophobic, repressed, beaten down, and hampered in ways Ava could only imagine. If her mother had forced her to take up housekeeping and cooking and sewing and babysitting as a way of life, a pattern for her future when she had hopes and dreams and aspirations of her own, she might have gone stark raving mad. No wonder Sheriff Mills was inclined to say the girls were runaways. Especially if the parents were pushing the outdated agenda on them the way Ava saw as she walked around.

Having seen enough, she went back outside to get a better feel for the town, the larger picture. How did the residents mingle and get along? Was there small-town hospitality? Did everyone know everyone else as she was imagining? Did everyone have personal knowledge about others like Jamie seemed to have about the missing girls? Some towns were like that. Some towns were comprised of *old families*. Families that established the town and had known each other for hundreds of years. The intimacy between a few families was to be expected, but Jamie wasn't from one of those families. She was a transplant, just like Scott had been.

Sometimes, the town gossip or busybody will have that kind of information about others. With all that Mills had said about Jamie, and most of it was not good, she hadn't once called her a gossip or a busybody.

As she moved back through town, working her way toward her rental on Pine Street again, Ava smiled to see that the residents and business owners had been out replacing and renewing signs for festivals and different celebrations for Halloween all through town.

One store was replete with every aspect of a harvest theme she could imagine, though with the recent fires being set, Ava would have opted out of the haybales and the strawmen and women in the big display window at the front.

Other stores had the icons of Halloween: Dracula, The Wolfman, The Mummy, Frankenstein, and the Bride of Frankenstein. Still others boasted generic fright-fares like ghouls and demons and vampires and zombies. Some of Ava's favorites were the ones smashed out in cute vintage décor, and she couldn't help but step into the old drugstore to get a better look. She found a jack-o-lantern, a black cat, and a witch's hat fashioned of thin wood and bought them. Molly would love the jack, her mother would like the hat, and she would keep the cat. If anyone suggested she get a pet again, she could always tell them she had a black cat.

Walking over to her rental, she saw signs for special events taking place every night through November first. There were themed parties for kids, teens, young adults, adults, and even at the nursing home. Near the end of the block, there was a sign announcing a potluck on Halloween evening at Penny's Floral Designs—Everyone Welcome! *Please bring 1 appropriately themed food with you!*

What was an appropriately themed food for a Halloween potluck? Ladyfingers? Graveyard cake? A pork roast tied and decorated to look like a human arm or leg? Or was it a much tamer potluck? Good thing she probably wasn't attending.

By six-thirty, kids were running around with plastic masks, and it was still almost a week before Halloween. That didn't seem to matter as the generic pirates, ghosts, robots with LED eyes, and even a Little Bo Peep wandered around huddled into their little groups laughing and telling scary stories before they had to get back home for the night. Several grumbled that they had to get to bed because of school the next day.

Sheriff Mills had not been exaggerating when she had said the folks in Woodsboro looked forward to the holiday.

CHAPTER FOURTEEN

Four Days before Halloween

A VA WENT BY THE LITTLE HOUSE AND DROPPED OFF THE DECORA-tions she had bought. It was almost time to meet the principal and a teacher at the high school. They had agreed to meet her there at seven—after church services ended—so she could ask them a few questions about the missing girls discreetly.

The high school gymnasium had been converted for a Halloween party. The signs all over town announcing the event proved it was going to be a big deal not only to the kids at the school, but to people in town, too.

Ava was impressed that the kids had built and painted elaborate props, a small stage, a photo-op area where attendees could get their pictures taken with the monster of their choice for only five dollars. A portion of the proceeds went to the school's art program, and the other portion went to the charity in town that helped the less fortunate with food, utility bills, rent, and medicine.

Most of the decorating was finished, and all the painting seemed to be done. A fog machine sat in the corner along with a tall helium tank. Beside that sat two large plastic totes filled with regular balloons. Another tote held Mylar balloons that were Halloween-themed and could be purchased for different amounts. Again, proceeds would be split between the two causes.

Mr. Nuss was a large man in his late forties with a military air and ramrod straight back. The ultimate high school principal. His piercing eyes never left Ava's when he spoke to her.

"You asked to meet us here on a Sunday evening to ask about a former female student who might be in trouble, Miss James. I'm sorry, but I don't understand the need for such secrecy. Are you a reporter? Because if you are, you can go back out the same way you came in." He motioned slightly toward the big door behind Ava.

"I'm not, Mr. Nuss, and I appreciate you and Mrs. Gaines meeting me here on such short notice. I'm not a reporter, and my name is Special Agent Aviva James with the FBI." She flipped open her badge and ID.

They exchanged a wide-eyed look.

Ava motioned to indicate the Halloween setup. "What's the security going to look like for this big party? The whole town is free to attend, right?"

Mrs. Gaines, the English teacher, shook her head. "Only the night before Halloween, and only between five and seven. The night of the school party, it's only students."

"And what kind of security will be in place to keep an eye out that they're all safe? That no one can just walk in off the street in a costume, or that the students can't just walk out anytime they please?"

Again, they shared that bewildered look. Mrs. Gaines cleared her throat. "Of course. There will be plenty of chaperones at all times, and the doors will be monitored all evening. No leaving and coming back in. No nonsense going on. Not on my watch. I won't stand for it. It's good clean fun for the kids who want it. Troublemakers should just stay home and not waste their time because I *will* call their parents to come get them if they act up."

Ava nodded slowly. She liked the cut of the teacher's jib, but it seemed that she maybe wasn't quite getting it. "So there won't be any police presence around inside or out?"

Mr. Nuss shook his head and his eyebrows met over the bridge of his nose. "No, of course not. This is a school function. There's no need for police. We've never had those kinds of problems before. Why are you asking? What's this really about?"

"I'm here to ask you about a few former female students, and I would appreciate your full cooperation. I'm investigating the disappearances of six girls over the last three years. I take it you know what I'm referencing."

They exchanged another look, and then Mr. Nuss nodded to Ava. "Come with me. Let's sit and talk." He led her to the opposite end of the gymnasium and they sat in folding chairs at a long table where kids had been making construction paper signs and covering them with black and orange glitter.

"So, I take it you know some of the girls who went missing?"

"We both did," Mr. Nuss said. "Charity Beaumont. She was troubled and had a dysfunctional home. It showed up here at school often."

"That's odd, because everything I read in her files said she excelled at her work and that she was trustworthy, dependable, a good friend, and an all-around good girl. I mean her GPA was…" she made a show of checking her notes, "a 3.7?"

Mr. Nuss looked down at his hands and shook his head. "I don't like to be the one to say all this, but Charity was troubled. Her grades were good, and when you could get her to commit to doing something, she usually would, but most of the time, she came up with an excuse as to why she just left you hanging instead."

"Her life at home was… *not good*," Mrs. Gaines reiterated. "At the best of times, her mom was intolerant and her dad was verbally abusive. And that was in public. Who knows how far it went at home?"

"Then why all the conflicting reports in the case file?"

Mr. Nuss leaned his arms on the table. "Agent, sometimes, people put on their rose-colored glasses when they're *remembering* someone. They prefer to remember them as a better person than they really were. Especially if they were less than nice to that person."

"You mean kids at school treated Charity badly? She was bullied? Picked on? What?"

"Take your pick," Mrs. Gaines sighed. "It really depended on what day of the week it was. She was beautiful, naturally smart, and a lot of the other girls just resented the hell out of her for that."

"Mix that in with her social awkwardness stemming from the way she was treated at home, and you had a recipe for disaster. It's just my opinion, but I truly believe she's a runaway. I wouldn't blame her at all if she did run away and never contacted anyone here again. Ever," Mrs. Gaines added with a nod of finality.

"What about Ashley Garland and Laura Halvorsen?" Ava asked, still shocked to learn such conflicting news about Charity.

Mrs. Gaines shook her head and tapped the table with one short fingernail. "Those girls were the epitome of wild. Especially Laura. If there was ever a wild child in Woodsboro, she was it. There was nothing she wouldn't do, or try to do. Nothing too outlandish, dangerous, or taboo."

"And Ashley was right there with her, no matter who tried to talk sense to her about it," Mr. Nuss added with a sad look. "If you don't believe us, Laura worked down at Sandy's in town. You can go down there and talk to them. Those girls were just as apt to hop in a car and take off with a stranger as not."

"We worried all the time what they might do, and what the other rebellious girls in town might try to do because they saw them doing it. They might be anywhere right now, and neither of them gave two hoots about anyone or anything here, so naturally, they wouldn't call or come back," Mrs. Gaines said.

"Not even their families?"

Mr. Nuss shook his head. "Maybe especially not her family in Laura's case. It was worse than Charity's situation, and there were rumors—"

Mrs. Gaines turned on him like a rabid dog, smacking one hand down on the table and causing a bottle of glitter to topple. "Leo," she exclaimed. "Rumors are like cancer. You should know that better than anyone."

Ava wasn't going to let up, though. "What rumors, Mr. Nuss? I need to know everything you know to do my job thoroughly. If there's a chance I can help even one of these girls..." Ava let the rest of the sentence go unfinished.

He pursed his lips tightly and looked down. "She's right. They're just rumors, and they don't bear repeating without evidence."

"Laura got into drugs and drinking in middle school, and she never looked back. She liked that lifestyle, and there was no helping her," Mrs. Gaines said firmly.

"I don't understand why the families are so concerned now. If they were so dysfunctional and things were going on that never should have been going on, why did the families demand that Sheriff Mills reopen the cases?"

"To put it simply, they need to keep up appearances. On a deeper level, maybe they feel guilty as hell about how they treated those girls, and rightly so. Maybe they think demanding justice for them somehow justifies being horrible parents and shitty human beings," Mr. Nuss said.

Mrs. Gaines closed her eyes and lowered her face toward her hands as if embarrassed. "And I know you're going to ask about Luna and Tina next. Let me tell you before you do that everyone in town knew them because they were *pagan*. They thought they were so different, so special. They ruffled a lot of feathers around town."

"They were always trying to be different than everyone else, draw attention to themselves, make a spectacle for one reason or another," Mr. Nuss interjected with a sour look to match the one on Mrs. Gaines' face. "Always with their baubles and their feathers and rocks trying to show conservative Christians in town how their beliefs were better because they had been around longer. People overlooked them for a long time, but then they started telling people that early Christians cannibalized the pagan beliefs and shit out Christianity and its accompanying holidays. That made a lot of people understandably upset, and a lot of people just didn't like them."

"That's also not exactly the picture the files paint of those two girls. They didn't seem like harsh or confrontational people at all," Ava pointed out.

"They might not have said things in those exact words, but that's the exact points they put across. They weren't confrontational, but they never failed to push their agenda when they were in town either. It was constant, and it rubbed people the wrong way after a while."

"Do you think someone here could have done something to hurt them because of it?"

"No," Mr. Nuss said. "But they might have grown tired of being ignored and shunned and denied at every turn and just decided to move on."

"Without even their cars? That seems like a stretch, don't you think?" Ava asked.

Mr. Nuss shrugged indifferently. That one movement let Ava know that he had a run-in with the women, with the *pagans*, and he didn't think highly of them. It didn't bother him at all that they were gone. And Mrs. Gaines' silence proved that she was on board with him in that respect.

"I said everyone knew them. Maybe I should have said that everyone knew of them, or about them. They were strange birds. Who knows what they might have taken into their heads to do?"

"What about Elise Abbot?" Ava asked, biting back on more logic that would have riddled Mr. Nuss' theories with holes big enough to drive dump trucks through.

He shook his head, and so did Mrs. Gaines.

"I didn't know anything about her. Just what others said after she disappeared," he said.

"And what was that, exactly?" Ava asked, totally expecting another conflicting story about another missing woman.

"That she argued with her boyfriend, Bobby somebody, and that she stormed off toward her house in the dark from the party they were attending, and that she was never seen or heard from again."

"And do you think when she stormed off into the dark that she just kept going? Maybe missed the turn to her house because it was dark, and ended up where? Maybe over in Maine? Down in New York? I guess she just got lost, right? And her cell phone died, so she couldn't call for help once she realized she was way off course. Oh, yeah, and all her money was at home, so she didn't have any money to get a taxi or rideshare, either. Got it. I'll be sure to note all that in the file. Thanks for your eye-opening information." She stood. Anger boiled in her chest at their blasé attitude toward all the missing girls.

"I'm sorry we couldn't give you what you wanted to hear," he said. "I thought you wanted the truth."

"You two act as if those girls asked for whatever happened to them. They didn't. I can assure you of that much. And it's so much easier for all of you to just say that they left of their own accord instead of taking the rougher route and trying to ask the harder questions to find out what really happened to them. Does it even matter to you that they were under the legal drinking age, and that the world out there is very, very dangerous—especially for young, attractive women." She leaned across the table. "And it's double dangerous for ones that are from troubled backgrounds."

Ava turned on her heel and stalked across the gym and out the door. For the next five minutes, she wished she had never opted to speak with either of them.

Later, in the bedroom of her rental, she was glad she had. It had opened her eyes as to how people in Woodsboro thought about the girls. Maybe not on the surface, but deep down, she knew how they felt about them, and it wasn't pretty.

She was even more determined to find out what had happened to them. It seemed that no one else cared enough to do it. It seemed others had sighed with relief after they had gone as if they had been nothing more than burdens.

CHAPTER FIFTEEN

Three Days before Halloween

AFTER SPEAKING WITH THE PRINCIPAL AND HIS CRONY THE NIGHT before, Ava went over the logged interviews again. They were mostly brief, and from a wide variety of people. She tended to read them only to glean facts. Names, locations, times, and so on. Over coffee, she read them again for tone, and she found that many of them were similar in tone to the conversation she'd had with Nuss and Gaines at the high school. It sickened her.

"Scratch a friend, find a foe," she muttered to the empty kitchen.

Why did it seem that some of the most offensive things could be found in small towns? Those idyllic places everyone pined away for. Was it because they were held to such idyllic standards from fiction stories that crimes *seemed* more offensive in small towns? Or, was it because it really showed how fractured and tainted human nature was? Even in small towns of only thirty-five-hundred people, there were all the atrocities and double standards, and deceits and betrayals that lurked in big cities. It just didn't matter the locale; humans could be horrible to each other.

Ava drove to the field where the corn maze had been three years prior. The last place Charity had been seen. The field where she had apparently evaporated into thin air.

She wasn't sure what she was looking for, but she hoped something would show up to give her some direction. The police files were completely devoid of any evidence, and so were the interviews.

It was just a regular field. Nothing at all special about it. One acre bordered on two sides by a thinly forested area that wrapped around the two sides. A deep ditch ran along the third side, and the area used for parking marked the fourth side. Beyond the parking area was the road. Beyond the thinly forested area were more fields owned by the same farmer. Again, nothing special. Crop fields.

The land was featureless with slightly rolling hills cut into rectangles for planting crops as she stood in the field and turned in a circle. She could see for miles in all directions except where the trees separated her field from the others. In the distance, mountains reached up toward the sky and stretched out to fill the horizon. Gnarly, naked branches like fleshless finger bones endlessly reaching for heaven.

A chill, stiff wind hit her, blasting her hair and whipping her light jacket back. Gasping, she pulled the jacket closed and turned sideways as she headed to the perimeter of the field. At the edge closest to the forested area, she peered into the shadows. She could see the fields beyond, and dread crept up her spine and tickled its long fingers outward over her shoulders. She squinted harder into the woods but saw nothing out of the ordinary.

She finished walking the perimeter of the acre without finding a clue to point her in any direction. Although she had not expected to find the smoking gun that would crack the case, she was still disappointed when she left and headed to the theater where Laura and Ashley were last seen.

The place was old and small. Its last update had probably been in 1990, and its seating capacity was about fifty from what Ava saw. She was accustomed to sprawling multiplexes with balconies and hundreds of seats. It was good to visit the places in town and try to put herself in the mindset of the girls as they were there.

Nothing stood out except the small size of the place, and that it had only one screen, which meant they only showed one movie at a time.

There wasn't much of a selection going on unless there was another hiding somewhere in town.

When she left, she drove to the road where the girls likely disappeared from. People saw them leave the cinema on foot. They were seen leaving the back way out of town and heading in the general direction of Laura's apartment. And then, nothing.

The road was tree-lined like so many other back streets in town. There were only two houses at the other end, and if someone had snatched the girls from there, it was unlikely that anyone would have heard them scream.

"But both girls were grabbed right here," she said, stopping the car and looking around at how close she was to town and the two houses at the other end of the street. If the girls had been panicked and screaming and fighting…

Maybe Nuss and Gaines were right? Maybe they just hopped into a stranger's car and sped off somewhere unknown? Maybe Ava had been wrong?

She couldn't believe that. Maybe Laura and Ashley had gotten into someone's car without a fuss, but they didn't run away. Who ran away and left all their personal things behind?

The question plagued her as she drove to The Great Hall where Luna Bradford and Tina Leeyung had gone missing. Again, it was a small place that could be seen from several other places. It wasn't completely obscured, not hidden away in some dark alley, or out in the wilderness. People drove by it on a regular basis. The residents saw the place on their daily commutes all the time. They saw The Great Hall, and they saw the parking lot where the women's cars were parked after everyone else had left that night.

"And yet, somehow, people came to the conclusion that Tina and Luna just decided to skip town and leave their vehicles behind," Ava muttered as she walked through the parking area where the cars had been.

She hadn't expected to find anything that would help out the investigation, but again, she got a good dose of perspective. One blood-curdling scream could have been heard from that location. It was almost a sure bet it would even echo.

Ava cupped her hands around her mouth and belted out one short, sharp vocalization. She nodded as the sound bounced. The residential homes were too far away down Baker and Moss for people to hear the screams maybe, but Sandy's Grab-N-Go was just across Baker Street. Its back faced The Great Hall's parking lot.

"And nobody heard or saw anything." She looked around another minute and then got back into the car to go to the place where Elise Abbot had gone missing from.

As she drove down Moss Street, on the right-hand side, she passed the turn onto Pine where her own rental sat, passed two vacant lots filled with scrub tangle and two houses at the end of the block. On the left side of Moss Street, she passed four houses. All the houses on Moss Street were older, but the owners had maintained them meticulously. Usually, the homes on the backstreets of small towns were the ones that looked like stereotypical trap houses, but not in Woodsboro.

Short Street was at the end of that block. Ava stopped at the sign to get a feel for the neighborhood. No one came out of their houses. No dogs bounded to the street to bark and alert that she was just sitting there—a stranger in the middle of the day—even though a beagle lay on a porch to her left.

Beagles normally barked if the wind changed direction, but not that one. It looked old and fat as it raised its head just enough to look at her. Holding eye contact for exactly two-and-a-half seconds, it lost interest and put its head back on its paws.

She turned right and idled down the road. The path Elise took that night started in the wooded area behind The Great Hall. That path would have taken her past Pine Street and let her out on Short Street.

Ava stopped the car at the outlet of the path and rolled down her passenger window. Her field of vision into the woods was unencumbered. The path was visible for several yards even with the dead leaves covering the ground—it was at least as wide as one lane of the street, it looked mostly flat, and Ava doubted there were many turns. It was nearly a straight shot from where she was to The Great Hall. Elise walked away from her boyfriend and the party and entered the woods not far from The Great Hall.

"If she had been snatched in the woods, no one would have heard her screaming." Ava got out of the car and stepped onto the path.

She walked about three hundred feet in and stopped to look around. The path was still clearly visible, flat, and wide. And visibility wasn't so bad, either. From three hundred feet, she could tell where the roadway was. There were no leaves on the trees. That meant there were none when Elise went missing, which meant she would have seen if someone was following her, or lurking around the mouth of the trail as she stepped out onto Short Street.

There was a streetlight at each end of Short Street. Maybe the lights weren't there when Elise went missing. Maybe she couldn't see that someone was there, but that would mean she couldn't have seen in order to traverse the forest trail, either. At least, not without some sort of light. It was safe to assume that being a residential street, the streetlights were working that night, and that the light from them reached a few yards into the edge of the woods on the Short Street side.

The houses on Moss were close enough that Ava could see the one at the stop sign, and the one across the way at the corner of Short and Moss where the beagle was lazing on the porch. If Elise had screamed...

But then, what if she hadn't? What if none of them had? What if they'd been drugged, or quickly snuck up on from behind and gagged so quickly they didn't even have a chance to cry out? It was another question to consider.

Ava got into the car and drove the few hundred feet to Elise's house at the end of Short Street. The road dead-ended just past the driveway in a shoddily paved circle just large enough to turn a car around on, which Ava did.

The house was a nicely kept two-story farmhouse trying to be modern. It wasn't working, but to each his own.

Driving back to her rental on Pine, Ava called Ashton. If anyone could see patterns in seemingly random events, it would be him. She spent fifteen minutes giving him the quick rundown of facts.

"Okay," he said, taking a deep breath. "All the victims are young females, between the ages of sixteen to twenty, with pale blonde to light brown hair. They all weigh between 100 and 120 pounds, which means they could be easily handled by your average size and strength male. All the locations they went missing from are sort of isolated, but still easily accessible by vehicle, and crowded around the time of the disappearances. Seems like there's a definite type of victim there. Definite type of attack he likes, too."

The portrait of the killer-slash-kidnapper came into sharper focus in Ava's mind. "Ashton, thank you," she said. "He's early to mid-twenties, white most likely, confident, fit, healthy, fits in with crowds, moves easily among them without standing out or drawing unwanted attention—"

"So, he's not deformed, ugly, rude, a real loner, or anything of the sort," Ashton interrupted.

"No, he couldn't be." She paced and thought about the man. "He can't even give off very strange vibes. You know, he can't give people goosebumps or weird energy when he's around them, or they would take special notice of him in a bad way. They'd remember someone like that being around, and they'd say something."

"If not to authorities, then to their friends, siblings, parents."

"Right. He's meticulous, and he plans things out. He's patient. Very patient and dedicated to what he sets out to do. Which in this case, seems to be kidnapping and maybe murdering young women. He strategizes, follows his plans through to the letter, he doesn't deviate from a carefully crafted plan, and he leaves no evidence behind."

"That means he's very smart, and you know what that means."

"He's very dangerous," Ava said.

CHAPTER SIXTEEN

Two Days before Halloween

IT WAS TIME TO START LOOKING AT THE MEN WHO MIGHT HAVE BEEN in the lives of the missing women and to eliminate as many as possible as quickly as possible. Halloween was only two days away. The next victims were already on someone's radar, and figuring out whose radar was Ava's task. If she were being truthful, it was more like her obsession.

It was a task she couldn't do alone in a timely manner. She would need help to narrow down the long list of suspects; otherwise, she would be searching out peers, friends, friends of friends, fathers, brothers, cousins, store clerks, ticket salesmen, and anyone else she could manage to put on the list. That would take roughly ten years to work through.

The next victims didn't have that long, which meant Ava didn't have that long.

Sheriff Mills was in her office sitting at the desk with a large cup of coffee, an open bottle of aspirin, and a half-full bottle of Pepto-Bismol in front of her. The dark bags under her eyes and the tension around her lips made it abundantly clear that she wasn't having a good morning.

"I hope to hell you're having a better morning than I am, Agent James," she said when Ava knocked at the open door. She motioned for Ava to enter.

"Can't say." Ava moved to a chair and nodded to the coffee and medicine. "Standard desk set, or is something up?"

"Nah, these came in a set with the stapler, sticky notes, and those nifty little primary-colored paper clips down at the Discount Dollar. Really get your money's worth these days." Mills smirked and twisted the cap off the bottle, turned it up, and drank a hefty dose of the sickly pink stuff.

Ava cringed internally. "Love to see what comes in the bathroom starter kits."

Mills guffawed and then put her hand over her mouth, cutting the sound off abruptly. "Damn. An agent with a sense of humor. Will wonders never cease?" She put the lid back on the bismuth and dropped the bottle into a drawer. "Need something, Agent James?"

"I came up with a profile of who might have taken the women, and I need some help with finding who might fit that profile. If you have time, it would help a lot."

Mills nodded solemnly. "A profile, huh?"

Ava nodded back.

"I've heard about you guys coming up with those. Do they really work? Aren't they just kind of generic? You know, white male, late thirties to early forties with mama issues. He was made fun of when he was in school and daddy was mean to him, or some nonsense like that?"

"A lot of people think that way, but that's because they don't understand how the profiling works. Sometimes, profiles *seem* pretty generic, but they're not."

Mills kept nodding and staring at her hard as if really trying to process and understand the worth of what she was saying. After the silence had long since grown uncomfortable, Mills smacked her lips, spread her palms, and thumped the blotter with them a couple of times as she sat back in her chair letting out a long breath. "Okay, regale me, Special Agent James. Let me hear your profile of this serial kidnapper, and I'll see what I can come up with for you."

Ava quickly flipped open her notes. Before she could start, Mills held up a hand and sat forward again, rocking the desk chair and testing its mechanical limits as bolts and springs squealed for mercy. "Hold up. Am I going to be able to ask questions to refine this profile just for my own sake?"

"Of course. Ask anything you need to ask," Ava said. She was only glad Mills had agreed without an argument. She read off the profile quickly and clearly. Mills listened intently as she drank coffee and fingered the bottle of aspirin.

"Okay, that was succinct and much shorter than I expected, but I do have some questions," Mills said, popping three aspirin.

"Shoot," Ava said.

"I would, but then there'd be a ton of paperwork and an investigation into why..." Mills dropped the aspirin bottle into the same drawer with the bismuth and looked up sheepishly at Ava. "Just kidding. It helps pass the time and keep me sane."

Ava grinned and gave a slight nod. Quick wit was always a good sign, but the dark humor she could have done without. Mills was an unknown for all intents and purposes, and saying things like that didn't come off as funny, it came off as a little worrisome.

"Anyhoo, why do you think the perp is male, first off?"

"Most serial kidnappers or killers are male. Very few females perpetrate these types of crimes, and even fewer become serials."

"So, we're just going on statistics here?"

"No. A male would be more likely, more logical, if you will. A male would have an easier time handling these women."

"We'll say it's a man. Now, why's he in his twenties? Why wouldn't you think he's older and wiser? He did get away with it, if he existed at all."

"He would have to fit in with the same crowd as the women did. He couldn't stand out, and if he was much older, women in their twenties would almost immediately peg him as an outsider, a creep, a pervert. No one came forward about any older man lurking around any of their groups, parties, or any gatherings that fit that description."

"I can live with that, I guess. Why's he have to be white?"

"Because most serial kidnappers and killers in the United States are white males. That doesn't mean there aren't other races who ultimately perpetrate these crimes, but again, it circles back around to him fitting in. I have noticed in my time here that the population of Woodsboro is predominantly Caucasian. Am I mistaken?"

Mills shook her head. "No, you're not mistaken. I guess I just never really thought about it, and I would bet that most of the residents here never really did either. You say this fella is fit, confident, and real smart, too?"

"He is. He must be. He left behind no evidence, drew no unwanted attention, and even upped the ante every year. He's likely a bit of a thrill-seeker, too, but he wouldn't let that override his meticulous nature. He likes to plan and strategize."

"Patient as Job," Mills said, rearing back in the rolling chair again and looking toward the window. "I know a few men who fit the profile—not now because they'd be either too old or too unhealthy."

The phone rang and a deputy knocked at the door, which was still open.

Mills held up a finger for him to wait a minute as she snatched the phone from its cradle. "Sheriff Mills here," she nearly barked. The lines around her mouth deepened and her brow furrowed.

The deputy shifted from foot to foot, and Mills shot him a warning look. He turned to look down the hallway and ran a hand over his thinning hair.

"I'll be right there," Mills said and dropped the phone back to the cradle. She stood. "What is it?" she barked at the deputy.

"It's trouble at the end of town where the haunted house is. There's a group of kids—"

She flapped a hand at him. "Ah, hell's bells, I'm headed there now. Damn townie kids." She turned to Ava. "I've got trouble. You're welcome to ride along, but I gotta go now."

Ava stood and followed. "I'll ride. You had me at haunted house," she said.

The phone rang again as they stepped out of the office.

"Shit on a shingle," Mills said. "Answer the phone," she yelled to the deputy. "If it's about the kids, tell 'em I'm on my way."

The deputy spun a one-eighty and darted into the sheriff's office.

"What's going on?" Ava asked.

"Group of town kids is pissed at a group of church kids and they're having it out over next to the haunted house. Townies are saying the churchies are trying to ruin Halloween for everybody."

Mills flipped on the sirens and lights as she accelerated out of the parking lot. It was unnecessarily fast. The town wasn't big enough to warrant that type of racing speed. She didn't bother putting on her seatbelt, and Ava hadn't either. Town wasn't that big. It was a three-minute drive at best.

Then Mills schooled her in just how deceptively sprawling Woodsboro was as she took side streets, rough-paved roads, blew through intersections and red lights and even through a parking lot to circumnavigate lined-up traffic at another light. Ava was tossed around like a marble in a washing machine while Mills' hefty stature and her grip on the steering wheel kept her anchored in the driver's seat.

A gut-wrenching seven minutes later, Mills slowed the cruiser and rolled into view of what could only be described as a teenage mini-riot. The adults trying to keep things civil were no more than ignored chaperones who each only held sway over one or two of the kids.

Mills blooped her sirens at the crowd and stepped out with the bullhorn.

Part of the Youth for Salvation group stopped shouting Bible verses at the haunted house workers about a hundred feet away and looked at the sheriff. The part of the group that was arguing with the townies did not shut up. They kept arguing and shouting, and things were going downhill steadily.

The townies hadn't physically hurt anyone. Yet. A few of them were getting in faces and throwing their arms and hands in the air around the heads of the church kids, though. Cheeks were red, eyes flared, and threats poured.

Mills blooped her siren again, and more of the Youth for Salvation group stood down. The townies were having none of it, though. They were fighting mad.

"Jessup Carter, June Hardy, Eric Hallowell, you three best get your asses on the other side of the street before they land in jail. You're too old to be getting in fights. Your daddies can't talk to the principal and get you out of it if you screw up out here in the real world," Mills said through the megaphone.

The three did as they were told and went to the other side of the street, where they continued to egg on the other, presumably younger town kids. Mills proceeded to blare the megaphone, and everyone shut up and covered their ears.

"Y'all better shut up, and I mean this second," Mills said. She followed the order with a few more names and threats to tell parents. "Now go on back home, or anywhere but here at this very minute, or you'll all spend Halloween night in the town jail whether you're underage or not."

Ava moved toward a young man who seemed to be the leader of the church youth group and smiled. He returned the smile warily.

"Hi," she said, looking over her shoulder at the dispersing townies. She turned back to the young man. "They're leaving. She'll probably make your group leave, too. You were all shouting some pretty serious accusations at the workers over there when we pulled up."

He nodded. "Someone has to call them out on their evil works, and all the adults in town seem to be too scared to do it. Maybe it's because they're not kidnapping and sacrificing older women; it's only the younger ones." He bobbed his shoulders and stared at her unblinkingly.

His boldness was admirable but shocking. It wasn't just a façade. No fake bravado hiding a chicken-hearted boy who quivered in his boots at the slightest noise. Some of the others in his group seemed to have obvious anger issues, others were only following the group, and still others seemed unsure of what they were really doing out there.

"You really think that's what's going on?"

Mills bulled through the thickest part of the Youth for Salvation group. She was greeted with gasps and vocalizations of dismay and shock at her rudeness. "I want you all to go home, or back to church, or wherever. Just like I told the others. I want you anywhere but here. I won't tolerate any more of this upheaval in my town. This nonsense will lead to no good and will get someone hurt."

"People have already been hurt," the young man said, turning to face the sheriff. "That's why we're here, Sheriff Mills. We cannot, in good conscience, allow them to continue to take our young women without consequences. The good Lord will pass judgment on them in His time—"

"Lucas, please, honey," Mills said with great, exaggerated exasperation. "Please, those men and women are only doing their jobs. You can't be out here harassing them while they're trying to earn a living. It ain't right. They've done nothing wrong, and we've talked about the missing girls—they probably ran away, or just up and left for a better life elsewhere."

"Is it their job to kidnap our women and sacrifice them to Satan? Are you condoning that? Is that your definition of 'just earning a living'?"

Ava put her hand on Lucas' arm. "Lucas, is it?"

He turned to her. "Yes."

"Young man, you best mind your tone with me," Mills said. "I want your *group* dispersed this minute, or I'll personally call for backup and see that each one of you is taken to lockup and your parents have to come get you." Her eyes turned stormy, and the tone of warning left her voice only to be replaced with a tone that was more akin to a dare. She was facing off with the leader of a youth group of a local church. Not a good look at all.

Ava nodded to Mills. "I need to speak with him."

Mills glared at her and then at him before turning her attention back to the youth group. They moved slower than she liked, so she barked at them again to get them moving. It worked. Ava motioned for Lucas to follow her to the corner of the street away from the commotion.

"Am I in some kind of trouble? I did nothing wrong. I didn't hurt anyone."

"No, you aren't in trouble, Lucas. I just wanted to know why you think the haunted house workers are kidnapping and sacrificing women to Satan."

"Dancing Devil Haunts?" he asked, raising his eyebrows as if that explained it all.

She shook her head. "Okay?"

"That's the parent company. Who even calls their company that? Who would glorify Satan that way?" He jabbed a finger toward the haunted house site. "Lucifer's Lounge. They call it that, as if it's a nice, everyday thing. It's just where Lucifer sits back in his easy chair and drinks coffee while watching the evening news. He's just like one of us. Nothing to fear here. Don't pay me any special attention."

"It's just a kids' holiday. It's all in fun. Granted, from the religious slant, I can see how it might be upsetting, but I don't understand how you can honestly believe they are kidnapping and sacrificing women to the devil."

"Okay, the same year this haunted house came to town is the same year Charity Beaumont went missing. You think that's just a coincidence?"

"She went missing from a corn maze, not the haunted house."

He struggled to keep his composure as he nodded. "I know that. Everyone knows that, but she disappeared nonetheless. In the months following her disappearance, a church burned down, and two farms were lost to the banks due to failing crops, which was something that had never happened before. One of the farms had been here since the early 1800s, and now, it's just gone. Developed into apartments, shopping malls, and a hunting lodge for tourists. Oh, and just before the next fall season, the Millers' six-year-old son shot and killed his three-year-old brother. It was an accident, of course, but Mr. Miller swore that he had unloaded that rifle and put the trigger lock in place just like he'd done a hundred times before. Both parents were in the house when it happened—they were in the kitchen arguing over what to have for dinner that night. I'd like to remind you that was only what happened in the *first* year after Lucifer's Lounge moved to town. Things have gotten progressively worse every year since, including that each successive year another woman than the year before disappeared and hasn't been seen since." He looked at the haunted house and then back to Ava. "This year, if I'm right, and I know in my bones that I am—God has told me that I'm right—four women will go missing on Halloween. I don't know what else to do to get the message out except these protests and shouting it from the rooftops."

"Well, you're scaring people, Lucas."

He barked out a caustic laugh. "Well, I hope so! I want to scare them. I want to scare them bad enough that they stay home and clutch their Bibles, get on their knees, and pray to God to protect and forgive them. Halloween isn't a Christian holiday, Miss…? I'm sorry, I didn't get your name."

"Agent James."

His eyes went wide. "Agent? As in Federal Agent?"

"FBI."

"Why's the FBI in Woodsboro, Vermont?"

"Trying to find out what's happened to those missing women. That, and keep the peace while I'm investigating. I know you're scared and worried for the women of Woodsboro, but don't cause any more trouble. Sheriff Mills would be well within her rights to charge all of you with disturbing the peace, harassing the workers and the town kids, and a whole slew of other charges, if she wanted to. And just between you and me, she might do it. She's stretched a little thin with all this right now, and the last thing any of us need is more distractions like this to deal with."

"You're really here looking for a serial killer?"

She shook her head. "No, I'm not looking for a serial killer, Lucas. I'm trying to find out what happened to those women. Totally different than looking for a serial killer. We've no reason to believe there's a killer at all."

"Right. Because for it to be a killer at all, there would have to be bodies."

"Right, and there are none. I came up to put that theory to bed and put everyone's mind at ease on that subject. Hopefully, while I'm doing that, I can find out what really happened. You'd like to know the truth about it, right?"

"Of course." He scoffed as if offended at her suggestion otherwise.

"Good. Now, if you, or anyone you know has any helpful information about any of the missing women, just give me a call." She handed him a card with her number on it. "Or call the sheriff and she can get in touch with me."

He grinned and shook his head. "I'd call you directly. The sheriff isn't known for being so friendly and inviting when it comes to this case."

Ava nodded. "Understood. Now, I'm sure those people really are just doing their jobs, so, I really need you to make sure your group doesn't heckle them and give them a hard time anymore. Can you do that?"

He shook his head. "You can say that because you haven't been here. You don't live here. If you just went over there and talked to them, walked through that place, you'd probably be shocked, and you might even find out that I'm right. I know Sheriff Mills has you convinced that we're a bunch of half-crazy zealots, but we're not. This isn't our norm. It's just the only thing I could think to do to draw attention to something we all feel is being ignored."

Ava looked over at the house and the site. It looked nothing out of the ordinary for a haunt. She had been around plenty of them, and that one looked like so many others that it was laughable. But something in Lucas' eyes made her take notice. Whether the place seemed sinister to her or not, whether the workers looked like normal everyday joes to her or not, they certainly seemed nefarious and evil to him. Otherwise, Lucas seemed to be a levelheaded young man with a high enough IQ to get him into a damn good university if he ever chose that path in life. He was articulate, confident, and his thoughts were well organized.

She stopped and looked at him again. That time through a new filter. It was the filter of her profile. He ticked a lot of the right boxes, but he also ticked a lot of the wrong ones. He would have stuck out in a crowd of partying, drinking, cursing, Halloween enthusiasts. He would have creeped out some of them with his religious talk and his bold, direct, unflinching eye contact. And he didn't seem to plan and strategize meticulously as the kidnapper would have. He admitted that he didn't know what else to do but cause the scene on the street and stand there yelling Bible verses and fire-and-brimstone threats at the workers.

"She's never said anything derogatory about any of you, first off, and this isn't being ignored. At least, not now. If I go talk to the workers and owners, will it ease your mind any?"

"It would ease my mind a lot, actually."

"Consider it done, then."

CHAPTER SEVENTEEN

Two Days before Halloween

LUCAS NODDED AND GAVE HER ANOTHER OF HIS WARY SMILES AS she started across the intersection toward Lucifer's Lounge. She couldn't figure how people could be so certain about the existence of God and Satan. There was no God without Satan, or vice versa. The whole thing gave her a headache. Some days, she believed in everything, and other days, she believed in nothing at all.

From across the street, the two-story house seemed decrepit and about to fall in on itself. The peeling white paint had turned gray, and windows had been boarded up or blacked out on the second floor. First-floor windows sported hellish paintings of smiling demons with screaming women in their clutches, drinking liquor, smoking cigars, and even one reclining in an easy chair staring at a TV as if he were possibly watching the news.

Had Lucas seen that? Was that what had sent him into a panic? There was nothing overtly terrifying or threatening about any of the decorations or the artwork. It was run-of-the-mill and borderline generic, compared to what she'd seen in the city. Nothing stood out except the name: Lucifer's Lounge Haunted House. Usually, haunts were rife with ghosts and ghouls and vampires and werewolves—the iconic Halloween staple monsters, but over the last decade, there had been a marked uptick in all things demonic. It was only natural for that interest to bleed over into haunted houses on the scariest night of the year. What haunt owner wouldn't enjoy a new cash cow to ride for a few years?

Workers struggled to set up the animatronics at the front where the crowd would gather later and form a line to enter the site. An intimidating tree that would undoubtedly move and speak in a threatening, guttural tone just to set the creepy mood. Just past that stood three witches at a bubbling, lighted cauldron. One stirred the cauldron, one cackled madly as her head tilted back, and the last stood with her lower jaw unhinged, head tilted at a severe angle while her body vibrated. Her voice came out sounding like that of a broken child's toy.

"Dammit," a man exclaimed as he jerked the power cord from an outlet box.

"Hello," Ava said, startling him.

"We're not open, if you couldn't tell," he said, scowling and turning from her.

"Agent James, FBI. Just need to speak with your boss. Unless you're the boss."

He turned to face her. His face paled, and he shook his head. "Nope. I'm Dallas. I'm just the prop super and emergency worker if there's ever an emergency during a tour."

"Where is your boss, Dallas?"

The man pointed at the entrance. "I guess inside. Don't keep up with them. Glad when they're not around, just to be honest."

"They?"

He nodded. "Nathan Helm and Melanie Gurdy." He gestured toward the house. "I need to get this bitch fixed." He turned back to the witch without asking the nature of Ava's visit.

She stepped inside the door. It was bright. All the lights were on—even lights no one ever thought about being inside a haunted house. Big rows of fluorescents overhead that flooded the rooms with brightness.

Nothing was left to the imagination, and every prop was revealed in vivid detail.

"So much for the suspension of disbelief, huh?" a female voice asked from the left.

Ava turned. "Hard to believe in ghosts and ghouls and demons when you can see the strings and power cords."

The woman—resplendent in tattoos and piercings, and with a shock of magenta hair—nodded. "We're not open, but I suspect you know that. You aren't supposed to be in here, but I suspect you also know that, so I'm tempted to believe you have some sort of business here. If it has nothing to do with Jesus saving my soul or the devil skewering me with his pitchfork, I'll give you five minutes."

"You know that whole pitchfork thing is just Hollywood, right?"

"Alright, you found your way in, find your way out. Don't make me call the sheriff." She put her hands on her hips and glared.

"I would, but I really do have business here. I'm not with any group... Ms. Gurdy, right?"

Shock registered on her face. "How'd you know my name? Who are you?"

Ava showed her badge. "Agent James. The sheriff and I were just settling the little disturbance across the street."

"FBI," she said with a cocked grin.

"That Catholic youth group was saying some really nasty things about your haunt and your workers, Ms. Gurdy."

She grimaced. "Mel, please. And you haven't heard the half of it, if you just caught today's latest ruckus. They've caused me so much trouble, you have no idea. They're the reason I've had to hire seven new people in the last week. Seven. These people don't have a clue what they're doing. Nate and I are having to train them." She jeered and shook her head. "They're helping us do their jobs, is more like it. This church stuff is ridiculous. Those kids need to be arrested or fined or whatever the sheriff can do. They are screwing with my livelihood here. Not to mention they've tried to destroy some of our props. I'm not too sure someone didn't try to burn down the house, too."

"Did you report any of this to the sheriff?"

"Yes. I made the reports myself. Of course, nothing ever came of any of them."

"People are scared, Mel. Those kids in the church group seem to think you and your employees had something to do with young women in town going missing since you came to Woodsboro."

"That's ridiculous. We run a haunted attraction, why would we have anything to do with missing women? And yes, I've heard them shouting that we're all going to burn in hell for sacrificing those women to Satan. I can assure you that we don't do that, either. I'm not saying that we're all perfect Christians, but most of us do believe in God and a few of us have a healthy relationship with Him." She pulled a small gold cross necklace up from the neck of her shirt, dangled it a moment, and dropped it back down her shirt. "And it didn't even burn my skin," she quipped.

"Would you mind if I looked around the place? I told the youth group that I would have a look around just to quiet their fears. They are determined that there is a kidnapping ring doing business right out of this place, and it's demonic, Satanic, in nature. If I can go back and tell them that I talked to you and some of the employees, saw nothing suspicious, maybe they will slack off the protests. Or at least do it quietly."

"I'll have to ask Nate. As far as I'm concerned, the whole group could come in and look around if it would shut them up. They're making me nuts." She turned and walked farther into the house.

The tall, lanky, and equally tattooed Nate agreed, and Ava did a quick but thorough walkthrough. The areas forbidden to the general public were only used for storage or electrical needs. One small closet space had a makeshift pallet of blankets where a new hire slept at night so he could be there in case someone broke in, but that only lasted two nights, and he refused to stay again after the people came onto the enclosed back porch and destroyed one of the animatronic zombies.

Ava thanked the owners and the employees she had spoken briefly with before leaving.

Lucas stood leaning against the church van when Ava returned. He pushed away from it, flapping his hand behind him and shushing the members inside. "Well? What did you find?"

Ava held out both hands and shook her head. "It's just a haunted house, Lucas. I promise. I went through every single room. There were banks of fluorescents on, and it was so bright in there that there weren't any shadows even. I'm telling you, the place is just for entertainment."

Disappointment crawled over his handsome features, pulling them and giving a hint of what he would look like in about twenty years. "Did you talk to any of them?"

"Oh, yes, I did. They are not impressed with all the antics out here on your end, either. You've cost them seven employees in a week. That's a lot, and they could probably take legal action if they really wanted to press the issue."

Mills ambled over with her thumbs hooked in her belt like an Old West sheriff. "Well, make any arrests, Agent?"

Ava shook her head. "Not a single one. They're all clean over there, Sheriff."

Mills bobbed her head once, looked at Lucas, and stepped up into the van. "Ya'll hear that? Nothing is going on over at that haunted house except entertainment. Just because it's not your cup of tea don't mean you can keep on with all this hollerin' and screamin' and raisin' hell with these ridiculous accusations. You hear me?"

Several heads nodded in unison. Lucas started for the bus, but Ava stopped him. "Not a good idea. She's right."

He jerked his arm away from her, clenching his jaw as he stared at his youth members through the open windows.

"Good. I don't want a Satanic panic in Woodsboro. I don't want any trouble from any of the youngsters in my town. There's enough unrest without you adding to it." She stepped out of the van and sighed. "Lucas, take 'em on back to the church or wherever they're supposed to go, and don't get them in trouble. Leave this stuff to us." She pointed to Ava and herself.

"We have a right to protest ungodly events, Sheriff," he said in a civilized, well-mannered tone.

"Yes, you do. Yes, you do, but that's not what you've been doing, is it?"

He dropped his gaze to the ground and shook his head. "No, ma'am."

"If your group decides to protest, you must do so quietly and peacefully," Ava said. "The owners and workers already have enough reason to take action against your group. The church surely wouldn't like being dragged through all that."

His cheeks burned and his jaw muscles worked. "No. We won't cause any more trouble. But I can't speak for the townies. If there's trouble, it won't be from us."

"Thank the good Lord in heaven," Mills said, patting him on the shoulder before walking back to the cruiser.

He turned to Ava. "Thank you for talking with them and looking around. I trust you and your judgment." He tilted his head in Mills' direction. "Hers, not so much."

Ava shook hands with him. "You've got a good head on your shoulders, Lucas. You'll do a great job with the youth group. I trust your judgment." She smiled.

He smiled. It was the first unguarded smile Ava had seen since meeting him.

She got back into the cruiser with Mills and immediately buckled her seatbelt.

Mills laughed. It was a big, jolly laugh. "The return trip won't be near as rough."

"Not much on taking chances." She patted the lock on the seatbelt and grinned.

Mills laughed again. "Where were we now? Oh, yeah. That profile of yours. I've been thinking, and I came up with a few men in town who might fit."

"That's great. Thank you," Ava said. When the hell did she have time to think about who fit the profile, though?

Mills handed her a badly wrinkled piece of paper with five names scribbled on it.

"I know it's not many, but that's all I can think of right away. At all, really. People around here just aren't geared to think that way, you know. They don't plan in the way that would allow them to cover their tracks completely. I'm not saying they're not that smart because some of them are smart. Maybe genius smart, but just not in that kind of way. We both know it takes a certain kind of person, a certain kind of smart to do these things and get away with them."

"You're not wrong about that. Are you telling me that you think these five could think that way? They are that type of smart?"

Mills vocalized something that sounded like a mix between a groan and a sigh. "I don't know, for Christ's sake. Maybe. They're the right ages. They're smart, cocky little shits, fit in with most crowds their age, and they're manipulative. I figure that plays right into that whole liking to plan and follow through with shit, because they always seem to get what they want in the end, no matter the cost to others."

"Yeah, that sounds about right. That would mean they're patient and they see things through to the end. Manipulation requires strategy. And the sociopathic tendencies seem to be present in spades, too."

"That's sort of a requirement for a man who's going to be a serial kidnapper or killer, unless I'm very, very wrong."

Ava chuckled. "You're not wrong, Sheriff."

"Didn't think so. I was one time, though."

"Really?"

"Yeah, and it was horrible."

"When were you wrong about?" Ava asked, playing into what she was sure would be a good story.

"Damnedest thing… I can't remember, but I know if I ever was wrong, it would have been horrible." She glanced at Ava and then burst out laughing.

Ava joined. It felt good to laugh, and it ended soon enough of its own accord.

"You know, Agent James, Woodsboro has its problems. I'm not blind, and I'm not an idiot even though some might disagree. Despite all the problems, I love my little town and most of the people in it. But in a town so small, I know way more about a lot of the residents than I ever wanted to know. That includes some of the families of the missing girls and some of the girls themselves."

"Do you know something you're not telling me, Sheriff? Something that might have bearing on this investigation?"

"Not in the way you're thinking. Laura Halvorsen. The wild child of Woodsboro." Mills sighed and readjusted her grip on the wheel. She shook her head as if deeply disappointed.

"What about her? Every town has a wild kid. Most towns have many more than just one nowadays."

"And I don't know anything about the ones in other towns personally, do I?" she bit.

"How about you let me in on what you know about Laura and let me decide if it has any direct bearing on the investigation one way or the other."

Mills tilted her head this way and that as if figuring out how best to say it. "She didn't have the best home life. Mama and Daddy aren't all they seem to be, and when Laura first went missing, they didn't even act as if they were worried. It was more of an inconvenience for them that people were coming around asking questions. Good ol' Ivory even ran one of my deputies off his property saying the sheriff's department was unduly harassing him and Deliah."

"They were angry that you were trying to find Laura?"

Mills nodded. "Seemed that way to a lot of folks including me. And before you get all worked up, I investigated Ivory. He didn't do anything to Laura. Well…" She scoffed, tilted her head sharply to one side and thumped the steering wheel with one hand. "He didn't kill her or dump her in the river or a big hole somewhere, let's put it that way. He did plenty to her. So did Deliah."

"Not a big fan of mysteries," Ava said. "What did they do to her? If I need to be arresting them, I need to know right now."

"No, I told you, they didn't kill her. That girl just ran out, and I don't blame her one damn bit. I might have been tempted to do worse if I were in her shoes. Thankfully, she didn't wake up that morning and choose violence, I guess. Mama Deliah was, and probably still is, a pill-popping alcoholic. Daddy Ivory is just a mean-ass drunk who would rather talk with his fists than his vocabulary after he's had a few Millers or a little Jack, if you know what I mean. Deliah doesn't care much what comes or goes as long as she's left to her pills and alcohol. Been in and out of rehab eight times over the last ten years. Guess there was never much hope that Laura would fare much better than her parents."

"That's a shitty way to look at a kid's future and not intervene."

"What could I do? I'm the sheriff, not the kid's aunt or sister or grandmother. My hands were tied all that time. All I could do was watch the decline of a family unit, the decay of another youth, the ruination of yet another life before it ever truly got started. You think that shit feels good? You see it every day, I'm sure, but you see it in a bigger city where your relationship with the people is sterile. You don't know them. I've known these people my whole life. We're neighbors, we've borrowed things from each other, had barbecues together, attended church and town functions where we sat side by side, so you don't get to lecture me on how shitty it was to look at Laura's future, make assumptions about it, and not intervene. If I could have, I damn sure would have. Make no mistake about that. There was never anything to be done from a legal standpoint. If Deliah put up with Ivory smacking her around while he was drinking, there was nothing I could do. He didn't lay a hand on Laura back then. That came later; when she was older. Teen girls come standard-equipped with a smart mouth and an attitude that could make a saint commit murder. By then, she had learned from her mother to keep her mouth shut about it."

"Then how do you know he did it at all?"

"Rumors have a way of getting around in a small town."

"And getting way out of proportion."

"When you've been sheriff for a while, you learn which stories are true and which are not. He was hitting her, alright. Not all the time because Deliah was fresh out of rehab again. He was actually giving Laura a break at the time. Maybe Laura just saw it as her break, her time to make a run for it."

"Did her father ever do more than that to her?"

She pressed her lips into a tight line. "You mean, did he ever molest her?"

Ava nodded. "That's exactly what I mean."

"Never that I know of, but there were stories about it. I asked Laura once, but only that once, and she denied it. Said she'd slit his throat in his sleep if he ever did something like that."

"Did she admit that he ever hit her?"

"No, but she never denied it, either. She just smirked, thanked me for the burger, grabbed her soda, and left the diner. We never really spoke again after that. She actively avoided me. I think she felt vulnerable, like I knew too much, and she didn't like that." Mills drove back into the parking area of the station and turned off the engine. "It's those sorts of things I know about all the families involved. Not all of the stories are bad, either. Like when Charity Beaumont graduated eighth grade and her mama had bought her the prettiest little dress and matching shoes. Took her to the salon and had her hair done. You know, the whole nine yards. That was the prettiest that girl ever looked, and you could tell she felt like a princess. Biggest smile in the whole room. She hugged me after graduation and thanked me for helping her get on track during the school year. I had caught her skipping school and had a long talk with her. I checked up on her once a week after that for the rest of the year. Sometimes, I would help her with homework for thirty minutes, sometimes I'd buy her a donut, or we'd just talk out here while she waited on her mama to pick her up. See where I'm going with this?"

Ava hummed. "I think so. It's all very personal to you, isn't it?"

"It is. I've exhausted all avenues of investigation here. I don't know what else these families expect me to do. I say the girls left, and I think they all had reasons to do it. If you find differently, so be it. Maybe I'm too close." She got out of the car and slammed her door. Looking over the hood at Ava, she smiled wanly. "At least I'm woman enough to admit that might be a possibility."

Ava stood there and watched Mills go back inside the building. Was it actually a hindrance that Mills knew so much about the girls and their family dynamics? Familiarity breeds contempt, and sometimes, it breeds exasperation and a tendency to look the other way in certain situations.

Maybe all the case needed was a fresh set of eyes, after all.

CHAPTER EIGHTEEN

One Day before Halloween

AVA ANSWERED JAMIE'S CALL BEFORE HEADING OUT THE DOOR FOR the day.

"What's up, Jamie? Is everything okay?"

"I don't know. Is it? I mean, where are you with the case, Ava? I'm worried that nothing has been done so far and more girls are going to go missing over the holiday. Tell me I'm wrong. Tell me I'm right. Just tell me something."

Jamie's voice was tight, and Ava had no problem envisioning the pulled, worried expression on the woman's face. "Well, to be honest—"

"God, just what I was afraid of. You haven't found anything, have you? Has Mills gotten to you, too? Has she convinced you that the girls all just ran away?"

"It's not that. The case has so many—"

"Mommy," Bailey wailed from somewhere in the background of Jamie's house.

Ava's heart skittered, and she sucked in a near-panicked breath. What had happened to the little girl? "Jamie? Jamie, what's happened? Is she okay?"

"Bailey, hold on, sweetie," Jamie said in a muffled voice that let Ava know she was talking but not into the phone.

"But I wanna go, Mommy. All my friends are going, and I got dressed up. See?"

The last word stretched out until it almost turned into another teary wail. It was something to do with a Halloween celebration, no doubt. Ava's heart settled back into its normal rhythm. Bailey wasn't hurt, just throwing a tantrum because she wanted to go do something, and her mother was likely set against it.

"I said to give me a minute, Bailey." Jamie's voice was sterner. "Sorry about that," she said into the phone. "Bailey wants to go to the harvest movie and dinner afterward tonight, but I'm too scared to take her."

"I want to go to the Halloween party tomorrow night, too, Mommy. It's not fair! Not fair!" Bailey yelled.

Everything went silent in Ava's ear. Jamie had hit the mute button. Ava wanted to tell her that it was okay to take her kid to the festivities, just let her be a kid, and have fun. But she couldn't. Not when the profile of the kidnapper was stuck in her head. Not when there was something about that profile that seemed wrong and bothered her so much.

Jamie was petite, but she was older than the targeted victims of the past. Bailey was much younger, but she had the same complexion and coloring as the past victims. If something went wrong, and the kidnapper's plan got foiled... Who was to say that if his Plan A failed, and he saw an opportunity, he wouldn't take it?

Ava couldn't take that risk. She couldn't tell Jamie it was safe to take her daughter out for a good time. Not in good conscience. Not even if it ruined Bailey's holiday, and she was mad at her mother for the next year. That was better than the possibility of either of them becoming a victim.

The line opened again. Jamie huffed and groaned. "You want to borrow an eight-year-old for the next couple of days and let me hunt down the killer?" She chortled dryly.

"Nope. This is one time I'll just stay right in my lane, thanks. She's mad, huh?"

"To put it in her words, she's *big mad*." She laughed. "It's not safe, is it?" Her voice was low and heavy with worry again.

"I can't recommend that you two go out to any of the functions for the holiday, Jamie. I just can't. I have the profile worked up, and… well, I just think it would be much safer for the both of you to stay home and do arts and crafts, have a nice harvest dinner for two, watch a movie there, whatever it takes. Just stay home. That's my advice."

"She's already big mad, guess it won't hurt to make her bigger mad."

"I'm sorry, but that's my advice. I just can't say it's safe when I'm not sure. Better safe than sorry, right?"

"Absolutely."

They talked for a little longer and then Ava ended the call. She needed to get moving. Time marched forward, and for some reason, it felt as if it were marching at double time. Maybe it was because the next day was Halloween, and she was no closer to finding out who the killer was than when she first arrived. Maybe it was the shorter days of autumn.

With the profile and her notes, Ava visited the men on the list she got from Mills, but she was certain none of them were the kidnapper. She had been around truly bad people before, and only one of the men she spoke with even had the potential to be a bad person. He was currently living in a house with five roommates, barely scraping by, barely able to pay bills and buy food. She could see him maybe lashing out and killing in a rage if confronted, but to target someone, plan it out, kidnap the target, and leave no evidence behind? Absolutely not. He was too spontaneous and hot-headed, and those types rarely got away with criminal deeds for very long. They were the types who got caught pretty quickly because they inevitably left things behind, or they talked afterward.

The sun was nose-diving toward the mountains in the west by the time she had finished talking to the men. Maybe Mills did know the people in her town well enough to know that none of them had hurt the girls. Then again, maybe she had overlooked someone who fit the profile because he didn't stand out in any way. And Ava was out of time. Halloween was descending, and she had nothing. Absolutely nothing to go on except a gut feeling that more girls were going to be targeted and taken. Would she be able to help any of them? Was it crazy to think it would happen again?

She stopped by The Grill and ordered chicken planks with fries, which she ate on her way to Lucifer's Lounge. Since the youth group was convinced the disappearances started because of the haunted house's arrival in town, she would go there and see if she could spot any nefarious people or activities at the site. Maybe the site owners and operators had pulled the proverbial wool over her eyes. Maybe they were a bunch of Satan-worshipping serial killers after all.

She doubted it, but she had checked out crazier ideas in her career.

The haunt had been open for a couple of hours by the time she got there, and the screams were in full swing. Youth for Salvation stood across the street holding their homemade signs high, quoting scriptures, and offering passersby religious pamphlets that surely invited them to become part of the flock of Saint Mary's Catholic Church.

They could have been doing worse than pandering for their church. Much worse. Most people took their pamphlets and kept walking while others simply sidestepped and acted as if the youth group didn't exist. Either action was okay by Ava so long as there were no altercations and the peace was intact.

Lucas met Ava at the edge of the group with a measured smile. "Everything is peaceful. We're doing just as we promised, so you don't have to babysit us. You can go do whatever you need to work your case." He stood so that he blocked her path farther into the group.

"That's great. I'm glad you're all upholding your end of the deal, Lucas. It's nice to know there can still be peaceful protests." She stepped around him and made her way into the group, which seemed to have grown by at least ten people since their previous meeting.

"Peaceful, but still not accomplishing much," he said. He looked at the stack of pamphlets in his hand.

"Hey, I saw at least four people take those with a smile on their faces before I ever came over. Maybe you're making more progress than you think." What else was there to do but try to appeal to him and his mission?

He shook his head. "They're still going in there, though. It's not stopping any of them. Some of them have even made rude jokes about our theory on the missing girls as if it could never happen to them, or never happen at all. It scares me for them. For all of us."

He looked over his shoulder at the growing line of people in front of the haunted house and shuddered deeply. "Lucifer's Lounge. It's literally written in giant red letters and lighted for them, and they still run headlong right into it." He turned to her. "Do you think if hell has flashing neon signs pointing the way people will line up to go there, too?" He had the weathered and beaten look of a battle-weary soldier even though he'd never seen a battlefield.

"I'm just here to do some people-watching, Lucas. I kind of need to be alone and unnoticed while I'm doing it." She didn't smile. It was one of those times when she knew if she wasn't firm, her request would be ignored.

He nodded. "I understand. You're using us as cover, aren't you?" He scoffed and shrugged. "We do have the best vantage point of anywhere on the street." He walked away, shoulders slightly drooped, flipping the stack of salvation papers against his palm, and looking for his next target.

Just like the kidnapper.

Ava searched the crowd of Youth for Salvation. They each wore their identifying shirts and blazers with their names embroidered above the left breast. They all had signs and pamphlets and determined expressions as they protested Lucifer's Lounge in a civil manner. Exasperation ran through the group like the ebb and flow of the ocean—steady and constant—but the youngsters stayed their course. That was commendable.

Having ascertained that each of the youth was legit, Ava moved to get a better view of the street and the people moving to and from Lucifer's Lounge. Some were in typical Halloween makeup and costumes; others wore plain clothes. Mostly, it was teens just out for a good time, and maybe a good scare. What teenaged boy didn't want to have his ladylove get a good fright and jump right into his arms, bury her face against his chest, and allow him to be the big, strong hero that protected her for a little while?

"Have you seen anything out of the ordinary yet?" Lucas asked from her right.

She turned to him. It had been nearly an hour. "No, not yet. Why, did you?"

"All of them are a little weird to me, so you're asking the wrong guy. Did you see the guy painted red with devil horns and the black pentagram painted on his forehead? He had black talons on his fingertips and everything. Tell me these people are *normal.*"

"Is anyone really normal, Lucas? I think that's subjective. We all have a slightly different definition of normal. If that guy ran around looking like that every day…well, maybe that wouldn't be so normal, but tonight? It's the night before Halloween, and he's obviously celebrating Halloween." She shrugged.

"So, if I came out on a saint's day dressed as a saint, that would be considered normal?"

"If it's a recognized holiday, I couldn't say it was abnormal. To each his own as long as he's not hurting others or himself. Right?"

"But celebrating Satan cannot be *okay.* It only leads to evil deeds."

Ava took a deep breath. "Lucas, I'm sorry, but this debate will have to wait. I need to be focusing on—"

"Right, right." He spun and walked away angrily.

The chaos ensued inside the haunted site, screams rose and fell in a rhythmic cadence, and nothing seemed out of the ordinary for the circumstances. People were coming out for cheap thrills, and it seemed they were getting what they paid for.

Another hour passed. It was eleven when Ava decided it was time to roam through town. The All Hallows' Eve festivities in Woodsboro ended at midnight, including those at Lucifer's Lounge.

By the time she made it to the Main Street sidewalk, she made her way through people dressed as all sorts of spooky creatures and iconic monsters. Nine out of every ten held the hand of a much smaller spooky or iconic monster, who inevitably clutched plastic pumpkins stuffed with candies and creepy toys to their little chests. There were no screams on Main Street. In the middle of town, the screams had been replaced with giggles and laughter and excited chatter.

As the sidewalks became more crowded, more adults were not in costume, and Ava studied those people hard. Still, nothing stood out as odd in any way. They all looked as if they belonged in Woodsboro. No one was up to anything nefarious.

At midnight, she walked back to her rental on Pine Street. Maybe All Hallows' Eve was safe, after all.

She stood in the open doorway until one. Everyone would have been home and getting their little ones tucked into bed by then, if they were lucky. If not, they were still trying to pry those plastic pumpkins out of their little hands, and silently wishing a plague of camel spiders on the people who handed them out to the kiddies.

Lying on the bed with her phone clutched in one hand, Ava stared up into the darkness until she finally drifted guiltily into a fitful sleep. What if she had been wrong? What if she had missed something that had been right in front of her?

When the phone rang, her grip tightened painfully around it as she sat up gasping and dreading the worst.

"James," she said hoarsely as she raked the hair back from her face and blinked to clear her vision.

"Agent, it's the sheriff," Mills said.

"Yes, what's happened?" She was fully awake and already at the edge of the bed reaching for her clothes as her pulse kicked into high gear. She had missed something. Something important, and now she was going to have to deal with the repercussions.

"Zoe Iversen's mother is frantic. Zoe is missing. I was sure it was nothing at first, but then Summer Tipton's dad called and said she hadn't come home either, so now I'm not so sure it's nothing. I thought I would go out and scout the local drinking spots for teens. You want to come with me?"

"Damn straight, I do. I'll be ready in five."

"Good because I'm almost to your front door now."

Ava hung up and yanked on her clothes, pulled her hair into a messy bun, and put on her shoes in less than three minutes. Mills pulled up just as Ava came out of the bathroom.

Three in the morning, and with less than two hours of sleep, Ava trotted to the car and got in feeling as if she had slept a full night. Adrenaline had a funny way of electrifying her and carrying her for a while.

Mills handed her a cup of coffee. "Thought you might want this seeing as how it's three in the morning, and I know you were out at midnight, and probably later, if I don't miss my guess."

Ava nodded, taking the cup. "Thanks. You knew I'd come, huh?"

"Didn't think you'd say no." Mills' cell rang. She answered, listened, tried to calm someone, listened some more, and then hung up. "Shit on a shingle. I think we might have a problem here."

"What?" Ava asked, her gut knotting and dropping.

"Parker Wilson is missing, too."

"You think the kidnapper—"

"No, no, nothing like that. Damn kids are lying around some damn campfire drunk somewhere and likely to burn themselves up, or burn down the damn woods. We need to find them, *pronto*."

Ava propped against the hood of the cruiser and watched as the sun crested the eastern horizon while Mills explained to another parent where she had found their kid and what said kid had been up to.

"Well, that's twelve," Ava said. "And not a single one of them was Parker, Zoe, or Summer, Sheriff."

"No shit, Sherlock," Mills said angrily. She got into the cruiser and slammed the door. "We're going by Bluebird for food and coffee and then on to Summer's parents' house."

Ava nodded. "A caffeine IV would be good right about now."

"Whatever gives me energy and not a heart attack right now will do."

CHAPTER NINETEEN

It Happened Again

"THE FBI?" MRS. TIPTON ASKED, LOOKING AT MILLS AND THEN back to Ava. "I thought you people were notoriously slow about getting involved in missing persons' cases."

"She was already here," Mills said, not giving Ava a chance to answer.

Mr. Tipton's eyes went wide. "That's right. You were working on the other missing girls' cases." He turned to his wife. "The ones who went missing over the last three years. The runaways."

"Maybe they're not runaways any more than our Summer is a runaway," she said, her face blanching even paler.

"Mr. and Mrs. Tipton," Ava said. "This is a terrible situation. If we could just get some information from you, we'll get back out to look for Summer. Maybe she'll turn up at a friend's house yet. Who knows, right?"

Mrs. Tipton shook her head. A tear shimmered down her cheek. "We've called everyone. There's no one left to call. She's a part-time model, Agent. Her life is here, and it's well-established."

"And she never ran wild, either. So, get that right out of your head, if that's what you're thinking," Mr. Tipton said.

"No, sir. Of course, not," Ava said. "When was the last time you spoke with your daughter?"

"I called around one-thirty this morning just to check on her because all the festivities were over and everyone was home by then. She was going to go to the haunted house, or maybe one of the functions in town, and I wanted to make sure she was back and safe before I went to bed," Mrs. Tipton said.

"And was she okay at one-thirty when you called?" Ava asked.

Mrs. Tipton broke down into a sobbing mess and shook her head.

Mr. Tipton wrapped his arms around her. "She didn't answer her phone. Naturally, we've called every thirty minutes since then, and she hasn't picked up yet. Not a call back, not even a text. Summer wouldn't let us worry like this. She just wouldn't."

Ava nodded.

Mills put her hand on Ava's arm and tilted her head toward the door.

In the car, Mills blew out a sigh. "Summer is just the most beautiful girl you ever saw. Ethereal would be a good description of her, actually, and that's not exaggeration."

"You think she just got a wild hair and she's drunk or smoked up on weed somewhere?"

Mills shrugged. "Anything is possible. Even the most responsible people can slip up, right?"

"Where to now? There are three other girls missing."

"You sure are getting good at pointing out the obvious. We're going to the Iversen's house. It's the closest."

Mrs. Iversen sat on the sofa crying when Ava and Mills entered the home. She was inconsolable, and she didn't seem to comprehend who was there or why. She didn't care. She just wanted her daughter home.

"Zoe is only sixteen. It's my fault. It's all my fault that she's gone." She crumpled to the side and put her face on the arm of the couch. Great huge sobs wracked her.

Ava cringed. The storm door was closed, but the inner door was open. She could step out and give the woman a minute to collect herself. But she didn't have that kind of time. She turned her attention to her husband instead. "Mr. Iversen, what did she mean it's her fault Zoe's gone?"

He harrumphed. "She's been in trouble over the last three weeks for her grades and behavior at school—"

"She was grounded, Richard. *I* grounded her from everything," Mrs. Iversen shrieked out between sobs.

He nodded and rubbed her back. "I know, honey, but any parent would have." He turned to Ava. "We let her go to the haunted house—"

"But I wouldn't let her take her phone," Mrs. Iversen cried loudly. "If I had, this would never have happened. She could have called for help, Richard." She pounded the arm of the couch weakly.

Mr. Iversen started crying and sat back, covering his face with both hands. "She's only sixteen, Sheriff," he said.

Mills nodded sympathetically. "I know, Richard. I'm doing my best here. We got some other girls gone missing, too. Do you think they might be together?"

He dropped his hands and looked hopeful. "Really?"

Mrs. Iversen raised her tear-reddened face. "What? You couldn't have led with that? Who are the others, and I'll tell you if Zoe might be with them."

"Summer Tipton, Nicole Rodgers—"

Mrs. Iversen flapped her hands at Mills to stop. "No, no, no," she said angrily. "She wasn't their type. They wouldn't hang around together, and as a matter of fact, Zoe thought Summer was a prissy bitch. Told me so herself once about a year ago when Summer started modeling."

"Ouch," Mills said. "Maybe they got over that?"

"Nope. Not Zoe. She could hold onto stuff like that forever."

"When did the other girls go missing?" Mr. Iversen asked.

"Last night or early this morning—" Mills said.

"So, the last time either of you saw or spoke to Zoe was before she left for the haunted house?" Ava asked, stopping Mills from sharing anything more with the Iversens.

Mills looked shocked, but she didn't push the issue.

Both parents nodded.

"Have you called and checked with her friends?" Ava asked.

"Do you think we're idiots?" Mrs. Iversen asked.

"No, ma'am, but I do know sometimes that in such stressful situations people often forget to—"

"Well, we didn't forget. As a parent, that's the first thing you do. *Before* you call the police, *before* you go into panic mode, you call all their friends and then you call all your family and all your friends, and they do the same."

"Yes, ma'am. Of course," Ava said. "Thank you for your time. We'll get back to you as soon as we know something." Her feet were already taking her toward the door. As she passed Mills, she nodded toward the door.

When the door closed behind them, Mills let loose. "What the hell was that in there?"

"What?" Ava knew exactly what.

"You cut me off and ran right over top of me while I was talking. I don't know exactly how things are done in the big cities, but around here, we don't appreciate rude outsiders. These people know me and trust me even when they don't like me. You had no right butting in."

"And you had no right talking to them about the other missing girls. That was none of their business. You don't discuss a case with others involved in the case especially. You only discuss it with people assigned to help you with the case—other officials, not with the general population. It's not an over-coffee topic of discussion, Sheriff Mills. That was unprofessional and could have put our investigation in jeopardy."

Mills started the car and grunted, clamping her jaw tight as she backed out of the driveway. "I'm not going to argue with you, but things are done differently in a small town. We all know each other around here, and the more informed we all are, the more likely we are to say something if we know something that might help the case, Agent James."

"I'm not going to argue, either. You can't discuss an ongoing case with these people at your leisure. We question them about their daughters, and we don't give them information about the other girls. That's just how it is."

Though it was obvious from the set of her jaw and the ice in her eyes that Mills didn't like it, she didn't say more. What could she argue? She knew better, surely.

Again, it crossed Ava's mind that being so close to the case and the people involved was a hindrance to Mills instead of a help.

Ruthie and Jerry Wilson sat at their kitchen table with vacant expressions.

"Mr. and Mrs. Wilson, I'm sorry to bother you at such a time, but I really need some information to help me find your daughter."

"Whatever you need," Mrs. Wilson said.

"How old is Parker?" Ava asked.

"Eighteen. She works in the office at the hospital five days a week, sometimes six or seven days," Mrs. Wilson said as if on autopilot. She slid a five-by-seven color photo of her daughter, Parker, across the table to Ava without making eye contact. "She's responsible, beautiful, and everybody loves her. She doesn't have a mean bone in her body, so she doesn't have any enemies."

"And no boyfriends," Mr. Wilson added. "Says she just isn't ready for that kind of commitment yet."

"What about girlfriends?" Ava asked as she took notes about the girl's appearance: light brown hair, green eyes, slim, petite.

"No, she wasn't gay," Mrs. Wilson said, a little hotly.

"I didn't mean it like that," Ava said quickly. "Friends that are girls. Does she have many? Close ones that she might be visiting without telling you?"

The couple shared a quick glance and then shook their heads simultaneously. "No," Mrs. Wilson said. "She's so busy, she just didn't have much time for friends."

"How tall is she?" Ava asked.

"Five-five. Why?" Mrs. Wilson asked.

Ava shook her head. "Just getting all the information I can about her. She looks rather slim, too. What? About a hundred-ten pounds?"

"One-fifteen. Skinny as a rail. I'm always trying to get her to eat more, but she just doesn't put on a pound. Hasn't since her sophomore year of high school. Is this important somehow?" Mrs. Wilson wrung her hands and narrowed her eyes at Ava.

"I just like to have all the details, Mrs. Wilson. Does she live here with you?"

"In a little apartment near the college," Mr. Wilson said. "Nothing would do her but to be independent."

Mrs. Wilson broke into quiet, snuffling sobs. She turned away and stood to hide her face from Ava and Mills.

"When was the last time you saw or spoke to your daughter, Mr. Wilson?" Ava asked.

"Yesterday afternoon. We called the sheriff this morning when I called Parker's phone and one of the haunted house workers answered it."

Ava snapped her head up and looked sharply at him. The haunted house again. It kept coming up. "Excuse me?"

"One of the workers answered her phone to let us know that it had been dropped by one of the big props near the back of the house. He said he figured she must have dropped it during the last jump scare when the group screamed and ran from there into the last room before the exit. He said the last room is just sort of a cooling area before they turn the group back outside so they're not running out panicked from the last scare of the night."

Ava looked at Mills, who arched her eyebrows and bobbed one shoulder in an I-don't-know gesture. Had Lucas been right after all? The haunted house had come up in three out of three missing girl cases, and it was still shy of lunchtime on Halloween Day.

"Did you go get the phone from the haunted house?" Ava asked.

"Of course, I did. I wasn't just going to leave her phone down there with a stranger. I drove by her apartment on the way back here, too. I was going to drop it off, but she wasn't there, and from the looks of it, she hadn't been since yesterday."

"I called her work, and she hasn't shown up or called out," Mrs. Wilson said in a watery, low voice.

"Was she scheduled to work today?"

Mrs. Wilson nodded. "Nine to five." She chuckled dryly. "She always said that was so Dolly Parton cliché. You know, because of the song?"

Mills smiled grimly, but Ava was lost. She didn't have a clue what they were talking about, but the conversation was lost for a few minutes as they bantered about it. Ava didn't mind because it stopped Mrs. Wilson's tears for a while. If she had to endure one more frantic, crying person, she might suddenly just wink out of existence.

Had her own mother cried that way when she had gone missing in Prague? Ava doubted it. Ava could only imagine her mother taking charge and rallying the troops to go out and beat the bushes until Ava was found.

But maybe Elizabeth had broken down. Maybe that was part and parcel of being a mother. Ava simply couldn't see her own mother doing so.

Mrs. Wilson followed them to the front door. "You do whatever you have to and find my baby, Sheriff Mills. You hear me? Whatever it takes."

Mills tipped her head. "You know I will, Ruthie."

Halloween Day in a small town was a busy time for the police. There were the mundane run-amok teens, cars that were egged, and then there were the inevitable fights that broke out because of the drinking. Every holiday seemed to be an excuse for excessive drinking all over the nation, but in small towns, they were reason to binge drink and get mean. People who were normally nice and peaceful suddenly became belligerent, violent, and the jail cells filled quickly with residents who usually didn't cause any problems at all.

Bloody noses, busted lips, blackened eyes, torn clothes, cursing, spitting, and even puking. It all came through the door, and most were in the age group between twenty-one and twenty-nine. A few temporary residents of Woodsboro Jail fell outside the average age range, but not many.

"Sheriff, I must say that I am sorely surprised at the sheer number of people you've already brought in. It's only four in the afternoon. What the hell happens here after the sun goes down on Halloween night?" Ava asked. She threw up a hand and shook her head. "Wait. Do I really even want to know? You don't even have room for more inmates at this point."

"Relax, Agent," Mills said. She raked her fingers roughly through her short hair and brushed past Ava on her way to the Drawer of Treasures for the Overstressed. "Soon as they sober up, I turn them out. No sense keeping 'em. The ones that haven't done anything real serious, anyway." She turned up the bottle of Pepto-Bismol.

"What?" Ava asked incredulously. "You *turn them out*, as in, you let them go Scot-free?"

Mills nodded as she dropped three aspirin into her hand, thought about it, and dropped another for good measure. "They're just raising a little hell, letting their hair down. Nobody will even press charges. Mark my words. If they do, I'll do my part, but if not ..." She shrugged. "Small town, Agent. Things are just different." She downed the four aspirin with half a bottle of water.

"If you so much as get a paper cut, I'll have to take you to the emergency room to keep you from bleeding out. You know that, right?" Ava eyed the bottle of aspirin pointedly.

"I have Super Glue and Gorilla Tape in the cruiser. Just use that. If I had to pay an emergency room bill, I'd have a heart attack and die anyway."

"Sheriff!" a woman yelled from the hallway. It sounded like she was running toward the office. "Sheriff!" she yelled again right outside the door.

A woman burst through the doorway with a man right behind her. They were dressed as if they were monied. Not like businesspersons, but as if they came from money. The woman's makeup was perfect, as was every strand of her slightly graying, light brown hair. The man had blond hair that had gone silver at the temples, giving him a distinguished look and accentuating his dark blue eyes, which held an expression of mixed worry and anger.

Mills hurried toward them, hands up as Ava stepped back and out of their way. "Mr. and Mrs. Rodgers, what's going on? What's wrong?"

"It's Nicole," the woman snapped. "She's missing."

Ava stepped closer. "Your daughter?"

Mrs. Rodgers cut her eyes at Ava, looked her over with a hint of disdain, cleared her throat, and turned her attention promptly back to the sheriff. "We didn't even know she was missing until this morning around nine when I went in to see why she was still lazing in bed. You know nine is far too late to still be in bed."

"Yes, ma'am," Mills said, leading them to the seats in front of her desk. "Have a seat so I can fill out some forms while you talk, please."

Mr. Rodgers made sure his wife was seated before he sat. "Sheriff Mills, we're not even sure when she went missing, or if she is missing yet."

"Tony, you know damn well she's missing," she hissed at him, her eyes narrowed. She gripped the cheap plastic armrests hard enough to make her dainty knuckles stand out and turn white.

Tony put a hand on her forearm. "Nancy, please calm down. You're not doing anyone any favors by being hysterical, dear."

"I'm not hysterical!" she screamed. "Our only child is missing!" she yelled.

"Please," Ava said, moving in again.

"Please, what?" Nancy spat. "Who the hell are you?" She turned to Mills. "Why does she keep interrupting?"

"Mr. and Mrs. Rodgers, this is Special Agent Aviva James of the FBI," Mills said, motioning toward Ava.

"Oh, well…" Mrs. Rodgers turned to face Ava with a calmness that was so sudden it was off-putting. "Agent James, my daughter is missing. What are you going to do about it?"

"When was the last time you saw or spoke to your daughter?" Ava asked.

"Last evening sometime, but I'm not sure of the exact time," Mrs. Rodgers said. "I found that she was not in her bed, and hadn't been all night, when I went to get her this morning at nine. Just like I said."

"She started calling Nicole's friends immediately after we searched the house and had the staff help search the property," Mr. Rodgers said.

Ava nodded. "How large is the property, exactly?"

"Let's not let the size of our estate play into this, please," Mr. Rodgers said in a tone of exasperation. "The important thing is that we searched every inch, and Nicole is *not* there. Anywhere."

Ava glanced at Mills, who kept her gaze averted. "Okay. Did you call Nicole's phone?"

Mrs. Rodgers cleared her throat and shifted in her seat. "No. No, we didn't call her phone."

"Why?" Ava asked.

"Because it wouldn't have done any good. It's not with her," Mrs. Rodgers said as she touched her hair and glanced at the floor.

"Is it at home?"

"Yes," Mr. Rodgers answered quickly. "It is."

"Where would she go without her phone?"

"One of her friends said Nicole had been at the haunted house last night with a boy," Mrs. Rodgers said. "She saw them sometime between eleven and eleven-thirty going inside the house, and she said Nicole's group was almost the last to go in."

"What was this girl's name?"

"Alexandria Perkins. She and Nicole have known each other for most of their lives. They're both seventeen, and they both are in line to inherit their parents' fortunes. They had a lot in common." The note in Mrs. Rodgers' voice surpassed pride and trekked into the territory of smugness.

"Who was the boy she saw Nicole with?"

"She didn't know for sure who he was, but she said he was good-looking," Mrs. Rodgers said.

Mrs. Rodgers and her husband looked at each other. It was one of those communicative looks. Ava witnessed the exchange of some hidden knowledge between the two, and she didn't like that they kept it from her. Not when their daughter was missing and it might be of use to the case.

"What's going on?" Ava asked, tapping the pen against the paper as she scrutinized the couple.

Mr. Rodgers cleared his throat and shifted in his seat before standing up and thrusting his hands into his pockets. "It might have been that damn boy she was sneaking around with a few months ago." He turned away from Ava to look out a window.

Mrs. Rodgers slid her hand around his forearm, and they exchanged another look. She sighed as she looked at Ava. "He got her pregnant, Agent James. Our Nicole is seventeen, unmarried, and two months pregnant. We didn't take it so well when we found out." She looked up at her husband as if for confirmation. He nodded for her to continue. "That's why she didn't have her phone. It broke. I caught her texting him to come get her one night after she thought we'd gone to bed. She was waiting by the front door for him. She was going to sneak off with him again after we had forbidden it. We argued, and the phone got broken. I refused to get her a new one until she came to her senses."

"We shouldn't have taken her phone, but we were only trying to keep her safe from him," Mr. Rodgers said. "He was no good."

"I've got everything filed, Mr. and Mrs. Rodgers," Mills said. "I'm sorry about your daughter, but maybe she just threw a tantrum and went somewhere to stay for a while to get a dig in at you. Kids do that sometimes, you know." She stood and ushered them out of the office.

"As a Rodgers, I highly doubt our daughter is throwing a tantrum or trying to get a dig in at us, Sheriff Mills," Mrs. Rodgers said in a scathing tone. "That's simply not how we handle things in our family."

"No, you just break cell phones," Ava said in a low voice as she shook her head. "That's a much more mature way of handling things." She grabbed her jacket and her messenger bag off the table in the corner.

"Where you going?" Mills asked as she strode back in.

"I need to make a call or two for some help here. Your town doesn't have the capabilities I'm going to need for this, Sheriff. I might grab a bite for dinner, too. Want to come with me?"

"Not particularly, but thanks. I think I'm going to work on finding these girls. Besides, somebody has to be here to rotate the stock of troublemakers in the cells as the new ones come in."

Ava nodded. "Ah, right. I almost forgot about them."

CHAPTER TWENTY

Remote Help

ASHTON ANSWERED ON THE FIRST RING. "HELLO?"

"That was fast," Ava said, shocked that he had answered so quickly.

"Oh, Ava. Hi." His tone dropped, and he sighed deeply.

"Sorry that I wasn't who you were expecting, but you don't have to sound so disappointed."

"It's not that. Well, I am, or I *was* waiting on another call, but I'm not disappointed to hear from you, just that it's not the call I was waiting on."

"And that was almost confusing. It's about new equipment, isn't it?"

"It is. A couple of things, actually, although they technically already shot one down."

"Well, don't give up, Ashton. I'm sure you'll get some of what you ask for." She wasn't sure of that. Not sure of it at all, and she didn't have time to dwell on it. "Listen, I need you to do something for me, if you have time."

"Sure. What is it?"

"Woodsboro doesn't have the capabilities to locate the last pings on some cell phones that I really need located."

"I can do that. I'd be happy to. Give me the numbers, and tell me how the case is going up there while I get the traces put into the system."

Ava gave him the numbers and updated him on the case.

"Sounds like you might have a big case instead of nothing. Isn't that what the sheriff up there kept saying it was? Nothing at all; just some runaways."

"Yes, and now she thinks these girls might be out drinking and just haven't called their parents or friends yet. I don't know if she's really that obtuse, or if she's being overly hopeful. She knows these families. All of them. She wants their kids to be okay, but maybe to a detriment."

"I understand that, but she's the police. She can't keep her head in the sand. Not if she wants to help them. Hopefully, they are all just being rebellious. I'll get these traces running and call you the minute something shows up."

"Thanks."

Ava hung up and then called Sal to update her as well.

"You have your hands full in that little town," Sal said.

Ava could hear Sal's pen scratching across paper and then the clackety-clack of the keys on the keyboard. Sal was working and undoubtedly had the phone wedged between her shoulder and her ear. "That's why I was calling you, Sal. Is there anyone on the team who might be able to come help me sort this out? Woodsboro PD doesn't have enough manpower to do the job efficiently and still monitor the town. With these four girls disappearing, the town is going to start panicking fast. They were already in an uproar over the others, but now? It might turn into mob mentality, and Mills will have to deal with that while I'm trying to sort out the real case alone. I just don't think that's feasible if I'm going to help these girls."

"Woodsboro doesn't have any reserve manpower you can call in to help you, or that Mills can call in to help her while she assists you?"

"Sal, do you know what her forensic team is here?" Ava pressed two fingers to her forehead where pressure had begun to build in the center just above the bridge of her nose.

The clacking on the keyboard stopped. "What?" she asked apprehensively.

"The county coroner, who took classes on how to collect evidence from a crime scene at the community college three counties over. She learned how to lift prints and look for DNA deposits and can bag, tag, and store it. One person. Only one. Her crime scene kit looks like a doctor's bag from the thirties."

"It's not even her specialty."

"Nope."

"Cross-training never hurt anyone, but in this case…" Sal groused.

"I'm not sure how I feel about it, either, but Mills keeps telling me that things are done differently in a small town, as if I know nothing about small towns and how things are done in them."

"She isn't breaking any laws with the way things are done, is she?" Sal's voice took on a serious tone.

Should she say something about how Mills discussed the case openly with whomever she pleased? Would that bring in a few more agents, get the Bureau involved to an extent that the missing girls stood a better chance of being found? No, it would only rain down an investigation of how Mills handled her business, get her in trouble, and the missing girls' case would be swept to the side. There would be more agents cluttering up the already crowded station and making it even more impossible for Ava to get anything done.

"No, she's not. The town is underfunded and doesn't have the capabilities I need to give this case the full attention that I feel it needs right now. Regardless of what Mills or anyone else thinks is going on with the missing girls, I think this is the work of more than one person."

There was a tense silence for a few seconds. Ava let it hang there as what she said sank in.

"You think there's more than one perpetrator now?" Sal asked.

"I do. There are four missing girls as of this morning. Four healthy, young women all taken within just a few hours. I don't think one person could have done that. Do you? I need someone to help me figure this out, and to catch whoever is doing this because they won't stop. Next year, it'll be five women. Left to the Woodsboro Sheriff's Department and their limited capabilities, this could go on unsolved indefinitely."

The next silence hung a bit longer. Ava gripped the phone tighter. Her only hope in being believed enough to get help with the case was Sal. Sheriff Mills wouldn't believe there was a single person taking the women, let alone more than one perpetrator. She certainly wouldn't allocate even a reserve deputy to help on the case. She would likely laugh and start working even harder to prove the theory wrong.

"Ashton is the only one who might be able to come, Ava," Sal said at last.

He wouldn't want to leave the office when he was waiting for calls about the petition for new equipment. Indeed, he might be too distracted to be spot-on with the fieldwork. "I just spoke with him. He's doing some remote work on the cellphone pings for me."

"You told me. He can access all that from Woodsboro. You know that. Dane and Metford are working another case. They won't be available. Santos is having a medical procedure done to help manage her migraines and then she'll be riding a desk for at least a week. Ashton needs something to distract him from all this tech stuff, and besides, he's sort of making everybody here crazy talking about it all the time. Metford told Ashton that he had a nasty stomach virus the other day just to keep him away, and I'm pretty sure Dane threatened to toss him down the elevator shaft if he brought up a spectrograph or some such, again. So, being forced to forget about this stuff for a while might just be good for him, and for the rest of us."

"That's fine with me. If he's available, I would greatly appreciate the help, and so would the people of Woodsboro, I'm sure. Four victims are a lot to negotiate, and as I said, I am certain we're dealing with more than one kidnapper. So far, there has never been a body recovered. I want to find these women, Sal. I don't want to be looking for bodies, if I can help it."

"I know. I'll send Ashton ASAP."

"Thank you."

It was almost six when Ava dialed the sheriff and then headed to Lucifer's Lounge.

CHAPTER TWENTY-ONE

Lucifer's Lounge

"I THOUGHT YOU WERE TRYING TO HELP ME KEEP THE PEACE, Agent," Mills said as she walked around the cruiser to face Ava on the sidewalk in front of Lucifer's Lounge.

Ava nodded. There was already a long line and a big, excited crowd formed outside the haunted house. "Priorities have changed, Sheriff. All the girls had one thing in common this time." She pointed to Lucifer's Lounge. "That means I need any and all evidence we can get from in there." She looked to Francis Conroy, the coroner and sometimes forensic team for Woodsboro Sheriff's Department. "Think you can handle the collection of evidence alone?"

Francis jumped a bit and she shifted the heavy black doctor's bag from one hand to the other. "I think so. Besides, I'll have Detective Graham and the sheriff to help, right?"

"Let's get her shut down before any more evidence can get destroyed then. Where are the deputies, Sheriff?"

"Pulling up as we speak." She jerked her head toward a side street where two cruisers approached.

"They'll need to do crowd control," Ava said. "Detective Graham, you and Ms. Conroy come with me." It wasn't the best team to take with her, but there was no time to do better. She had to work with what she had.

Thirty minutes later, Nate and Mel stood at the side of the entrance red-faced and livid as the deputies ordered the last of their would-be customers off the property for the night and stretched police tape around the perimeter.

"You know this is the night of the year," Nate said as he waved one finger in the air wildly, "that we work so hard for. The *one night* that brings in most of our money. Halloween night is what we do all this for, and now we're just shut down? And for what? We're up to all the codes, we've broken absolutely no laws, I bought the property and I pay the taxes," he ranted at Ava and Sheriff Mills.

"Nathan, we have four missing girls," the sheriff said flatly. "They were all here right before they went missing. It's…" She glanced at Ava before finishing, "…*procedure*. We'll try to hurry, but I'm not making any promises that you'll be able to open back up tonight." She walked toward the door and clapped him on the shoulder as she passed. "That's just how it is."

"We didn't have anything to do with those girls getting gone!" he yelled at Ava. "We didn't even know them! We barely know anyone around here. We run a damn business here! That's all." He looked at Mel, and she nodded.

"No one is accusing you two of anything. I need to ask all of your workers and you two some questions. It would be simpler if everyone was here in a group. If I have to question you one at a time, it could take through tomorrow." She cocked an eyebrow.

"Marcelle, get all of them over here now," Mel told the barker without looking at him.

The man spun on his heel, stepped to the side of the house where he was still within sight, cupped his hands around his mouth, and yelled for the workers. If past lives were a thing, Marcelle had surely been a town crier. His voice rang out crisp and loud, and Ava was certain that even over the din of a scared crowd, it would have easily been heard.

The workers filed around both sides of the house and a couple came from inside. Ava motioned for them to stand in a group so that she could see their faces when she spoke.

"Mel, do you have security cameras?" Ava pointed up toward the eaves.

"No, we don't. That's why we had someone stay here when the youth were trying to vandalize everything we had. We don't have the funds for that sort of thing."

"Yet," Nate said. "And if we keep getting shut down like this, we probably never will."

Ignoring him, Ava pulled up file pictures of the girls on her phone. "Does anyone know this girl?" She held her phone out and walked around so that everyone could see. All heads shook. She stepped back and looked up at them. "Parker Wilson. That's her name." Still, no one knew her.

The reactions seemed genuine. No one seemed to shift their gaze, avert their eyes, do any sort of grooming gestures, or self-soothing gestures that would indicate any kind of guilt or deception.

Repeating the same process for Zoe Iversen, she got the same responses. Then she held up a picture of Nicole Rodgers, and immediately, two of the female employees recognized her.

"I saw her here with her boyfriend," the first worker said.

"You don't know he was her boyfriend," the second said.

"They were holding hands, and at one point he had his arm around her and was practically licking her ear," the first retorted.

"Hey," Ava cut in sharply. She shoved the picture closer. "You're certain it was this girl?"

The first woman nodded. "Yes."

The second woman nodded. "She's rich. I think her name is Nicole Rodgers, but don't hold me to that because it could be another first name, but I know her last name is Rodgers."

"How do you know that?" Ava asked.

"Because her family is stupid rich and she makes sure everyone knows it. She's younger than me, so I didn't go to school with her, but I know who she is, and yes, she was here with a sexy guy who I didn't recognize."

Ava held the phone out to the others again. "Her name is Nicole Rodgers."

"I said don't hold me to that," the woman said.

"That is her name," Ava said, not looking back at her. "Does anyone else know her? Remember her being here with anyone?"

Everybody shook their heads. She went back to the two workers who had spoken up. "When was she here with the guy?"

They looked at each other for a moment. "Maybe last night or the night before," the first woman said. "It's hard to remember. We get a lot of people through, and the dates just kind of blend together because of the times we work." She looked back to the other woman, and she nodded in agreement.

"I need your names."

"Julie Rice," the first woman said.

"Sarah Hoyle."

"Are we in any trouble?" Julie asked.

"Not at all, but I might need to ask you more questions later." Ava pulled up Summer's picture on the phone and held it out to the crowd. The response was unanimous. Everyone recognized the picture except the owners, Nate and Mel.

"That's Summer Tipton," Marcelle said with a wide smile. "Everybody knows her, or at least recognizes her."

"She's gorgeous," Julie said. "If you're a girl around here, you grew up wanting to be her, or at least be like her."

"And if you were a guy, you wanted to be *with* her," a man said. That was followed by low, male laughter.

Ava turned to that group. "Summer is missing. Have any of you seen her?"

The man who had spoken cleared his throat. "She was here. Couple of times this season. The last time was within the last day or two." He nodded toward Julie and Sarah. "Like they said, though, it's hard to know exactly when because we work weird shifts. It was either last night or the night before, though, because I didn't work the night before that."

"What's your name?"

"Steven Murphy."

"I'm going to need everybody's name and contact information before you leave this area. Just form a line, and I'll get it."

Afterward, Ava took a deep breath and put away the pen. Just as she started toward the front door, Mills came out.

"Anything?" Mills asked.

"Not much. Just confirmed that Nicole Rodgers was with a *sexy* man that no one recognized, and that Summer Tipton is gorgeous and unforgettable and very much admired among her peers. What about you? Figure out what's going on yet?"

"I still don't think we have a serial killer on our hands, but I'm willing to admit that something is going on, and I just don't know where to even begin. Graham and Conroy have been all over the house. Do you have any idea what a nightmare it is to investigate a haunted house? No pun intended. We have two hundred sets of prints to run—all of them from different people. I don't even want to guess at how much DNA we have." She shook her head as if already defeated.

They walked toward the house. "Anything stick out as suspicious or odd?"

Mills chuckled low. "Other than ninety percent of the things in there?" She grinned crookedly.

Realizing what Mills meant, Ava returned the grin. "Yeah, other than all *that*."

Mills pulled a plastic bag from her coat pocket and held it up for Ava. "We found this strip of fabric with traces of what Conroy is sure is chloroform on it stuck under the edge of one of the heavy props in the very last room. Other than that, though? Nothing."

CHAPTER TWENTY-TWO

Checking Out Lucifer's Lounge

THE CLOTH WAS NOTHING SPECTACULAR. NOTHING THAT WOULD
have stood out to many people. It could have been a strip of cloth
off one of the robed costumes worn by the scarers at the haunted
house, or maybe from a costume worn by one of the many customers.
Ava opened the bag. The faint odor of very sweet pineapple and alcohol
lingered on the cloth.

"Oh, I wouldn't do that," Francis Conroy said, moving toward her
fast with one hand out as if to snatch away the bag. "You shouldn't
inhale that."

Ava shut the bag quickly, wondering if she had inadvertently done
herself any harm. "It smells sweet. Really sweet with alcohol."

"That's chloroform, Agent." Conroy reached for the bag. "Here, let me just make sure it's sealed up real tight." She smiled tightly.

"One little whiff can't knock me out," Ava said.

Detective Graham scoffed and shook his head. "Indeed not. People got that crap all wrong. It takes a lot of that on a rag being breathed in for several minutes to knock a person out, and even then, the result is quite unpredictable."

"Really?"

Mills chuckled. "Graham knows a little about everything. He's our resident nerd."

"Got one of those myself," Ava replied.

"But he's right," Conroy said. "It can make a person unconscious for twenty minutes, or maybe for hours. There's not really any way to gauge what it will do. It can even kill people."

"I thought chloroform was something used back in the 1800s. I didn't realize we even still manufactured it," Ava said, taking the bag back from Conroy.

"It's in pesticides, refrigerants—"

"Chlorinated drinking water supplies," Graham interjected, raising his eyebrows, the corners of his mouth pulling down in a way that deepened and elongated the wrinkles on his cheeks and made him look even older.

"It was used in a case in the early nineties. A man used it to sexually assault and sometimes kill teen girls," Conroy said. She gasped, her eyes widened, and she looked at Mills. "You think that's what's going on here?" She pointed at the bag with the cloth in it.

"Show me where you found it," Ava said.

She followed Conroy, Mills, and Graham into the haunt and through the warren of rooms. Along the way, a couple of workers fell in behind them and stood in the doorway as Ava circled the big, wooden prop.

It was a simple design. A stereotypical Halloween-shaped coffin tilted at about a thirty-degree slant. Oversized. Attached to a wooden platform that was a couple of feet high.

She raised the lid. A fake corpse lay there in repose with black roses on her chest and a creepy Mona Lisa smile on her lips. A sign below the spray of black roses read: *Dearly Departed Delilah wishes you a peaceful journey through the doorway to the otherworld.*

Ava looked at the door below the exit sign. "Turn off the overheads for a minute."

The lights went out. The room was thrown into complete darkness except for the very dim red glow of the exit sign and the ghostly gray glow *otherworld* that had been painted on the door below it.

"Lights."

The lights came back on, and she turned to the workers in the other doorway. "Why would it have been so dark in here? It doesn't make sense if Dearly Departed Delilah here had a sign for the customers to read."

"There's a fog machine and faint green lighting from under the thick mist when the haunt is in business," the shorter man answered as he pointed to a corner where the fog machine was artfully hidden behind a fake mantel.

"This is where you found the cloth?" Ava asked Conroy as she pointed to the corner of the prop.

"Yes. That thing is heavy."

"You have gloves I can use?" Ava pointed to the black bag hanging at Conroy's side.

She pulled out two pair. "Latex, or vinyl?"

Ava took a pair at random. "Doesn't matter." After pulling them on, she bent and grabbed the slight protrusions on the corner of the prop and lifted. She got it off the floor, but only with a lot of effort, and when she put it back down, it rattled and clanked because of the dummy in the casket and the movable lid.

"Told you it was heavy," Conroy said.

Why would someone have lifted such a heavy prop? Why was the chloroform on the fabric and then stuck under that thing? Refrigerants. Pesticides. Fog machine.

Ava glanced at the workers in the doorway and then turned to Conroy, Mills, Graham, and Deputy Marsh, who had opened the 'otherworld' door to peek inside. "I want you to check the underneath sides of all the props for fingerprints and DNA. Anything and everything is evidence. Got it?" she asked Conroy and Graham.

Conroy nodded. Graham huffed.

"Why?" Mills asked. "What have you thought of?"

"What if someone chloroformed the girls and hid them under the props until they could get them out without being seen later?"

"One man couldn't do that," the short man in the other doorway said, sneering as if it were the dumbest thing he'd ever heard.

Ava spun on him. "Excuse me, what was your name again?"

"Owen King. One man couldn't do that alone. Your theory. How would he chloroform the girl and then hold that heavy prop up with one arm and slide her under it with the other? See what I mean?" He smiled indulgently.

"Right, right. Now, go on and get out of here, please. This is now an active crime scene. If there are any others in the house, they need to leave, too. Immediately. Go on," she said, waving her hand toward the side exit nearest where Owen stood. "Deputy Marsh, get Latham and Marty. You three stand watch at the three main doors and don't let anyone inside. I want everyone kept out. *Everyone.*" She looked at Mills when Marsh didn't immediately jump to action.

"Get to it, Marsh. Now. She's right. This is an active crime scene until you hear different from me or her. No one comes in for any reason without permission from Agent James or me." She turned to Conroy and Graham. "And why are you two still standing there? You need silver-lined invitations to do your damn jobs? Come on. Get a wiggle on." She held out her arms as if herding sheep toward a pen, and moved them toward the first room of the house. "Let's get these damn props overturned and checked out."

Ava took the room in again. Dread gripped the base of her spine. There could be more than two perpetrators. It could be a group. A coordinated effort among friends. That thought made her a little nauseated.

She walked back through the house to get a look at some of the props. Most of them were heavy, or at least awkwardly shaped, but they all had similar aesthetics to the workmanship. In the front room, Mills stood by and supervised as Conroy collected samples from a large, overturned easy chair and side table.

"You seem to have this under control," Ava said. "I am going out to speak with the owners again. I need to know who made these props."

"Sure you don't want to help us wreck the devil's living room?"

"I'm sure he has a target on my back for plenty enough other stuff. I'll leave you holding the bag on this one." She flashed a grin and stepped out of the house, shutting the door behind her.

Nate and Mel sat with their backs against the short wooden fence a few yards away looking dejected and overwhelmed. Nate shot to his feet when he spotted her. "What the hell? A crime scene? Are you serious? It's a haunted house, Agent James. It's set up to *look like bad shit happened in there.* That's kind of the whole point."

"Well, this time, bad shit really happened in there. Unless you have a legitimate reason for having chloroform." She looked at each of them in turn. "Well? Was chloroform part of your scare tactics? Just a prop? What?"

"The only chemicals we have are first-aid and the fog machine," Nate said, his face going pale.

"And my epi-pen," Mel said, pulling it from her back pocket. "But I keep it on me. There's no chloroform in there anywhere. That's shit from like the Victorian Era, right?"

"Obviously not. I need to know who built those props. Did you do it, or did you hire someone? How does that work?"

"We hired a local company to do it. Small company." Nate pressed his fingers to his forehead and squeezed his eyes shut. "Two brothers. They're young." He snapped his fingers and looked at Mel. "You remember their names?"

"Elite Woodworks. Something, something Elite Woodworks," she said, looking up at the dark sky.

"Humphrey," Nate said. "That was their name. Corey and Devin Humphrey Elite Woodworks."

Ava wrote down the name. "Two brothers, you said?"

"Yes," Nate said. "Mid-to-late-twenties. They said they had been working with wood since they were old enough to tie their own boots. Their family was into logging, and that's where they got their start."

"They're good at what they do, but they're cocky little bastards. Especially toward women. If you're planning on talking to them, you might want to take the sheriff or one of the deputies with you," Mel said.

"Did they give you any trouble?"

"I didn't like dealing with them if Nate, or some of the other men weren't here. They're big guys. You'll see. And they get too close for my comfort."

"She said they were *aggressively charming*," Nate added.

"They just gave me the creeps, and it didn't help that they were both over six feet tall and three feet wide at the shoulders. It was like having two Paul Bunyans hulking over me," she said, scowling hard at him.

Ava considered all this. "Thank you."

The Humphrey brothers went on the short list of suspects. The very short list. They fit the profile, they would be able to handle the petite women with the greatest of ease if they were as big as Mel stated, they knew their way around the house, and it was likely that they knew the layout of the props down to near-exact measurements because they had placed the sets. That would make it possible for them to move around in near-darkness, or maybe even complete darkness.

Mills shook her head and put her hands on her considerable hips. "No. Now, I don't know what they told you about the Humphrey boys, but you can't really take anything they say about locals to heart anyway.

They're not from here, you know. The Humphrey boys are just the sweetest boys you'll ever meet, and I would advise you against going over there and talking to them as if they were your prime suspects in some case that might not even be what you think it is."

Convinced more than ever that the case needed a fresh set of eyes, Ava smiled tightly at Mills. "Alright, Sheriff. Thanks for the advice. I still have to talk to them, though. That's just how this works."

It was far too easy to form opinions based on emotions rather than facts when one was too close to the people in question. Mills had lost her objectivity on the case.

And it was up to Ava to solve it.

CHAPTER TWENTY-THREE

Corey and Devin Humphrey Elite Woodworks

THE HUMPHREYS, LIKE SO MANY OF THE RESIDENTS OF WOODSBORO who didn't live in town, owned a sprawling amount of land. Mountains bordered it on two sides, and rolling hills ran into the distances in the other two directions making the place seem much larger than it actually was.

The house was a large three-story farmhouse-style. A guest house stood a few hundred feet behind it and seemed much newer. The workshop was attached to a wood mill, and every manner of logging equipment sat on the property past that section of property.

A handsome young man stepped out of the house and sauntered down the path toward Ava's car with a smile that could have shamed a stadium spotlight. He was very tan; presumably from working outside much of the time considering his profession. He raised a hand in greeting.

"Hey, there. Help you?" he asked.

Ava stepped out of the car. He was indeed a little over six feet tall. As he neared, she had to think that Mel had only exaggerated a bit when she had said the brothers were three feet wide at the shoulders, too. She saw how easily two men that size could have intimidated a much smaller Melanie.

"Yes. I'm looking for Corey and Devin Humphrey Elite Woodworks. Am I at the right place?"

"You most certainly are." His smile broadened as he pointed to a large wooden sign, of course it was wooden and handmade, at the side of the workshop that displayed the name prominently. "What can I do you for, officer?"

"Officer?" she asked. "I haven't even introduced myself yet." Her first thought was that Mills had called ahead to warn them, and her blood pressure edged up a few notches.

He pointed to the side of her badge barely showing at her belt. "It kinda catches the eye when the sun glints off it like that."

Feeling a fool, she uncovered it completely. "Special Agent James, to be more accurate. Is your brother here, too?"

"He is. What's this about?"

"I need to speak to both of you, please. Out here preferably." He seemed nice enough, but she was not gullible enough to go into a small space with two unknown men his size. "Which brother are you, by the way? Corey or Devin?"

"I'm Corey. Devin's my little brother." He pulled out a cell phone and tapped out a quick message. "He'll be right here. He's just in the house. Want me to flip on the outside lights? It's kinda dark out here."

"That's an understatement. That would be fine, thanks."

"There's a picnic table just over here. We can sit while we talk if you want."

She shook her head. "No, thanks. I prefer to stand. You two can sit, though. That's fine. I know it's pretty late, and you're probably tired."

Devin came out of the house and down the path washed in the same dim light as his brother earlier. He was just as handsome, but he was even bigger than Corey, and his smile even broader and brighter as he thrust his hand out toward her.

"Hey, there. Devin Humphrey. Corey says you wanted to talk to both of us?"

She didn't shake his hand. Instead, she showed her badge and stepped to the side a half-step to be sure the picnic table was between her and the brothers. "I do want to speak with both of you. I'm Special Agent James of the FBI. I was investigating the disappearances of six young women over the last three years. Since yesterday, though, four more young women have gone missing from Woodsboro."

"That's terrible," Corey said. "We hadn't heard anything about anyone going missing recently, but we knew about the others. Everyone's heard about them."

"We stay to ourselves working out here a lot," Devin added. "Sometimes, it's a week between visits to town for anything."

"That's odd for men your ages, isn't it?"

"Is it?" Corey asked, chuckling. "Why would it be? We're entrepreneurs. That means we work for ourselves and that we have to work twice as hard as most people."

"Besides, have you seen Woodsboro, Agent? There's not really a lot for anyone over the age of twelve and under sixty to do there. You have the theater, the park, Graphic Fiction Addiction, two party supply shops, coffee shops, restaurants, and the senior center. Not much of an exciting selection."

"Don't forget the Feed and Seed Hardware," Corey said, chuckling along with his brother.

"This isn't a joke," Ava snapped.

The men went serious and glanced at each other.

"Sorry," Corey said. "We know it's not a joke, but honest, this is how we've always lived. I don't understand why it's any concern to an FBI agent that we don't leave home very often."

"Did you build the props at Lucifer's Lounge?"

They looked at each other again. "Yes, we did. Most of them when they first bought the place," Corey said. "What's that got to do with anything?"

"Did you also place those props in the house for the owners?"

"Of course. That was part of our job. The owners were too skinny, they couldn't have moved the props without hurting themselves, or without some sort of wheelie system that would have required them to widen the doorways of the house, so we agreed to place the sets and props for a little more pay."

Devin nodded in agreement. "Did someone get hurt on one of them? Because we're not responsible for that, you know."

"It's safe to say that you would know your way around that house." Ava eyed them levelly.

They both nodded.

"Wait a minute," Corey said, holding up a hand. "Where did these recent women go missing from?" Devin started to speak, but Corey shushed him.

"Where do you think they went missing from, Mr. Humphrey?"

He shook his head. "We built the props, but we didn't snatch any women."

"Who all thinks we had something to do with this?" Devin asked.

"It's not part of my job to gauge the community's suspicions. It's my job to follow up on any leads I have, and this was one. You both fit the profile, not just for this, but for the other missing women. You are obviously physically capable of doing something like this with ease. You have all this property, all this equipment, a few different vehicles that could be used to transport the victims. You admittedly know your way around the haunted house well."

Corey shook his head and smiled. Contradictory actions that caught Ava's attention immediately.

"How many other people out here in the willywags fit that same description? Before you answer, really think about it. Be honest," Corey said. "I understand why you would find us suspicious, I guess. Because of the haunted house thing, but that was just a job. Our main stuff is pretty boring. Cabinets, doors, chairs, and tables. The occasional dresser. You're more than welcome to check out the workshop, or any other building."

"Hell, you can check out the house, if you want. We don't have anything to hide," Devin said. "We don't even know who is missing, but we'd be more than willing to help you find them."

"And if searching our place helps you move on and get on with the investigation, so be it," Corey added.

Their words were genuine. No hint of deception. Corey's mismatched headshake and smile were the result of the situation, perhaps. She pulled up Zoe's picture on her phone and held it out to them.

They shook their heads.

"Zoe Iversen?" she asked.

"Sorry, I don't know her," Corey said.

"Me neither," Devin said.

She showed them another picture. It was Parker Wilson, but she didn't offer a name, just the picture.

Corey squinted, then nodded, seeming to confirm it more to himself than to Ava. "I think I know that girl. She works in the office at the hospital, but I don't know her name. I saw her when I had to go a few months back. A piece of wood splintered off a log I was putting through the planer and did this." He pulled up his shirt, exposing a jagged scar on his right side just under his ribs. "Hurt like hell, too." He dropped his shirt. "She was in the office when I went back to make a payment after that, too."

They didn't recognize Nicole Rodgers, but did recognize the last name, just like everyone else in town.

When they saw the next picture, they both blanched and looked at each other.

"She's missing?" Devin asked.

"She is. Do you know her?"

"I would think most people do. Not personally, but yeah, everyone probably at least recognizes her pictures. She's kinda famous around here. That's Summer Tipton, the model. Beautiful girl. She's in a lot of the local magazines. Regional stuff. Hard to forget. Just look at her."

"When was the last time you saw her?"

"Ain't seen her in person in over a year," Devin said. "It's not like we run in the same social circles, or something. And we've never talked. I just saw her in town."

"How can you be so sure it was over a year ago, then?"

He chuckled. "Because I was finishing taking down the Fourth of July stage in the park that we had been commissioned to build for the town celebration. The town pays us to put that thing up every year and then we take it down and store it until the next year."

"Couldn't that have been this past Fourth?"

He shook his head. "Nope. Right after I saw her, I loaded the stage steps onto the trailer, and I left. Not even a mile later, the steps fell off the side when I hit a pothole, and they broke. This year, I had to build a whole new set of steps at no charge because it was my fault the others broke. I wasn't paying attention and I didn't strap them properly."

"And I think he saw Summer Tipton, got all flustered and giddy, and that's why he forgot to strap them, so I teased him about it," Corey said, grinning. "And like I said, we're more than willing to let you look around any time you want. If it takes time to get a search warrant, don't even worry about it. We'll sign papers or waivers or whatever. Whatever it takes to help those girls. We hope they're found safe and sound."

"And we don't care a bit to help search. I just can't believe Summer and the Rodgers girl are missing. You just don't think things like this happen to people you even kinda know," Devin said.

She had nothing concrete. Everything was speculation. She thanked them for their time and left disappointed.

Mills and her small crew were still at Lucifer's Lounge, as were Mel and Nate.

"Well, I'm elated that you didn't come dragging those boys back here in cuffs, Agent," Mills said. She yawned loudly.

"I don't think they did it, Sheriff."

"Nope. I don't think they did either. I called in Greenlee so he could bring by a fresh load of caffeine. He should be here soon. You look like you could use strong coffee, too."

"I could use a good solid lead is what I could use," Ava said. "Did you find anything new?"

"About a hundred new prints so far. Some DNA, but not from the undersides of those props yet. Most of them are rough wood, and Conroy is having trouble with them."

Ava inhaled and then exhaled deeply. "Right."

A taxi pulled up and the back door opened. Ava squinted to see who it was and then smiled as she walked toward Ashton.

"You would not believe how happy I am to see all these geek toys," she said. Relief washed over her, and tension rolled out of her shoulders and upper back.

"And just like that, she leaves out the geek who operates all the magnificent toys." He dropped his head and pulled the two field bags out of the trunk. He set them on their wheels gently and extended the handles.

"You know I'm glad to see you, Ashton. Did Sal send you by Express Mail, or what?"

"She might as well have. I had everything at the office, and left as soon as you called." He pulled his bags toward the house, looking up, to the sides, all around, taking in the whole scene as he talked and walked. "I'm going to get aerials before I go inside."

"In the dark?"

"Night vision." He grinned. "The wizard has arrived. You are no longer working in the Dark Ages of Technology, Ava."

"We might not be working in the Dark Ages, either, if someone would toss us a little bit of that funding, Mr. Wizard," Mills said loudly as she stepped out of the house with a sour look on her face.

Ava crinkled her face. "Uh-oh." She turned to Mills. "Sheriff, this is Agent Dwight Ashton, he's our tech wizard. He's come to help us out. Agent Dwight Ashton, this is Sheriff Wanda Mills."

Ashton smiled and offered his hand. Mills shook it but didn't smile.

"Nice to meet you, Sheriff."

"I was serious about that funding."

Ashton dropped his hand back to the handle of his bag. "Okay, I'm going to get to work now, Ava. The sun should be up in a couple of hours, and I'll get aerials of the surrounding land that I can zoom in on and search later. I'm staying at the rental with you, by the way. I hope it's big enough for both of us."

"It is. We won't be there long enough for it to matter anyway."

CHAPTER TWENTY-FOUR

Lucifer's Lounge and the Four Missing Girls

THIRTY-SIX HOURS LATER, MILLS THUMPED INTO HER SEAT AT HER desk and held up a hand to quiet Ava. "Please? One minute. Just one minute that someone isn't yammering in my face or in my ear to do something, get something, move something, look at something. Jesus, right now all I want is one minute of peace and friggin' quiet so I can hit the reset button." She dropped the hand to the desk, looked at Ava, and pressed her lips into a pencil-thin line.

Ava nodded and held up a finger. One minute. But she couldn't give more than that. They needed to move, and they needed to keep moving fast. She turned to look out the window and crossed her arms as the seconds ticked by. She silently counted them. She was unable to do otherwise. How could the sheriff sit idle even for that short period when there was so much going on with the investigation?

"Okay," Mills said after forty-nine seconds. "Let the deluge begin anew. What do we need to do now?"

"I need to know if your people got the hair samples for the missing girls yet. We need those. Now. And Parker's blood type. We have the others' blood types."

"My men are working on it. They ain't had a break yet, either, Agent, and they're tired, too. Believe it or not, we're not machines like you and your Mr. Wizard out there. We don't run on caffeine and willpower. They've gone to the girls' houses, and their parents' houses for those who still lived at home with their parents, and they'll have to give some sort of reasoning for wanting hair samples. The parents are going to want to know what progress has been made. These things just take time. We're not incompetent, just considerate."

"In this case, being considerate might cost some young ladies their lives, Sheriff. The quicker we move, the more likely we are to get these girls back safely. We already found blood at the haunted house that matched the blood types for the three girls we have on file: Summer, Nicole, and Zoe. We have hair. If we could just see if it looks to be the same thickness and color as any of theirs…" Ava held up her hands. "Maybe it is, maybe it isn't, but it would get us a step closer."

"Can't you send it off for DNA testing?"

"Yes, along with all the other DNA collected at the site. That should only take roughly a year to get analyzed."

"Put a rush on it."

"On which samples? Which ones are more important? The hair? The DNA found on the back of the mantel where the fog machine is? Or that found inside Dearly Departed Delilah's casket? Oh, or maybe it's the DNA swab from under the prop in the storage room upstairs."

Mills held up a hand again. "Okay, I see your point. We don't know which sample might be *the sample*."

"Right. We need them all analyzed. But, if the hair is similar enough to one of the girls' hairs, we can send that off and put a rush on it because some of it still had the roots attached." She leaned on the desk. "I really need those hair samples, Sheriff."

"I'll have Latham bring them out to the rental, if that's where you'll be."

"Thank you."

Ava went back to help Ashton. He sat hunched over the screen of his laptop when she entered.

"I think I found something here," he said.

She hurried to join him and he pointed to something near a wooded area.

"What is that?"

"A deep ditch that runs along a gravel road." He put his thumb and forefinger on the screen and then pulled them apart, zooming the image. They both leaned closer and squinted.

"Can you clean up the image at all?" she asked.

He dragged the laptop to him and worked on it for a few minutes, adjusted his glasses, and looked up at her. "I think it's a pair of glasses."

"Let me see."

He handed her the computer, and she zoomed the screen. "You might be right. I think the sunlight is reflecting off the lens, but it could just be a piece of broken glass, too, couldn't it?"

He shrugged. "Not very likely. The shape and refraction of the prisms—"

She held up a hand and shook it. "Okay, no. We should just go out and check the place physically. Bring your equipment."

He put the coordinates into the GPS. They drove away from town.

"These roads are skinny and winding, and I am so glad I don't have to drive them in the winter," Ava said.

"Or in the rain, or in high winds," Ashton said with a slight grin.

"Or after dark as a general rule because these people also do not believe in streetlights."

"Okay, we're close. It's just up there on the right. It'll be a gravel road," he said, pointing.

Ava turned onto the gravel road. She pulled onto the gravel just far enough that she was off the paved road and not blocking traffic, and then she parked.

"Be careful where you step," she said as they got out. "There might be evidence if those really are glasses."

"Did any of the girls wear glasses?"

"Parker Wilson."

He motioned ahead. "The glasses should be just about forty feet up there."

Ava saw them first. The glasses clung to a dead sprig of grass on the inner slope of the ditch about halfway down. One lens was gone. "They haven't been out here very long," she said.

He agreed as he photographed them. When he finished, Ava bagged the glasses and put them in her pocket.

"You think they were Parker's glasses?" he asked.

She shrugged and then nodded. "I do. Can't help it."

He turned and looked up the gravel road. Several cows milled around in a large pasture. A barn stood in the far distance, and beyond that, a barely discernable rooftop peeked over a hill. "Big farm."

"Most of them are, out here."

"If she was killed, she could be anywhere."

"Why would she be out here anywhere, though?" As soon as it was out of her mouth, Ava's hand went to the bag with the glasses in it. "Because her glasses were out here, but the missing lens wasn't."

"Right. If there had been a struggle out here, I think the killer would have taken the glasses. He would have picked them up to keep from leaving behind evidence. Since the struggle happened elsewhere, I don't think he realized the glasses fell off her face."

"You mean, you think he brought her out here to dump her?"

Ashton nodded. "I'm going to use the drone and just have a look over all this property. It will only take a few minutes."

Ava watched the screen with him as he guided the drone. Fifteen minutes later, Ava pointed to the upper left side of the screen. "Right there, Ash. It's a body."

There were a dozen or more cows grazing, but none of them were near the body of Parker Wilson as Ashton flew the drone low over her.

"It's her. It's Parker Wilson," Ava said. "We need to secure the scene. I'll call Mills."

CHAPTER TWENTY-FIVE

Cow Patties Preserve Evidence

A T THE END OF THE DAY, ASHTON PROPPED AGAINST THE CAR AND waited for Ava to join him. "Did Mills put out the public request for help?"

"Radio and TV appeals for any information. She said the hair samples were at the house waiting on us, too." Ava got into the car and started the engine. "She even said Conroy would come over and help us if we needed an extra set of eyes on the evidence."

Ashton shot her a doubtful look. "I don't know. I think we can do it for now. I would rather her be doing her job with the body, and only doing that for now."

"Me, too. That's her specialty."

"Let's go over what we have from the scene," he said. "I have a partial tire track in two piles of cow crap that were in a straight line and only fifteen feet from the body. I put the tread pattern into the system already to see what kind of tire it might be from, and what kind of vehicle it might be on."

"We have the glasses with the missing lens. The search team did *not* recover the missing lens, so it must be somewhere other than the pasture, the ditch, the gravel road, or the wooded area on the other side of the ditch."

"It also wasn't on Parker's body," Ashton added.

"Whoever killed her washed her down before dumping her," Ava said.

"Yes. There wasn't a single usable trace of anything on her. Just the dirt and grass from the field. Even her hair seemed to have been cleaned."

"You took strand samples?"

"I did."

They arrived back at the rental on Pine Street. A sealed box sat on the porch wrapped in yellow police tape.

"Are you kidding me?" Ava got out and snatched the box up to show Ashton. "Incredible. You know what Mills would say about this?"

He shook his head.

"Things are done differently in a small town." She unlocked the door and shoved it open. "She still didn't want to admit there might be a serial killer loose in Woodsboro even after we found Parker. I argued with her for nearly half an hour to get her to even put out the public request for information, and to tell people to be cautious."

"Things *are* done differently in small towns. You know that."

"Don't defend her, Ashton. Do you see this evidence? It was just left sitting outside in the elements. Anyone could have tampered with it. An animal could have carried it off. Anything." She pushed the door shut behind him.

"But nothing happened to it. It's fine. Let's just compare the hair samples to what we have and get on with this. Don't waste energy being upset over something that can't be changed."

"I hate it when you logic me. You know that, right?"

"Everybody does." He held out his hand for the box.

After several minutes of sorting and then examining, Ashton nodded solemnly. "This is the hair found under the prop at the back of Lucifer's Lounge. This is the sample I just took from Parker's body in the field, and this one is from her brush." He offered them to her and pointed to the window. "Look at them in the natural light first and then under the microscope."

"They look the same to me," Ava said.

"Now, look at them under the microscope. I have three hairs, one from each sample, on the slide already."

She looked. "They are all Parker's, aren't they?"

"They are, but I'm still sending them all to have DNA tests."

"We want this by the book as much as possible, so please do that. But now we know whoever killed her took her from the haunted house tour, hid her under that prop, and then she ended up dead and dumped in that cow pasture."

"We just need to find out who did it and why."

"And if they still have the other three girls." Ava turned away from him to look out her window. In such a small town, how could a serial killer kidnap four girls in a few hours and not be seen?

"The tires are from a Ford Escape. Reports just came back," Ashton said.

She spun to face him. "Great. How common are Ford Escapes in this part of Vermont? Can we trace it?"

His fingers flew over the keys. "Give me a minute. I'm looking." He navigated through several pages, filtering results. His face dropped. "They aren't the most common vehicles in the area, but common enough to be a great big pain in the butt to narrow down." He typed furiously again for several seconds. "There are hundreds in the state, probably."

"You've got to be kidding me. How many Ford Escapes can there even be on the roads?"

He scoffed and tilted his head. "You do not want to know."

"We've got to narrow this down."

"I could narrow it using your profile parameters."

"That's good. He'd own the car, not borrow it because he wouldn't want any time or use restrictions on the vehicle and would want to be able to ditch it if necessary, without having to make up a cover story to tell the owner."

"Exactly. I'm running the first search just for owners who are men." He hit the button and sat back.

Ava's phone rang. She answered and listened to Mills on the other end.

"Two hundred and sixty-two men in a twenty-mile radius," he groaned as she took the phone from her ear. "Now I'll run it for men aged—"

"Save the list progress. We need to get to the station. A fifteen-year-old girl just went in and said she saw a silver Ford SUV going to the cow pasture last night. We need to talk to her now."

At the station, Mills took them to the tiny interview room where the girl sat on a futon with a cup of hot chocolate. Her eyes were big, her face pale, and her parents were nowhere in sight.

Ava turned to Mills. "Where are her parents?"

"No," the girl said loudly. "I don't want them to know I'm here. I'll catch hell if they know I'm here. Or, if they know where I was last night."

Ava sighed. "I can't question you without your parents here."

"I'll just tell you what I saw, then." The girl rose off the futon and set her cup aside. "Please?"

Mills jerked her head toward the door, and Ava followed.

"I can't question her without her parents here. She's only fifteen," Ava said.

"She's a witness, and she's here of her own free will. She doesn't want her parents to know where she was because she was with her boyfriend last night. If they find out, they'll—"

"I can't."

Mills pushed a button on the wall to speak to the girl. "Lilian, why don't you just go ahead and start talking, honey? Just say out loud what you saw like I was in there with you, okay?"

Lilian nodded. "Me and Denny was out in the woods by the cow pasture there. You know, the one between the Watson farm and the Blevins farm? Well, anyway, we saw a silver Ford SUV going to the cow pasture. A man was driving, and he dumped something out there. I didn't go see what because I was too scared. Me and Denny, we just went ahead and left. We only went out there because nobody ever comes out there after dark, and neither of us wanted to get caught. We were supposed to have gone to that haunted house and then to my cousin's house for a lame Halloween party, but we didn't want to go bobbing for apples and do stupid scavenger hunts for candy all night. I just thought the man from the SUV dumped a dead sheep from Watson's farm. I didn't know why that would be happening, but it's just what I thought at the time, and we left. Was that okay, Sheriff?"

"It was fine, honey. You just hold quiet a minute now." She turned to Ava. "There, you didn't question her. No rules broken, and no more time wasted. I thought that's what you wanted."

"We still don't know how many men there were, what they looked like, where they went after dumping the body, nothing. Ashton already found out the tire tracks came from a Ford Escape. Her story just confirms it, and gives us a color."

Mills pushed the button again. "Lilian, did you get a good look at that man?"

"No, I didn't. He was too far away. But he had that body wrapped up in plastic when he took it out of the bed of the truck, and he must have been really strong because he handled it like it was nothing. Anybody who's ever handled a dead sheep knows that even a dead sheep is hard to handle, and that was a... *woman*." Her face visibly paled.

"What did he do with the plastic?" Mills asked.

"He kinda wadded it up and took it with him. It was thick and made a lot of noise. The clear kind. It wasn't black, or anything. He put it in the back of the truck and put something on it to hold it down."

"And did you see which way he went when he left? Did he go away from or toward town, honey?"

"Oh, he drove away from town. Pretty fast, too. Me and Denny figured we'd hear about a bad wreck on the news by this morning. Figured somebody'd be scraping him off a tree somewhere."

Ava cringed.

"Well?" Mills asked Ava.

Ava simply turned away, motioning for Ashton to follow her.

"I can narrow the search by vehicle color now as well," he said.

"Do it."

She went to Mills' office to wait for her.

CHAPTER TWENTY-SIX

The Pond

MILLS PUT OUT A BOLO FOR A SILVER FORD ESCAPE, AND SHE renewed the request for any information from the public.

"You have to tell Lilian's parents that she was here, that she is a witness in a murder investigation," Ava said.

"And I will, but not right now. Let the girl come to terms with it first. She knows her parents and how to handle them better than we do. She'll do what's right. She's got a good head on her shoulders."

"Really? She was out in the woods after midnight with her boyfriend because she has a good head on her shoulders?"

"No, she did that because she's a teenage girl. Weren't you ever one of those, or were you magically born in a twenty-something body with the soul of a crotchety old maid?"

Ava recoiled before she could stop herself. Ashton cleared his throat. Mills held eye contact across the desk, daring Ava to prove her wrong, or to engage more. This was her world, and no matter what, she was going to defend her decisions to the end.

And maybe she was right. Maybe Ava was being too rigid. It hadn't been that long ago that she had bent the rules somewhat to accommodate her own familial needs. She dropped her gaze briefly as her fingers touched the scar above her eyebrow. It was a grim reminder of that time.

"So, you haven't always been so uptight and by-the-book, eh?" Mills asked in a bemused voice as she relaxed back in her chair.

"I have to go. She's only fifteen. It's not right to question her and not tell her parents. They need to give permission for their daughter to be questioned. You know that."

"And they will. They're good people, too, Agent James. Everything will be in order."

Ava stood and headed for the door. "It's just not done in the proper order, and that could come back to bite this case in the ass when it goes to court. I don't know about you, but I don't want it on my conscience that a serial killer gets away with it and let loose because I didn't go by the book." She walked out without waiting for a reply.

Ashton got in the car without saying anything. When they were on the road, he turned to look at her.

"Go ahead, get it off your chest," she said.

"What?"

"You think I'm being too uptight, too, don't you?"

"That's not my call to make. You're lead. I'm just following, but I am glad we heard what Lilian had to say. I can narrow that search even more now and get us closer to finding the killer."

She sunk her face into her hands for a second. "Hungry?"

He let out a soundless chuckle. "You're hanging out with Metford too much if you think food's going to solve this."

"I know." Ava pulled in at The Grill. "They have good chicken planks, but they're deep-fried. The fries are good, too." She blew out a deep breath. "Sorry. I didn't mean to blow up back there."

"It's because she said you were acting like a crotchety old maid, isn't it?"

Ava burst out laughing. "Wow, you really have no filter sometimes." She opened her door and stepped out. "We'll order to-go."

"That's fine with me."

They went in and ordered their food. While they waited, they sat at a table close to the front.

"Do I really?" she asked him.

"What?" he asked, confused.

"Act like that."

He pursed his lips and shifted his eyes to the side.

"Come on. Be honest. You didn't have any trouble in the car being honest."

"You do sometimes, but I just figure it's because of some past trauma that you've experienced and that's how you learned to cope with the triggers you encounter in everyday life and on the job. It's just a trauma response. Lots of people have them. It's not uncommon in people who have gone through very traumatic, life-threatening, physically violent experiences such as—"

"Whoa, pump the brakes there, Ash. No need for all that. Put it in park, thanks." She tucked hair behind her ears and concentrated on keeping her face from turning completely red. "A simple yes would have sufficed."

"Okay. Yes. Sometimes you act like a crotchety old maid with a bad temper." He grinned and gave her the tiniest glimmer of a sarcastic expression and head tilt.

"Mills said nothing about the bad temper."

"No, that was me. I just added it. Thought it could use a little spicing up. I'm disappointed that Mills left it so flat and colorless, seeing as how she is such a colorful character and all." He turned toward the counter. "Where is that food? I need to get back to the computer."

As if he had summoned her, the waitress strolled to the counter with a bag and held it up. "James, Ashton."

Mills called Ava's phone. She put it on speaker and laid it on the table between her and Ashton. "Go ahead, Sheriff."

"Tip came in five minutes ago. Silver Ford Escape was seen around two this morning near Timson Road. That road only leads to a pond where nobody fishes. There's nothing else back there but that damn stagnant pond."

"Timson Road?" Ava asked, shoving her food aside and already grabbing her things.

"Yes. It's past where Parker's body was found."

"We're on it. Thank you, Sheriff." Ava hung up and headed for the door.

"Wait, I need my CSI kit and the field bag with the drone," Ashton said.

Ava stepped to the living room and snagged the handle of the field bag in question. "I have the drone bag. I'm going to the car."

"Right behind you."

Timson Road was five miles from the pasture where Parker's body had been dumped. That was five miles of winding, rough-paved road with deep ditches on either side. Five miles that took them farther back into the woods and farther away from town—any town.

Ava turned left onto Timson. Undergrowth and gnarly branches squealed down the driver's side paint as she aimed the tires for the weedy wheel ruts.

"Nobody's been in here in years," she said.

"Without GPS nav, the killer had to know this road was here. It's out in the middle of nowhere."

"It's likely someone from Woodsboro, or who knows a lot about the place," Ava said.

The trees and scrub opened up on both sides about twenty-five feet along the road, and the way was clear.

"It's like someone cut the scrub and wild growth back here," Ashton said.

"There's the pond." Ava pointed ahead and to the right.

A hundred feet ahead, she stopped the car in front of the swampy water. The body of water was small. Maybe twenty feet across at its widest.

Ava picked up a long stick, held it up beside herself. It measured from the ground to her shoulder. "Long enough." She moved carefully to the edge of the sludgy water and eased the end of the stick in. One slow swipe from left to right, and it snagged something. "Glove up. I got something," she said, moving to the other side of the water.

"This isn't very scientific," Ashton said as he bent to retrieve the item.

"You mean it's not something a crotchety old maid with a bad temper would do."

He shot her a look and stood with the item in his hands. Long, slimy strings of algae hung over it, but it was obviously a woman's small purse with a thin shoulder strap.

"It's a clutch," she said. "I bet there's a wallet and ID inside."

Ashton nodded, lips pursed tightly as he moved stiffly back to the plastic he had spread on the dirt. After photographing the purse, he cleaned off the muck and opened it.

"Summer Tipton," he said, laying the driver's license beside the purse on the plastic.

"What?" Ava asked, bending to look at it. "Oh, Jesus."

"Yeah. That means she's probably dead, too."

"And the same person took her as took Parker." Ava looked back at the water and snaked the stick back into it. "There might be more in there. It's not deep."

An hour later, the purse—and three more just like it—were bagged and tagged, and Ava and Ashton were back in the vehicle heading for the station.

"You know we're looking for three more bodies now, right?" Ashton asked.

"I know, but there's still a chance he's not killed all of them."

"Why else would all four purses be in a stagnant, remote pond? This guy doesn't waste time. Or, rather, these guys. We've established it must be more than one."

She nodded, hating that she must admit she had failed to save even one of them. She had been right there in Woodsboro. She had known in her gut that the previous victims were dead, and had suspected that four more would go missing, and still, she had failed to save any of them.

Ava added the purses to the growing box of evidence at the sheriff's office.

"That means they're all dead, doesn't it?" Mills asked from the doorway. Her voice was barely above a whisper.

Ava nodded as she placed the last purse in the box. "Most likely."

Mills stepped into the room looking as if she might puke and held out a piece of paper. "Another tip came in. Somebody got a good look at the boy with Nicole at Lucifer's Lounge."

Ava took the paper. "Black hair, dark blue eyes, sexy as hell, chiseled jaw, six feet tall, muscular, about one-ninety. Jeans and leather jacket with dark brown work boots that looked new." She looked at Mills questioningly. "That's very detailed. Almost too detailed, isn't it?"

"It was from a girl at the haunted house. She was checking him out because she knew he wasn't from around here, and she thought he was hot. She was jealous that Nicole Rodgers, the rich girl who would never have to work a day in her life, had scored such a sexy bad-boy." Mills held up a hand. "Her words; not mine."

"You got her name, I hope."

"Nope. The tip line was set up so people could give anonymous tips if they wanted. I thought that would get us more information, and I don't want to hear a bunch of bitching about it. I made the call, and that's just how it is. It's not breaking any of your precious unbreakables."

"I wasn't going to bitch about it. It's fine. Do you have a sketch artist?" Mills laughed.

"Right. I'll give this to Ashton and have him work up a sketch. When he's finished, put it on the news and on flyers. Get them around town ASAP. This guy is just wanted for questioning right now, he's not a suspect. That's the line we're putting out, but we all know he might be one of the killers. There are at least two, and maybe three at this point."

Ashton took the description. "How am I supposed to know if I've got this right? I need the person who gave the description to check it after I draw it."

"I know. Talk to Mills after I leave. Maybe she will be nicer to you. She doesn't hate you."

"She doesn't hate you, either. You just... rub her the wrong way," he said in a lowered voice.

"I'm not rubbing her any way. Just talk to her. She probably knows who the caller was. I'm going to see Conroy about Parker's body."

"Got it." He turned on his heel and headed toward Mills' office.

Conroy's eyes lit up when she saw Ava. "Hi," she said excitedly. "Wow, have I got news for you."

"Good or bad?"

"I don't know. Just news. Come on over." She went to the coolers and opened a door. She pulled a table out and reached for the cover over it.

Ava put her hand on Conroy's arm. "This is Parker Wilson, right?"

"Who else?" She chuckled and pulled the sheeting back to reveal the body. "Okay, what is the first thing you notice?"

"She's young and she's been murdered."

"Well, duh. I mean besides that."

"I'm not a big fan of guessing games, Ms. Conroy."

"Right, right. Well, here. Just let me point it out to you. You like bulleted lists? Never mind. She doesn't have any defensive wounds at all. Let that sink right on into the old gray matter."

"She was killed quickly?"

"Nope. She was strangled. That's a terrible way to go. There's definitely going to be a lot of fighting and struggling when someone is trying to strangle the life right out of you."

"But not in Parker's case." Ava looked closer. "Are you sure that's what killed her, then?"

"Oh, yeah. That's what did it. She was stabbed in the chest ten times post-mortem. Her body was hosed down thoroughly before being dumped in that cow pasture, but…" Conroy hurried off holding one finger up that Ava should wait right there.

Why she had to stand over a dead girl and wait for Conroy's big reveal was beyond her, but she took the opportunity to check the wounds and really look at Parker's face. Such a pretty girl with a whole lot of living left in front of her. Generations would never exist because some sick bastard had killed Parker before she ever had the chance to even live her own life.

There indeed were no defensive wounds at all. No bruising, no abrasions, not even the slightest scratches that indicated she had struggled before death. The only bruising was the ligature mark around her neck.

"Could she have been drugged?" Ava called over as Conroy rifled through a file cabinet.

"Maybe. I have a test out. Won't know for sure just yet though."

Conroy came back. She held out a plastic bag and a report file. "The killer was very smart and very careful. There wasn't anything left on the body after he hosed it down. I figure he took his time cleaning her off. But I found a tiny bit of DNA on this cubic zirconia earring. I've filled out the paperwork to have it tested, but it's my guess that it belongs to the killer. It was somehow transferred onto the earring after he hosed down the body but before he wrapped it in plastic and dumped it in that field." She handed the file and the bag to Ava.

"Thank you. I'll put a rush on it."

"I could be wrong, but I could also be right. Never know." She covered Parker's face again and shoved the metal bed back into the cooler unceremoniously before shutting the door.

Conroy was definitely unique. Ava had never met anyone quite like her, and she didn't know how she felt about the woman. She was good at her job, but she had her quirks.

CHAPTER TWENTY-SEVEN

Body Number Two

BY THE TIME AVA GOT BACK TO THE STATION, THE SKETCH HAD BEEN printed onto flyers and was slated for the news out of Burlington at six that evening.

"Did Mills get you in touch with the caller?" Ava asked Ashton.

"Already had her on the phone when I walked into the office." He grinned and shook his head. "I think she likes needling you. You must have ruffled her feathers on the first day, or something."

"Jamie ruffled her feathers before I was ever in the picture. I think that's what happened. Have there been any callers on the sketch?"

"A few hits. Mostly just random people who remember seeing the guy at the haunted house that night, but none of them knew his name, or where he was from. Nothing we didn't already know. One guy did say that he thought he remembered Nicole calling him Charlie, but he couldn't be sure."

"I say that we go back to the haunted house and gather up all the workers who were there the night before Halloween, and question them all again," Ava said.

"I think that might be a good idea."

It took less than an hour to get all eight of the workers who worked the closing shift that night together at Lucifer's Lounge. Mel came, but Nate did not.

Ashton held the sketch of the mystery man. Everyone looked at it and shrugged their shoulders or shook their heads.

"Okay, does anyone recognize this man? He is about six feet tall, muscular, about one-ninety. Black leather jacket, blue jeans, work boots. Came through the night before Halloween, and might have been in the last tour group, or almost the last tour group."

"Some of us saw him, but we don't know who he is," a woman said.

"Did you see who he was with?"

She nodded. "We already told you he was with that girl that was missing. The rich girl. Nicole Rodgers."

"Did any of you see which way he went after the tour?" Ava asked them.

They shook their heads.

"We didn't notice anyone lagging behind after the last group, either," a man said. "That would have drawn our attention."

"Yeah? Why's that?" Ashton asked.

"Because of the way we have to lock the place down. We're the two who are responsible for doing that, and there's a procedure to it. To clear the place, we start in the attic, and we work our way down to the first floor. One of us stands at the stairs and the other locks the front door, and checks the front rooms. Then we both check the back rooms and move out the back door and lock it. We noticed nothing out of the ordinary that night."

Ava moved closer to the two men. "Everyone else has a hard time remembering specific nights because of the weird hours and shifts. How can you be so sure that night there was nothing odd?"

"Because there's been nothing out of the ordinary any night. That's how."

She sniffed and leaned toward them a bit, wrinkling her nose. They pulled back, looking at her as if she might have lost her mind. She sniffed again.

"Lady, what the hell?" the man asked.

"It's Agent James, thank you. And, does my nose deceive me, or is that skunkilicious odor clinging to your clothes, your hair, and seeping out of your pores indicate that you have been enjoying the Devil's Lettuce?"

They recoiled and their faces turned ashen.

"Is it at all possible that you could have been listening to the sweet whispers of Mary Jane that night while you locked up after the last tour?"

"No way," they said in unison.

She nodded. "Right. You look shocked, but that smell. Something about it makes me not believe you for some reason."

"We weren't smoking while we were at work. Yes, we smoke at home and sometimes before we come in to set up props, but not while we're on the clock. I swear," the man said.

His friend held up the Boy Scout sign and nodded solemnly. "Me, too. It's legal, man."

Ava shook her head and turned to Ashton. "I'm done here."

Ashton thanked everyone, handed them flyers, and went to the car as well. "Where are we going now?"

"The station. We'll be close if another tip comes in."

"I want to narrow that Ford search by the first name Charlie, too."

"How long is the list right now?"

"Fifty-seven white males between the ages of eighteen and thirty who own a silver Ford Escape."

"That's still a lot."

"The first name will shave off a lot."

Back at the station, Ashton put the new parameter into the search, and the results came up zero.

"Looks like the first name shaved off more than a lot," she said. They tried every variant of the name they could think of—Charles, Chuck, Char, Chaz… but came up with nothing.

"Maybe I need to tweak the profile?"

She shook her head. "I think the profile is solid, Ashton. Maybe this Charlie guy isn't one of our killers."

"The chances are better that he is one of the killers. Maybe he's just not the one who owns that particular vehicle. I'm going to look over the list that's already populated since the other parameters are there. I'll narrow it somehow."

"How?"

"I don't know. I'll figure it out."

"I will leave you to it. I'm going out front to see what's going on with the tip lines."

He gave her a nod of acknowledgment, and she left the room.

Before she could reach Mills, the front doors burst open, and a heavyset man dressed in overalls stumbled in wild-eyed and looking scared half to death.

"Whoa, there, buddy!" Marsh yelled, making a dash for the man. "You alright, Jonesy?" He helped the man to a seat.

"No, man, I'm not. Not at all. I just found a body. I think it's a woman, but I was too damn scared to look."

"Where, Jonesy?" Marsh asked.

Ava hurried to them. "You found a body?"

The man nodded. "In my corn silo. I think it's a woman." He shook his head and scrubbed at his face with both hands. "There was so much blood everywhere I couldn't be sure."

"Why didn't you just call 911?" she asked.

"No cell service," Marsh and Jonesy said simultaneously.

"There's no cell service on most of my land, lady. It's a dead zone." His eyes went wide. "I didn't mean…"

"It's okay," Ava said. "What's your name, sir?"

"Victor Jones. Everybody calls me Jonesy."

"Good. Okay, Jonesy. I'm Agent James with the FBI. I'm going to go check out your silo, and I want you to stay here with Deputy Marsh."

"Not a problem. I don't want to see more than what I already did."

Ava got Ashton, and they met with Mills in her office. "I'm going to need Detective Graham, Conroy, Marty, and Latham to come with us. You can leave Ginny and your reserve deputies in charge of the tip lines."

"Go on ahead. We'll be right behind you."

"The corn will shift, and you'll get sucked down into it," Mills said. "You have to use the lifeline harness system that's in place, or you get slowly crushed to death and suffocate. It's really that simple, Agent."

"Fine. You're right," Ava said. She hadn't wanted to take the time to strap into the harness system. The body was several feet down and toward the center of the large silo. Jonesy had been right—there was a lot of blood on the corn. It looked as if someone had splashed it all around the body, but there was none on the body.

Once in the harness, Ava gloved up, took the camera, her specimen collection supplies, and started toward the body. She couldn't see a head, and as she drew closer in the very dim space, she realized why. There was no head.

The victim was female, and it looked as if rats had torn and chewed at her body. The overwhelming odor of corn almost overpowered the smell of the blood and of the hot, decaying body, but not completely. Putting her hand over her nose and mouth, Ava moved slowly around the body, wondering which of the missing girls she was looking at. As the corpse's feet came into view, she knew she was looking at Zoe Iversen. Her head had been placed between her ankles.

Ava took pictures and samples. She made sure the scene was taken care of and that they had what they needed before they lifted her out of the silo. Once out, she put the evidence in a box in her car.

"Sheriff, I need to know that you will make sure this scene is finished by the book. I'm going to go talk to Nicole's parents. They need to know what's going on. There's still a chance we might be able to get ahead of this and save the other two girls."

"You can count on me, Agent." Mills said. She looked humbled and pale as if the severity of the situation had finally hit her.

Ashton stayed behind to make sure everything was done by the book, and to make Ava feel more secure about the situation. In a perfect world, she could have called in a backup team of agents.

But, as she absolutely hated to admit, things were different in a small town.

CHAPTER TWENTY-EIGHT

Old Money, Young Scandal

T HE RODGERS' ESTATE WAS JUST THAT—AN ESTATE. IT WAS BY FAR the largest and grandest property in Woodsboro. The house was more along the lines of a mansion. An old English Manor. Ava half-expected a butler to open the door, but Mrs. Rodgers answered.

"Agent James," she said. "Has something happened?" Tears welled in her eyes, and her chin quivered. She pressed a hand to her mouth.

"No, Mrs. Rodgers. It has, but not with Nicole. That's why I wanted to come and talk to you and your husband. I need some more information."

Mrs. Rodgers opened the door wider and motioned her in. "Of course. Please, come inside. Tony isn't here right now. I don't expect him back until tomorrow."

"He's gone?"

"Yes." Mrs. Rodgers led her to a sitting room on the right side of the grand entry hall.

"While his daughter is missing, he's… gone instead of being here? That seems a bit odd, doesn't it?" Ava took the proffered seat across the dainty table from her host.

"He's out looking for her. He thinks he can find her. Thinks he knows her better than any law enforcement personnel can ever hope to know her. He is going to every place she ever visited or spoke about, and some that are just popular hangouts for kids her age."

Ava opened the file and took out the sketch. "Mrs. Rodgers, some people saw Nicole with a young man the night she disappeared. We got a pretty good description of him, and a sketch artist made this. Does he look familiar at all to you?"

Mrs. Rodgers' face tightened. She jabbed a finger into the center of the face on the paper. "That's him, alright. That's the man who got her pregnant. I knew she was still sneaking around and seeing him even though we took her phone and cut off her internet privileges. How was she still in communication with him?" She shoved the paper back to Ava. "We're old money. Both of our families—mine and my husband's. We were raised to be traditional, and we take our values very seriously. It's the foundation of our lives. We tried to instill that in Nicole, but it just wouldn't take for some reason." She pointed at the paper again. "Because of *him*. She is set to inherit two pepper canneries in the South, two more in Tennessee, and a paper mill as soon as she turns twenty-one. All she has to do is play by the rules until then, and those businesses are hers to do with as she pleases. The family has plenty more to give her later, but those are her testing grounds, so to speak. She was doing okay, and then that damn Charlie showed up and ruined everything."

"Charlie?" Ava asked, indicating the sketch. "That's his name?"

Mrs. Rodgers nodded curtly. "That's the name he gave us. I, for one, never trusted anything that boy said or did. He could have been anybody. We made her break up with him and stop seeing him just as soon as we found out she was pregnant."

"Why not file charges against him?"

She looked horrified. "And bring the family scandal out into the public like that? Absolutely not. It would humiliate Nicole and tarnish her name for the rest of her life, not to mention the Rodgers name in general. The family reputation must be protected as well as our daughter. If not, her generation and the next will surely be the last to thrive from it. She was only seventeen when she fell pregnant. That's too young to be having children, and too young to be getting married—which we would never agree to under those circumstances anyway."

"Why? If he got her pregnant, wouldn't you want him to step up and take responsibility?"

"You don't come from old money, established money, do you, Agent James?"

"Obviously not, or we wouldn't be having this conversation," Ava said, restraining the bite from her remark.

"Of course. I don't mean to sound rude, but if we had agreed to let them get married, that boy would have undoubtedly just run through with her entire inheritance. It was painfully obvious that she couldn't say no to him about anything."

"How did you get her to break it off with him, if she was so smitten?"

"By threatening to throw her out of the house and disown her, if she didn't do as we said." She looked away and clasped her hands under her chin.

"Would you have done that?"

"Of course not. Are you a fool on all counts? We love our daughter more than anything in the world, Agent. I would never leave her homeless and penniless. Why do you think we worked so hard our whole lives to keep the Rodgers empire running strong and true, and to keep the name and reputation sparkling in the public eye?" She put her hands flat on the table and leaned toward Ava for emphasis. "For our daughter. To ensure she had everything she ever needed in life after we were gone. It was a threat to get her to conform. It was for her own good, though. That boy was no good. I could tell it from the first time I saw him. It was the eyes. Something was off about them."

"I'm sorry, Mrs. Rodgers. We haven't heard anything else about Nicole other than finding her purse, but we're hopeful."

"You found another body, didn't you?" Her voice was as flat and lifeless as the expression in her eyes.

"Why would you say that?"

"Why else would you be here when you could have just called me? That sketch is on the TV. And you just have that look in your eyes that says you've seen something horrible and you're worried. Which of the other girls did you find?"

"I'm not at liberty to discuss the case with—"

"Oh, the hell with it. I'll know within the hour. You don't need to tell me, although I was hoping it would be a bit of *quid pro quo*. I told you some things that I was not thrilled to be sharing today because I thought it might help you find my daughter. I would appreciate it if you kept that story to yourself as well you keep the details of the case away from me."

"I will, Mrs. Rodgers. What was Charlie's last name?"

Without missing a beat, Mrs. Rodgers said, "Hess. He's a senior at the university over in Hamilton."

"Where's that?"

"About three hours west of Woodsboro."

"Name of the university?"

"Felton University. Did he take those four girls? Did he kill Parker Wilson?"

"Mrs. Rodgers…" Ava exhaled deeply. "I can't speculate. He's a person of interest, and we need to ask him some questions, just like the news and the flyer says. That's all. Thank you for talking with me. If you think of anything else that might assist us in our investigation…" She stood and walked to the door, ready to get out of that huge, rich house where every footstep echoed through the vast emptiness.

"Will do. You get that bastard, Agent. If he hurt those girls, don't hold any mercy on him. No one would hold it against you if he never saw the inside of a jail cell." She nodded but didn't move to show Ava out.

Ava hurried out the door, through the entry hall, and out the front door. Who could stand living in such a cavernous home where every footfall was a reminder of just how alone they were and just how empty their lives were?

She called Ashton on her way back to the station. They had just finished up at the crime scene, and Conroy had taken possession of the body. Everything had been done by the book.

Ava gave him the new information about Charlie.

"I'll put it in the system and see what comes up. Should have something ready by the time you get there."

When she walked through the doors, Ashton held out a file.

"The only names close to Charlie Hess are Steven Hess, fifty-two. Robert Hess, forty-eight. Josiah Hess, seventy-three. Their pictures and government-issued IDs are printed in there for you, but—"

She took the file. "They aren't the young, handsome man people saw with Nicole."

"I seriously doubt it."

She opened the folder and looked at the pictures. Shaking her head, she closed it again.

CHAPTER TWENTY-NINE

Making Connections

"**W**HAT DO YOU SAY WE GO TO THE CORONER'S?" AVA ASKED AS she walked back toward the front door.

"She won't have much, if anything yet."

"All the better. I can't just sit here."

Ashton followed her out the door and to the car with his field bags and shoulder bag containing all his equipment.

"You could have left those in the sheriff's private office," Ava said. "Nobody would have bothered it. They probably don't even know what most of that stuff is, let alone how to use it. I don't even know what most of it does."

"That's okay. I feel better taking it with me." He put it in the back of the car and then got in the passenger seat. "Never know when another call will come in, either. Might need it on the fly."

"You're not wrong. What did they do with all that corn?"

"Mr. Jones loaded it into two tantum dump trucks and sent it to an incinerator. There was nothing else in it except rat feces and bugs."

"The corn with the blood on it?"

"It's with Francis… uh, Ms. Conroy. All of it they could get, at least."

"There was no blood on the body, and even the rat bites had no blood. It's like someone bled her out and then threw her blood all around her body on the corn."

They arrived at the coroner's office to find Conroy in her high state of energy buzzing around as she had been before. Ava had a sneaking suspicion that the woman imbibed too many energy drinks.

"Lordy, Lordy. You two sure don't ask much, do you? I barely got the body on the table and started examining, and here you are with your hands out? I don't know how fast you want me to work, but I'm only one person, and I haven't slept in about sixty hours now."

"No, Ms. Conroy," Ashton said. "We just came by to see if you needed any assistance and to see how far you had gotten." He smiled broadly.

Ava stopped and took notice of his reaction to the strange woman.

Conroy pressed a gloved hand to her chest and smiled sheepishly. "Really? You came to help? Nobody has ever done that for me before."

He nodded eagerly. "If you need it, I don't mind a bit."

"Dead bodies don't creep you out, or make you want to barf on your shoes?"

He shook his head. "I can think of a thousand things I'd rather be looking at, but I seriously don't mind. I can handle it just fine. Hazard of the job, I guess."

Ava bit the inside of her jaw to staunch her response. It was like some awkward teenage mating dance between two of the strangest kids in class. If that class just happened to be taking place in an autopsy room. Where there was a corpse. A headless corpse.

She cleared her throat. "Could we possibly move past whatever this is and get on with the examination?"

"Right, right," Conroy said. She motioned toward the little side room. "You can wash and put on your PPE in there if you really want to help."

Ashton glanced at Ava and then went to put on the shields and apron and gloves.

Conroy lifted Zoe's arms one at a time, pointing to her forearms and hands. "There are several defensive wounds on her hands and forearms.

Two, three, four broken fingernails possibly from a struggle, or possibly from trying to claw her attacker. Could have been trying to crawl away from him, too, as the palms present with several abrasions and small cuts." She moved down the body to the feet and legs. "Bruises and cuts on the shins and tops of feet. Maybe from kicking at someone or something." She sighed and moved to stand over the center of the body again. "Rats and possibly other small rodents got to her though, which really messes us up. There is a fair amount of decomp present, but also there are more small animal bites than I can possibly count all over her body. They really did a number on her."

Ashton returned and went to the foot of the table. "What was the manner of death?"

"Homicide. Even a small-town dummy like me knows that," Conroy said.

"Cause?" He rolled the head to the side and looked at the ragged decapitation wound.

"Well, if the strangulation didn't do it, I would just bet a dollar that getting her head cut off did."

"So, no a definitive conclusion yet." Ashton put the head down again. "What about tests for the chloroform?"

"What about them?"

"I suggest using a chromatographic mass spectrometric analysis to test for it in the bodily tissues since there's a lack of blood. You could do that for both victims."

Conroy laughed and shook her head. "We don't have a mass spectrometer. Those are way above our budget. I have to get any of that fancy stuff done up in the city, or borrow the equipment, and I seriously doubt anyone within a hundred miles has one that I could actually borrow. So, I'll have to get the tests done in the city. They might get to my requests sometime before I retire, but I seriously doubt it because we are of no consequence to them way up here in Woodsboro, Vermont."

"You have to send samples to Albany, don't you?" Ashton asked.

"How'd you know?"

"Lucky guess. It was either there or Burlington. They are the two most likely to have the equipment and facilitate requests from here."

"What about New York?" Ava asked.

Ashton and Conroy laughed simultaneously. It was bitter laughter.

"Okay, sorry I had a suggestion."

"New York can't get their own tests done in a timely manner most of the time. They couldn't get to any out-of-state requests for the next century," Conroy said.

Ashton nodded in agreement. "I might just have one you could borrow," he said with a sly, small smile.

"No, you do not," Conroy gasped.

The small smile broke into a wide grin. "In my field bag."

"Where's that? Back home?"

"In the car."

Conroy looked from him to Ava. "He's joking, right?"

"It's been my experience that Ashton lacks a humor gene or two. It's very unlikely that he's joking."

"I'll be right back." He took off the shields, apron, and gloves, and rushed out the door. He was back through the door in less than a minute with his field bag in tow. He took out an object that Ava had never seen before and set it on a side table.

"I cannot believe that you actually have a portable mass spectrometer. I'm so freaking jealous. I wish I worked for the FBI."

Ashton and Conroy worked to get the samples prepared for testing from both subjects while Ava watched. Ashton showed Conroy how to start the test and then they walked back to join Ava.

"How long will that take?" she asked.

"Just a few minutes per," Conroy said.

Ashton smiled at her. "What about the blood on the corn? Was it Zoe's blood?"

"No, it wasn't. I tested it as soon as I got here. It was pig's blood. I did a dozen tests, and they all came back as pig's blood."

Within several minutes, they had the results from the spectrometer tests.

"Zoe and Parker have traces of chloroform in their systems. There was very little blood left to test, but it was there in those little samples we did get," Conroy said. "However, there was none in their hearts, lungs, or livers."

"And exactly what does that mean?" Ava asked.

"They were exposed, but the exposure wasn't excessive. Not enough to cause death," Ashton supplied.

"Just enough to knock them out. Someone was strong enough to hold that rag over their faces while they struggled and inhaled for probably five minutes. Maybe longer. They were unconscious. But chloroform is hard to gauge, and I bet that's why Zoe here has all those defensive wounds. Poor girl woke up and fought like hell trying to save her own life." Conroy's eyes rolled toward the head at the end of the table sadly. "God, I hope she didn't wake up while that was happening. Makes my heart ache thinking about it."

"Thank you, Ms. Conroy," Ava said.

"Oh, it's Francis, or Frankie, please. And you're welcome. Come back anytime."

Ava left without another word. The woman had a way of making even the most mundane situation seem awkward.

Ashton hummed lightly under his breath while Ava used the laptop to research Charlie Hess some more.

"Ash, listen to this."

He stopped humming and rolled his chair closer. "What is it?"

"There was a boy named Charlie Hess who was adopted by the Dawson family at age fourteen after his father signed his rights over to the mother, who then died. The father's name was Stephen Hess, spelled with a p-h. He would be fifty-two now. The Steven Hess in the file you gave me is fifty-two. I think they're the same man."

"But his name is spelled with a v."

"I don't care. I think it's the same man." She pulled out the picture of Steven Hess. "I think this man signed away his rights to his son. Gave him to his mother, and then the mother died. Why didn't he go back for his son after she died, though?"

"Because he probably isn't the right man."

"Charlie Hess was adopted by Theodore and Gretchen Dawson of Hamilton, Vermont. Ashton?"

"Yes?"

"Search Charlie Dawson in that vehicle search and see what you get."

He did. "No Ford Escape, but he is in here. Only one, too. He owns a brand-new Ford pickup and a Toyota Camry. He's twenty-two, and he's a senior over in Hamilton, Vermont at Felton University."

Ava snapped her fingers and grinned. "Matches what Mrs. Rodgers told me. I think we need to take a little road trip."

"That's not a little road trip. That's three hours west of here, and only if the traffic and weather are reasonable."

"Then we best get started."

CHAPTER THIRTY

Three for Three

"I T'S A FRAT HOUSE. WHY AM I NOT SURPRISED IT'S A FRAT HOUSE?"
Ava groaned as she parked in front of Charlie's address.

Ashton shrugged. "Lots of people are in fraternities during their
college years. I'm more shocked that he's enrolled at Felton University
and Nicole's family still had such a low opinion of him."

"What does the university have to do with anything?" She turned off
the engine.

"Felton is one of the highest-ranked medical universities in the
country. Not just anyone can apply and get into Felton. I've been checking his school history. His grades… he's a certifiable genius. A member
of MENSA. He could have gone to an Ivy League if he wanted to. I don't
know why he didn't."

"Do MENSA boys usually dress in black leather jackets, jeans, and work boots, and get their underage girlfriends pregnant while they're lying to her and her parents about who they really are?"

Ashton huffed out a long breath and closed the laptop. "I didn't say he was a saint, just a genius."

"A dangerous one, if you ask me."

Ava knocked on the door, and Charlie answered with all the swagger and confidence of, well, a frat boy. "Well, hello there. Can I help you, beautiful?" He smiled at her lecherously and almost acted as if Ashton wasn't there.

Ava rolled her eyes and flashed her badge. "Agents James and Ashton, FBI. We need to speak with you about your girlfriend, Nicole Rodgers."

His eyes went wide. "Nicole? She's not here. She lives in Woodsboro." He looked worried. "And we're not exactly supposed to still be seeing each other."

"But you are, aren't you, Charlie?"

He shifted from foot to foot. "What's this about? Did her bitch mom send you to scare me away? I love Nicole, and she loves me."

"We are federal agents, Charlie," Ava snapped. "People don't *send* federal agents to scare people away from their daughters. Nicole is missing, and we have some questions for you. We can come in and ask them here, or we can take you with us back to Woodsboro and talk there. Up to you."

He gave her a cocky grin that lasted about two seconds, glanced at Ashton, and jerked the door wider. "I guess you're coming in, then. Nicole isn't missing."

"Is she here?" Ashton asked.

"No, but I wish she was. At least we could be together. She's probably at one of her friends' houses hiding out from her parents. They're real assholes. They won't let her have access to the internet, and they broke her phone because she was talking to me. Real pieces of work, those two."

"I assure you," Ava said, "Nicole is missing. She has been since the night before Halloween."

"No." His eyes jittered strangely and then tears shimmered in them. "Are you sure about that?"

"Four young women went missing the same night," Ava said. "Two of them have been found brutally murdered already. We think Nicole is in real danger."

"No. I mean, that can't be right. Her family is so rich no one would dare lay a finger on her." He swiped the back of his hand across his eyes and sniffled. "This is their fault. Pompous assholes. They hated me so bad that they wouldn't let us see each other. I wanted to take her out for Halloween, but they wouldn't let her go anywhere near me. I went to a Halloween party here in Hamilton that night. I was so depressed that I got totally hammered."

"And I suppose there are witnesses who can back this story up?" Ava asked.

"About fifty people can verify that I was there the whole night." He started naming names and counting them off on his fingers.

"Whoa, Charlie, hold on a second. Why'd you lie about your last name to Nicole's parents? You told them your last name is Hess."

He looked as if he'd been kicked in the shin, but he recovered with lightning speed. "I didn't want them to find out I was adopted and that my dad had just signed me away like I didn't matter. I was just a throw-away child to him. My mom died. She overdosed. You think my dad came back into the picture just because I was all alone? Nicole's parents hated me bad enough. I saw no need to give them more of a reason. If they researched Charlie Dawson, my adoption records would have come up pretty damn quick. Charlie Hess doesn't even exist."

"That makes no sense at all," Ava said.

"Did to me," Charlie countered, looking smug and suddenly unconcerned that his girlfriend was missing.

"I'm going to need the names of all your fraternity brothers, Charlie," Ava said. "We have some questions for them, too."

Charlie gave her the names. Rattled them off without hesitation.

"Thank you. Did you know that Nicole was two months pregnant?"

Charlie blanched and looked as if he might vomit. He stared at her questioningly, one hand unconsciously clenching his gut.

"Well, did you?" she asked.

He shook his head but said nothing.

"Oh, I thought she would have at least told you that. Her mother is pretty upset, and her father is livid. Can't really blame them, though. She is only seventeen, and you're what?" She flipped through some pages as if looking for the information.

"Twenty-two," he muttered. "I'm twenty-fucking-two. You know how old I am."

"That's right." She smiled tightly. "Twenty-fucking-two with a missing and pregnant seventeen-year-old girlfriend whose parents despise the ground you walk on." She closed the notebook. "You stay close, okay? We will *definitely* have more questions for you. Right now, we need to go find…" She opened the book to the list of frat brothers. "Ah, yes, Ethan Coldwell, age twenty-one. We have some questions for him now. If you hear from Nicole, you'll let us know right away, won't you?" She held out a card with her information on it.

He took it with a glare. "Of course."

"Good boy, now, Charlie. Bye." Ava cut her eyes at Ashton to follow her lead as they left the frat house without another word.

"That was harsh," Ashton said.

"Needed to be. We have to get to Ethan before Charlie does. We need to question these guys before he has a chance to coach them."

A young man walked toward them, heading in the direction of the house they had just exited.

Ava took a chance. "Excuse me, are you a member here?"

"I am." He smiled, looked her up and down, and ran a hand over his hair. "And who are you?"

She gave him a winning smile and flashed her badge. "Agent James, FBI. This is my partner, Agent Ashton. We just talked to your frat brother, Charlie. What's your name?"

He blinked but recovered quickly enough. She looked at her list and back to him. "Name?" she repeated.

"Ethan Coldwell."

"First name on the list. Must be our lucky day. We have some questions for you. Do you live here?" She pointed to the house.

"Uh, I do. Third floor."

"We should go inside and talk." Ava motioned to the door.

Ethan opened it and waited for them to follow him inside before shutting it again. "Should I get Charlie?"

"No, we've already spoken to him," Ashton said. "We only need you at the moment."

"What do you know about Nicole Rodgers and Charlie Dawson?" Ava asked.

"They were seeing each other. Dating, I guess you'd call it. They were hot and heavy into each other, but her parents put a stop to it. They didn't like Charlie at all for some reason."

"Maybe that she's underage?" Ava pointed out.

He shrugged. "I guess. Why's this such a big deal?"

Ava had to actually, physically bite her tongue at his attitude. These frat boys were unbelievable.

"She's missing since the night before Halloween," Ashton said, wisely taking the lead.

"Maybe she ran away from those parents of hers. Last I heard they broke her phone and restricted her from the internet. They were keeping her locked up like some prisoner, or something."

"I've been in their home," Ava said. "It's nothing like a prison."

"Having all your freedom stripped away would drive anyone away from you no matter how much money you had."

"At seventeen, you don't have adult freedoms and privileges," Ava said hotly. "Where were you the night before Halloween?"

"Why do you need to know where I was?"

"If you refuse to answer, we can always take you to the station in Woodsboro and detain you for questioning. That can be a very long time. Much longer than if we were holding you and wanting to actually charge you with something," she said.

"I was with Charlie at a party here in Hamilton, if it's really any of your business."

"How long did the party last?"

"We were there until the dawn. Everyone at the party can vouch for it. We didn't do anything wrong, you know. It's our senior year. He was heartbroken because he couldn't see Nicole, and we wanted this to be the best of our college years. We wanted this party to really be memorable. It was a real bash. Something to remember for years to come."

"Right. You wanted it to be legendary," she said.

"Yes. You do understand. That's exactly what we aimed for, and that's exactly what I think we accomplished." He laughed, nodding enthusiastically.

"What kind of car do you drive, Ethan?" Ava asked.

He stopped laughing. "Chevy Equinox." He pointed out the window to the black car sitting in the parking lot. "Right there."

"Thanks."

"Is that it?"

"For now, Ethan, but don't go too far. We'll probably have more questions for everyone close to Charlie in the next few weeks."

"Weeks? Seriously? I can't go to my aunt's in Maine for Thanksgiving?"

"I wouldn't bet on it," Ashton said. "No one knows where Nicole is."

"I told you she probably ran away, and I wouldn't blame her."

"Three other girls went missing the same night," Ava said. "Two of them have been found murdered so far. I don't think Nicole ran away."

"Murdered?"

"That's right. Did you know she was two months pregnant?"

His reaction was much the same as Charlie's had been. His face paled, and he fell silent, only shaking his head by way of response.

"Yeah. She was. It seems that she didn't tell many people, which really shocks me. Her parents knew, though. Maybe that's why they didn't like Charlie so much, huh?"

She turned around and headed for the door again.

Ava and Ashton spent most of the day talking to a few others on the list. Each one of them confirmed Charlie's original story about his and Nicole's relationship and his whereabouts on the night of her disappearance.

"He couldn't have gotten to all of them before we did, could he?" Ava asked Ashton as they drove back toward Woodsboro.

"Texts. He could have typed one and sent it to the whole group," Ashton said matter-of-factly.

"But could he have done so before we saw Ethan? His story was the same as everyone else's."

"That's a bust. I don't think he could have, but maybe. Chances are very slim he could have conveyed all that information and that Ethan could have retained it in such a short time. It was only a minute at most."

"That's what I thought. If they were coached, it was done before today."

"They didn't seem to be coached, though. Their stories seemed natural."

Ava's phone rang. "Jeez, that's never a good sign," she said, digging the phone from her coat pocket and punching the button.

Ashton snatched the phone and pointed to the road. He put the phone in the holder on the dash and pushed the speaker button.

"Hello? Agent James, can you hear me?" Mills asked.

"Yes, Sheriff. I can hear you. I'm driving."

"We found Summer Tipton's body. You need to get back here. It's bad."

"Worse than Zoe?"

"Much worse."

CHAPTER THIRTY-ONE

Summer's End

IT WAS LATE EVENING WHEN AVA TURNED DOWN THE GRAVEL DRIVE in Woodsboro. The sun hung low in the west, and the shadows stretched long and thin from the mountains like dark fingers reaching toward the east, clutching insubstantial fingers at the land, wanting to devour it.

A slight bank rose on the left side of the drive. An old picket fence bordered a yard on the right. Farther ahead, on the left and past the slight bank, a clutch of bare crabapple trees shivered in the wind as they kept watch over a pond that had once surely been the pride of the homeowner, but no longer. It was full of fallen leaves and rot from the wild growth.

The long, ranch-style house on the right had, at one time, been horse stables. Though beautifully remastered into a house, it had also fallen into disrepair, and nature was taking back what had been hers all along, slowly erasing all evidence of man's intrusion on her perfection.

The drive widened just past the house, and several cruisers came into view along with the big, red barn. It was in true New England style. The main part was at least three stories tall with small, oddly placed windows and a steeple in the center of the tin roof. The second section that ran perpendicular to the main section was two stories with evenly spaced windows, large double doors at the small end, and small doors on the long sides.

The back of the barn looked like a myriad of other barns Ava had seen while in New England. Nothing to raise suspicion. It was just an abandoned, well-built barn on an abandoned farm with other well-built structures that were slowly being overtaken by vines and bushes.

"She's in the barn," Ashton said.

"I know that, Ash." Ava let the SUV slow to a crawl as she maneuvered around the cruisers and up onto the grass.

The grassy hills swept upward and away from the barn. They were running from the atrocity inside. Running toward the mountains. No doubt, Ava would want to join them shortly. Everything inside her wanted to stay inside the car and not see what horrible things had been done to the beautiful girl who had been a model, the beautiful girl so many people had admired and looked up to in Woodsboro. The girl who'd never hurt anyone and inspired so many without ever meeting them personally.

"Ava?"

"Yeah?"

"Are you okay?"

After a long moment, she realized she had been sitting in the car staring up at the rolling hills with the keys in her hand and not moving to get out. Sucking in a sharp breath, she turned to him. "Yeah. I'm fine. Let's go."

She was anything but fine. She was far from fine, but how was she supposed to tell Ashton or anyone else that? When she had been on Molly and her mother's case, she had seen enough horrors to last anyone a lifetime. Was she really ready to add to that? Zoe's body had been shocking, but Mills had given her the highlights of Summer's injuries, and she didn't know if she was ready to handle the scene or not.

Ashton got out and headed slowly toward Mills and the others. He glanced back twice at Ava. She sat with her fingers curled around the handle and her palms sweating. "Ready for it or not, you have to get out of this car and go do your job," she muttered to herself.

She opened the door and was thankful for the cold, bracing wind that instantly cooled her overheated skin.

Mills met her, blocking her path a bit. "It's bad. You need to brace yourself, hon. It's the worst I've ever seen."

"Have you been crying?"

"Hell no, I'm still crying. I'll be crying every time I think about this for as long as I live."

Ava blinked at Mills, not knowing how to react to her show of emotion. She took a few deep breaths and pulled on a mask and gloves. Ashton had already gone inside. She couldn't leave him in there alone. All Mills' people were outside with her, and they all looked as if they had been sick and crying and weren't going back in anytime soon.

Keeping her eyes trained on the ground, Ava stepped through the doors and to the left so that she was out of the sightline of Mills and her crew. She lifted her eyes, and for a moment, she couldn't make out what she was even looking at. It looked like a red sheet that had been cut in an odd shape and a large, weirdly shaped pinkish thing lying on the ground underneath it. The two were attached at a few points.

She took a few steps, and her guts turned to hot liquid.

Summer Tipton was lying on her stomach, spread-eagle. A board had been placed under her chin to hold her face up. The skin of her face had been peeled from her chin to her forehead. Her pale blonde hair was twisted around a wire that led to an overhead beam. The monster that had killed her had performed the blood eagle on her back, attached the wings of her flesh to wires, and attached those wires to support poles in the barn to keep them spread. The flesh from her calves to her buttocks had been left untouched.

"Jesus," Ashton said, gagging. "Her breasts are over here with the flesh from her stomach. He peeled it all off like skinning an animal."

He rushed out the door, gagging.

Ava stood rooted to the spot, unable to look away, unable to draw a full breath.

The only conscious thoughts in her head were that her parents didn't need to live knowing what had happened to their daughter, and that the monster who did this needed to suffer.

She didn't know how much time passed. At some point, she became aware that the sun was coming up, and they were still working the scene, and that people were still sniffling and puking.

The dissociation got her through the work and allowed her to sleep for a few hours later that night, but it didn't keep her from the nightmares in which she relived terrible events from her own past, and it didn't keep her from waking up screaming as she tried to save Summer from the faceless butcher in the barn.

"Ava!" Ashton yelled as he ran into the small bedroom of the rental. "What's wrong? Are you okay?" He flipped on the overhead.

Ava sucked in air and covered her eyes. "Yeah, turn that off, please." Her heart hammered, and her hair was stuck to her head with sweat. "Just a bad dream."

"Need anything?"

"Sorry I woke you. I'm fine." She turned away and dropped her feet over the edge of the bed. Sleep was done. So was the dissociation. Had she talked in her sleep? It wouldn't have been the first time. If she had, how much had Ashton heard?

CHAPTER THIRTY-TWO

Digging up the Past

I T WASN'T EASY TO KEEP THE AWKWARD FEELING AT BAY AS ASHTON sat in the passenger seat on the way to the station with his laptop open. Was he pretending to work so he didn't have to talk to her about how she had woken up screaming? That was silly. There was no rule that said he ever had to mention it. She didn't either.

"Ashton, what are you doing over there? You've not said ten words all morning."

"Running that Ford Escape with Theodore and Gretchen Dawson as possible owners. No hits on his name. And…" He sighed. "No hits on her name, either. I'm going to run it with Steven Hess."

That was good. At least his silence had nothing to do with something weird she might or might not have said in her sleep, which he might or might not have heard. Why was she worried about it anyway? Regardless of what she may or may not have said, she had woken them both up screaming. That was probably enough to freak anyone out.

"Hey, about last night," she said. Her mouth went dry, and her vocabulary bank scrambled and reverted to that of a toddler. Her hands tightened around the wheel. She was going to freak out and leave herself hanging in an even more awkward position when all she'd meant to do was apologize for scaring him awake so she could get over feeling so awkward around him.

"Don't worry about it. My dad was a vet. He had PTSD. It was really bad when I was a teenager. Lots of people have nightmares after traumatic events, and if what we saw yesterday wasn't traumatic, nothing is. No worries." He went back to his computer. "Actually, I'd worry if you had kept on acting like a damn robot. I prefer the outbursts of human emotions to that."

"I had to shut down to get through that. Don't you do the same?"

He glanced up and shook his head.

"How can you work a scene like that and *not* shut down, shut off your emotions, dissociate yourself from it? I'd go crazy."

He shrugged. "Steven Hess. Bingo. The silver Ford Escape belongs to him."

"Get the directions to his house. We'll pay Mr. Hess a visit."

"I thought you were going to see Mills," Ashton said.

"I can call her. I was just going to tell her to be sure her teams did a thorough job by the book. They should check every building at that farm. Whoever did that to Summer, they got dirty, and they took their time. Maybe they left trace evidence somewhere in one of the buildings."

Ava called Mills as she drove and gave her the rundown for the day. It didn't take long. Mills wasn't in the mood to argue anymore. She did whatever Ava asked, no questions, no quips, no stalling.

"Steven Hess' address is just outside Woodsboro. Only an hour away at most," Ashton said.

"All the better."

Steven's house was a small, rundown one-story with peeling paint, an unkempt yard, two broken-down trucks, and a boat that had a tree growing out of it in the side yard. It was a property that immediately sent up red flags and put Ava on edge.

Steven was sitting on the porch when they pulled up. He eyed them suspiciously but didn't get out of his chair.

"Mr. Hess?" Ava asked from beside the car.

"Who's asking?" he called from his chair.

"Agents James and Ashton, FBI." She held her badge up. Ashton followed suit.

"Got no business with the law. What do you want?"

"Need to speak with you about your son," Ashton said.

"I don't have a son," Hess replied without missing a beat or changing expression.

"Charlie Dawson," Ava said. "The son you gave away when he was only a teen."

Hess rubbed a hand down his face. "Shit, come on up. What's he done now?"

Ava and Ashton went to the porch to relay the news about Nicole to Hess.

"We just need to know a little more about your son, Mr. Hess," Ava said. "What happened when he was younger? Why'd you give him up?"

Hess glared at them. His mouth drew down into a deep frown, and his brow furrowed. "Charlie ain't right, but if you've talked to him, you probably noticed. He's crazy dangerous. I signed him over to his mother because he was crazy dangerous even when he was a kid. There was an incident with the neighbors' little boy. That little boy almost died by *accidental hanging*. He was only nine. Charlie was eleven, and I think he did it. Crazy. Just like his mother's side of the family. They were all dangerous crazy, but she didn't seem so bad until after he was born. We split up, and she wouldn't stop until I signed over my rights. Almost killed me a few times. Child support wasn't enough for her. Nope. She burned down my other house with me still inside. Ran me off the road and over a bank where no one would ever see me, let alone help me. I'm almost positive that she coached him into putting something in my coffee and making me sick at least once later on, too. After that, I signed over my rights. Let her have the boy. All his bad came from her and her side of the family. No one on my side ever did anything like that."

"Does Charlie come to visit you often, Mr. Hess?"

He shook his head. "Thank God. He comes when he needs something."

"Like to borrow the Escape," Ashton said, nodding toward the vehicle.

"Yeah. Like to borrow my car."

"Why would he need to borrow your car? He has vehicles of his own," Ava said.

"I don't ask. I don't want to know what that boy gets up to. I just hope he graduates and moves way the hell and gone away from me."

"Has he been borrowing your Escape over the Halloween holiday?" Ashton asked.

"Yeah. Some before Halloween, too. He always brings her back clean and with gas in the tank, so I don't bitch about it. I wouldn't anyway. Don't want to make that boy mad. God knows what he might do to me. I'm an old man living alone out here in the woods now, and I don't think I'd stand much chance against him if he took a notion to do something. His mother took those notions a lot. She was violent right up to the end. I think Charlie probably had something to do with her death. No one ever took me seriously back then, though."

Ava thanked him for the information and left.

"You think he's just jaded?" Ashton asked in the car.

"Can't tell. Maybe, but we can't afford to dismiss any of it just yet."

They drove to Felton University to speak with Charlie again. Ethan gave them the address to Charlie's parents' house, where they could find him.

"He doesn't know Charlie was adopted?" Ava asked as they drove to the Dawson house.

"He might not know any of Charlie's real history," Ashton replied.

The Dawson house was stereotypical suburban from the neighborhood, the living room décor, and placement of furniture. Everything about the Dawson home screamed cleanliness and order.

"I'm sorry, but Charlie isn't here," Mrs. Dawson said politely.

"We need to speak with you and your husband as well," Ava said. "Could we come in for a moment? It won't take long, and it's very important."

She showed them into the living room. She and Mr. Dawson sat on a couch. Ava and Ashton took the seats facing them. Ava relayed the story about Nicole going missing, and the other girls being found dead.

The couple was horrified, but Mrs. Dawson looked abnormally uncomfortable.

"Mrs. Dawson, is everything okay? You seem…" She lifted her hands and one shoulder as if she didn't quite know the word.

"Charlie was troubled growing up is all," she said.

"He had a rough life," Mr. Dawson added quickly, putting a hand on his wife's leg to silence her.

"What do you mean, Mrs. Dawson?"

She shook her head. "He had a rough life is all. Would you like some coffee, or some tea?"

Ava shook her head. "Where is Charlie now?"

"He was heading back to school," Mr. Dawson answered.

"You just missed him," Mrs. Dawson added.

Ava groaned.

CHAPTER THIRTY-THREE

Updates and Links

"CONROY IS RUNNING THE SPOT OF BLOOD WE FOUND ON A DOOR-knob," Mills said.

"From which building?" Ava asked.

"The house. It was on a back door. It wasn't the same blood type as Summer, so we know it wasn't hers. Jesus, that poor girl."

"Did you already inform her parents?"

"'Course I did." Mills dropped her head. "I think I'll hear that woman's scream haunting every silent moment in my life from now until the end of time. Can't you get more agents up here? This bastard needs to be caught before he can do any more harm."

"I've called my boss, but there are no more agents right now. We're assigned to this case, and in the Bureau's eyes, it's being taken care of.

There's progress being made." Ava put a hand on Mills' shoulder. "We'll catch him."

"I hope you're right, but I'm afraid some of my hopefulness faded right along with my youth, Agent James." She handed Ava a file. "We found a partial tire track that matches the one from the cow manure where Parker was found, too. It's the same person doing all this, isn't it? You were right all along."

"It's the same vehicle, but there are two or more people doing these things. I'm sure of that."

"Is it that Charlie character that was sneaking around with Nicole? The little shit that got her pregnant?"

"I don't know. We're checking the leads, Sheriff. That's all we can do. Was there evidence that the killers had been in the house at the farm?"

"Yep. The dust and dirt inside had been walked through, but whoever did it was smart enough to wipe out their shoeprints with an old straw broom. There were no fingerprints or anything else on the broom, either. My people dusted every surface that could have held a print, everything that wasn't covered with layers of dust and dirt and cobwebs, but that speck of blood on the doorknob was all we found."

"I'll get Ashton to pull all Charlie's medical records so we can check his blood type against that sample." Ava turned to leave the office.

"Agent James?"

Ava turned. "Yes, Sheriff?"

"I owe you an apology."

"It's okay. Let's just work the case."

"Not without owning that I was wrong. I wanted so badly for my town to be safe and clean and good that I just didn't want to admit that horrible things like this could ever happen in Woodsboro, and look where it got us. If I had listened to you sooner..." She exhaled deeply.

"No, not me, Sheriff. I wasn't the first one to bring all this to your attention."

Mills cut her eyes back to Ava. "Dammit. You're right again." She drummed her fingers on the desk. "I need to call her. I should call her, shouldn't I? That was rhetorical. Don't answer that." She stood and pulled her jacket from the coat rack. "This whole swallowing your pride and admitting your wrongs thing sucks sometimes."

"Where are you going?"

"To see Jamie Hall. I owe her a rather big apology."

"She's going to want an update on the case, too," Ava said, walking beside her down the hallway.

"I figured that. She's going to make me eat it."

"Probably." Ava stepped into the room with Ashton.

"I deserve it," Mills said and kept walking.

"What's going on?" Ashton asked.

"Mills is going to go apologize to Jamie."

He looked up sharply. "Really? Your friend? The Jamie who got this case started?"

"The same," she said solemnly. "I need you to pull all Charlie's medical records with an eye out for his blood type. They found blood at the farm that doesn't match Summer's."

"I'm on it."

CHAPTER THIRTY-FOUR

Mark it with a B

MILLS RUSHED BACK INTO THE STATION. "AGENTS, WE GOT ANOTHER body!" she yelled as she came down the hallway.

Ava and Ashton stepped out to meet her. Her cheeks puffed in and out like bellows, and red splotches bloomed high on her cheeks and forehead.

"We got another body at the old Rustic Crust off the highway. Marsh just called in for backup." She motioned for them to follow her. "I'll call Bob and Francis on the way. Let's go." She turned and hurried for the door.

"Is it Nicole?" Ava asked as they exited the station.

"I don't know, but I'm betting it is. Dammit. Dammit," she exclaimed as she threw her door open. "Son of a bitch!" She slammed the door and spun out of the parking lot.

Nicole's body had been stuffed inside one of the industrial brick ovens. The killer had carved a large B on her lower belly. There was a single deep puncture wound just below her sternum. Bruises ran down both her sides, under her belly, and across her chest. She had been strangled to death. Paper money—twenties, tens, ones—had been stuffed in her mouth and down her throat, and a quarter had been laid on each eyelid to keep them closed.

"Stupid little kids playing hooky," Graham grumbled. "Bet they wish they'd just gone to school today instead of running into that building to avoid Deputy Marsh."

"If they had, who knows how long before Nicole was found?" Ashton said tensely.

"Well, now they're probably scarred for life. You think it was worth finding her today? It would've been no different if she'd been found a week from now by some drunk adult who wandered in to sleep it off. Or some homeless person looking for a place to get out of the weather."

"She's here now," Conroy said with finality. "Nothing to be done for it except move forward and work the case. Stop bellowing, please."

"I'm not bellowing; I'm making a damn point. I got kids their age. They'll never be right after this."

Mills put a hand on his shoulder. "Robert, go to my office and sit down for a minute. Maybe get in the second drawer down and have a little sip while we work, okay? I'll call you if we need you."

Graham left the room.

"He has two grandsons. One is twelve, and the other is fifteen. He's awful touchy about them. I saw how you looked when he said he had kids that age. Man in his sixties shouldn't have teeny-boppers, eh?"

Ava shrugged. Ashton didn't respond at all.

"Anyhoo, back to Nicole here."

"She was alive for a lot of this," Ashton blurted.

Conroy and Ava stared at him for a moment.

"Unfortunately, yes, she was," Conroy said.

"She was alive while they did this to her?" Ava asked.

Conroy nodded. "But that doesn't mean she was conscious. She has some defensive wounds, so she was conscious at some point."

Ashton shook his head and pointed to her wrists. "Those are ligature marks. They tied her wrists." He pointed to her ankles. "And someone held her ankles. That's why there aren't more defensive wounds."

"They tortured her to be sure. Sick bastards, no doubt. I just can't figure why the precision to all bruises. And why the one, single puncture below the sternum. It looks like it might have been done with a screwdriver or an icepick. The B carved in her belly might be the initial of one of their names..." Conroy's voice faded.

Ava and Ashton exchanged a knowing look. Ava shook her head. "That's not what it is. It's a reference to an old nursery rhyme. Nicole was two months pregnant."

Conroy gasped, her eyes went wide. "*Pat-a-cake, pat-a-cake, baker's man, bake me a cake as fast as you can. Pat it and prick it, and mark it with a B, put it in the oven for baby and me,*" she recited flatly. "It was someone who knew she was pregnant."

"So far, only her parents admit to knowing," Ashton said. "Were there any prints on the body?"

"No, but there might be a useable partial on the quarter from her left eyelid." Conroy handed him the lifted partial. "I'm guessing you can run that a lot quicker than I can."

Ashton took it and went to the other side of the room. "I can check it against someone's I already have in minutes. All I need is a high-res picture."

"Did you get all the paper money out?" Ava motioned toward Nicole's mouth.

"I did. They shoved it pretty far down her throat. Wouldn't surprise me to find more in her stomach. Who knows what they put this child through before they finally killed her."

"Is strangulation what killed her?"

"That's my preliminary finding."

"Did they put the money in before, or after?"

"Hard to tell, but seems to me maybe both."

"The print belongs to Charlie," Ashton announced.

At that point, Ava was not shocked. No one was shocked.

CHAPTER THIRTY-FIVE

Shock and Chaos

CHARLIE WASN'T ON CAMPUS. NEITHER WAS HIS BEST FRIEND, Ethan. None of the frat brothers who were at the house knew where Charlie had gone. Most of them thought he was in class, and the dean had no clue he wasn't there.

"I'm not running a nursery school, nor am I a warden, Agents," the dean said. "The students are free to come and go, and if they choose to miss a day here and there, well, they are adults. They are the future. They are our up-and-coming doctors and lawyers and surgeons and politicians. I think they can make those decisions."

Ava and Ashton walked the parking lot by the frat house.

"Wonder if the dean realizes she's defending a psychopathic serial killer?" Ashton asked.

"I wonder if she even cares," Ava said. Her phone rang, and dread ran through her like a tidal wave as she answered and put it on speaker.

"The blood from the doorknob at the farm did not belong to Charlie," said Mills.

Ava's heart sank. "What?"

"It's not Charlie Dawson, or Hess, or whoever the hell he really is. But who else knew Nicole was pregnant?"

Ava and Ashton stopped walking and stared wide-eyed at each other. "Ethan Coldwell."

"Are you sure?" Ashton asked.

"It has to be. There's nobody else that fits. Ethan Coldwell," Ava repeated, more to herself than to anyone else.

"That's what I said. Conroy is finished with Nicole. I have to go inform the Rodgers family about their daughter now. Are you coming?"

Ava cringed. "I'm at Felton. Ashton and I came here with a warrant for Charlie, but he's not here. Neither is Ethan."

"Christ on a crutch, I thought you came out here to help me with the hard parts, Agent James," she barked.

"And I am, Sheriff," Ava retorted.

"Then why am I going to the Rodgers' house by myself while you're staring at air on some fancy university campus three hours away?" The phone went dead.

"She hung up on you," Ashton said.

"You think?" Ava dropped the phone to her side. "Nothing to be done about it. We all have our jobs. We need to find Charlie. Maybe he went back to see the Dawsons again. Either way, I need to let them know what's going on." She dialed Mrs. Dawson's number as she seemed the one more eager to talk to them about Charlie before.

"Hello?" Mrs. Dawson's voice trembled. The thread of fear running through it was palpable.

"Mrs. Dawson?"

"Yes, who is this?"

"This is Agent James, is he there?"

"Yes, I remember you, Agent James." She took a small, tremulous breath and seemed to hold it.

"Are you in danger?" Ava asked, lowering her voice to barely above a whisper.

"Yes, my husband is here."

Ava motioned to Ashton to get to the car. They hurried toward it. "Gretchen, stay calm. We are on our way." They were too far away to get there in time to do much good. "I understand, but now really isn't a good time at all. We're getting ready to run some errands over Woodsboro way. Maybe tomorrow afternoon?" She had barely spoken the name of the town.

"Do whatever you can to stall, but stay safe. We will find you if you have to leave. Do not raise his suspicions, and don't make him angry with you." Ava shoved the key in the ignition.

"Okay, Agent. See you then."

The line went dead, and Ava turned the key, revving the engine to life. "He's with them, and they're in trouble. We have to get to them."

"We need backup, Ava. We don't know what we're running into here," Ashton said.

"Call state police, if you want to, but you know they won't make it in time to help us much. Mills is our best bet, and her crew is stretched thin, besides, we don't even know where they'll be for sure."

"Charlie and Ethan know the game is up. They're going to be as dangerous as cornered lions. They'll come out fighting, and it'll be dirty."

"They were getting ready to leave the house. If they get the Dawsons out of that house, there's no telling what will happen to them. Four girls are dead already, I don't want the Dawsons on my conscience, too. And there's no guarantee they were going to Woodsboro. If they were, we don't know where in Woodsboro."

She floored the gas, breaking every speed limit to the Dawson residence. The front door stood halfway open as they cautiously walked to the porch and called out. There was no answer and no movement from inside.

Ashton pointed out skid marks on the pavement in front of the garage. Someone had left in a hurry. She nodded, but they went into the house with guns drawn. They had to check that no one was in there, and that there were no victims left injured or dead.

Once the house was cleared, they got back in the car and followed the direction of the skid marks out of the driveway. Ava stopped at the stop sign. She looked left and then right. Which way had they gone?

She pounded the steering wheel. "Goddammit!" she screamed. "Give me a fucking break just once." She hit the wheel with both palms again. "Four girls are dead. Isn't that enough?!" she yelled out the windshield at the sky. Who was she screaming at? God? The universe? Did it matter?

Ashton put his hand on her arm. "Ava, the roads out of town are all closed. They can't get far. The state police are involved now. Roadblocks with their pictures and pictures of the Dawsons are at every roadblock. Head toward Woodsboro. By the time we get there, it will be locked down, too. There's only one way from here to Woodsboro." He pointed right.

She inhaled through her nose and blew it out through her mouth. "Right." She turned and drove with pain thrumming through her palms.

Speeding, she entered Woodsboro without realizing it. Several minutes later, she slowed. "There was no roadblock, Ashton."

"It's okay. Just keep going. She said they were going to Woodsboro, and we haven't passed them so far. They had to go this way."

Ava followed Ashton's direction. It was logical. She knew it was, but everything inside her screamed frantically that they were letting two killers take two more victims while they drove randomly and calmly down back roads through the country.

She stopped at a stop sign and looked on with dismay. "The road goes in three freaking directions from here," she said.

The view was unobstructed for miles in all three directions, and there was no sign of a car.

Ava's phone rang again. She flipped it over. "Shit, Gretchen," she said, fumbling phone in her attempt to answer it.

CHAPTER THIRTY-SIX

Brave Mama

AVA GRABBED THE PHONE AND PUNCHED THE BUTTON TO ANSWER it. Immediately, she hit the speaker button. Before she could say anything, she heard a woman's voice, small and muffled, and watery as if crying.

"Charlie, I love you, son. I don't care what you've done. I'm your mother, and I'll always love you." It was Gretchen Dawson, and she was crying but trying to hold it back. Her breath was hitching badly.

"Shut up, *Gretchen*!" Charlie screamed. "You are not my mother. You're the substitute *cow* that gave me a place to stay until I could get out on my own. You were never anything but a simpering, cowering puke too afraid to get out and experience the world on your own!" he roared.

"Shut up, Charlie!" Ethan yelled close by. "Jesus, you're too loud, dude. Keep it the hell down."

The voices echoed as if they were in a very large and empty building, or perhaps a cave.

"Son," Mr. Dawson said. "Please, your mother and I have always loved you as if you were our own flesh and blood. We only wanted what was best for you. We can help you get through this. Whatever you've done, we'll help you."

Fists hitting flesh cut Mr. Dawson's words off.

Gretchen cried loudly. "Charlie, stop, please! You're killing him!"

"I'm not, but I could. Is that what you want, *Gretchen*?"

"Of course not," she sniffled. After several silent seconds, she asked, "Son, why are we in the old slaughterhouse? Are we hiding? Do you need a place to hide for a while?"

Ava pressed the mute button. "Get the directions to the old slaughterhouse."

He pulled up the directions on his phone and called out the turns to her as they continued to listen to the conversation happening on the other end of the phone. How long before Charlie figured out Gretchen had her phone on? The reception cut in and out sometimes for several seconds. During those intervals, Ava's heart forgot to beat.

When she was about three minutes from the slaughterhouse, the reception cut out, and she hoped the call wouldn't drop. That had been her great fear since the first time it cut out. When it came back on, Gretchen and Theodore were screaming in unison. Her heart burst into a furious pace, and her hands tightened involuntarily around the wheel.

Their screams weren't from pain, though, they sounded more from shock and fright.

"The slaughterhouse is up there on the right," Ashton said, pointing to a road. "The access road is going to be long. Probably the length of a football field at least, maybe more. I'm calling Mills for backup."

Ava adjusted her speed and took the turn. The pavement only ran a hundred feet or so and then the access turned to dirt. The compound loomed in the distance looking like something out of a Mad Max movie in the middle of a barren wasteland and surrounded by concrete barriers and high fences with hurricane wire. She'd never seen a slaughterhouse, and had thought it to be only a single building. A smallish one. She had been very wrong.

She counted seven buildings, and all of them were oversized. The slaughterhouse had been an industry before it had shut down, not a small-town, mom-n-pop business at all.

"Sheriff, we're at the old slaughterhouse, and we need all the backup you have immediately. Charlie and Ethan are here, and they have Mr. and Mrs. Dawson inside held hostage somewhere."

"Dear God. I'll call everyone. I'll be there in ten."

"Make it five." He hung up and unbuckled his seatbelt. "Do you have riot busters?"

"No, this is a loaner. Mills will have some in her cruisers, I'm sure. Which building? I thought there'd just be one."

"That one," he pointed to the side. "Easiest access, but many sections, lots of exits. Stop here so they don't hear us."

Ava stopped a hundred or more feet away from the Chevy, and they got out, leaving the doors open. Gretchen was still crying over the phone, which Ava left in the phone holder on the dash. At least she was still alive.

The large door opened easily, and Ava and Ashton entered quietly. It was a long room to the right of the open courtyard. There were three doors down the right side, two down the left, and one straight ahead. The lights were on, but many of the bulbs were blown or only worked at partial capacity, buzzing loudly in the ballasts.

Charlie stepped into the room from a doorway on the right. Gretchen yelped as he dragged her with him. He had an arm around her waist and a knife to her throat. He grinned at Ava as he pressed the knife into Gretchen's neck.

"Charlie, don't do this," Ava said. "You don't want to hurt her. You need to let her go."

"No, I don't, and you know nothing about me. Maybe I do want to do this. Maybe this is my life's mission." He pressed the blade harder, and Gretchen's eyes bulged as she pressed back into him.

"Charlie, don't make me shoot you," Ava said. Time slowed just a tick, and Charlie's face came into sharp focus. The light glinting off his teeth, the way his eyes glistened when the fluorescent above flickered, and the slight indentation just above the brow ridge all became visible points that drew her focus. "Let Gretchen go."

Movement outside another doorway drew Ashton's attention, and he swung toward it, his gun aiming true. "Whoever is there, show yourself," he ordered. "Move in here where I can see you." He took one step to the side for a better view.

"Ethan, man, come on in here. No use hiding. You think they don't know about you, too, by now?" Charlie said, gurgling jovially.

Ethan came in, dragging Mr. Dawson the same way Charlie had dragged Gretchen. He pressed the barrel of a snub-nosed .38 under the shelf of Mr. Dawson's jaw and grimaced at Ava and Ashton.

"Let them go, boys," Ashton said, still aiming at Ethan.

"No. They're insurance so you don't shoot us," Charlie said.

The wail of sirens broke the tense standoff. Charlie's head jerked in the direction of the sirens, the blade in his hand slipped, and blood poured from Gretchen's throat. She screamed and grabbed her throat, falling to her knees and out of Charlie's shocked grasp.

Mr. Dawson spun away from the gun at his throat, elbowed Ethan under the chin, and lunged toward Charlie to knock him away from Gretchen. Ethan regained his footing, aimed, and pulled the trigger.

Mr. Dawson was flung to the side as the bullet hit him in the side of the head.

Ava turned and fired at Ethan, hitting him in the arm as he dropped the gun. Ashton kicked the gun away, and tackled Ethan to cuff him.

Mills ran in, gun drawn. "Police!" she yelled, her voice booming and echoing as loud as the gunshots.

"Over here!" Ava yelled back.

Charlie bolted out the door at the back of the room, and Ava gave chase. Mills followed while the others rushed to render aid to the Dawsons. He turned left and immediately back to the right and then ran straight ahead.

"Stop, Charlie!" Ava shouted.

"He's going nowhere," Mills said. "All the exits are up that way." She poked a thumb over her shoulder. "Ain't that right, Charlie? You just ran yourself right into a very fitting room, and there's only one way out."

Mills and Ava walked to the doorway.

"The Lazaretto. A quarantine for very sick animals. Animals that are so sick, they can't be around the others," Mills said.

Charlie put his back to the wall, dropped the knife, and slid laughing to the floor as Ava and Mills walked toward him with the cuffs.

CHAPTER THIRTY-SEVEN

The Slaughterhouse Six

AFTER CHARLIE AND ETHAN WERE HAULED AWAY FROM THE slaughterhouse, Mrs. Dawson was rushed to the hospital in critical condition. Mr. Dawson had become part of the crime scene.

The other rooms of the slaughterhouse had been Charlie and Ethan's playground for years, it seemed. The cooling room, the offal room, the tripery, and the skins room contained corpses, or what was left of them.

The previous women who had gone missing from Woodsboro had been killed and put on display with their IDs attached to them as if they were tagged trophies.

"Why did you kill all those girls, Charlie?" Ava asked.

Charlie smirked at her.

"Are there others besides the ones we found?" Ashton asked.

Again, he only smirked.

"The families need to know what happened to their daughters. If there are more, you should at least let us know so we can tell the families and they can stop their useless searching and wondering. Give them some peace," Ava said.

"Like a decent human being," Ashton said.

Charlie laughed.

"You know you're going away forever, right?" Ava asked.

"Really?" It was the first word Charlie uttered.

"Yes, you are, and so is your friend. Doesn't matter if you never speak another word. You'll never be a free man again, Charlie."

"We'll see, Agent." His grin bordered on evil.

The brothers at the Felton University frat house were more than willing to spill the beans on their brothers after learning that they had been sharing their lives with psychotic serial killers.

Jason Monroe knew the most about Charlie and Ethan. He had gone to school with them all through college.

"I had heard their dark jokes a few times, but I didn't think anything about it. I thought it was all because of the horrible double date they had back when they started college."

"What kind of dark humor?" Ava asked.

"They would say stuff like they should just kidnap women and make them pay for wasting their time and money. They'd joke and say that if they did it to women they didn't even know a few towns away, they would get away with it. I never thought they were serious, though. If I had, I would have told somebody."

"So, it wasn't weird to you that they never really dated anyone, and that they kept talking about stuff like that?" Ashton asked.

"Not really. I mean, all guys say stuff like that sometimes. It's just a macho thing, I guess. But none of us really mean it. It's just so we sound tough in front of the boys, or something. And just to be honest, I sort of thought they had a thing for each other and just didn't want anyone else to know. I thought they just used that old bad double-date story as sort of a cover for why they were always bad-mouthing girls."

"Looks like they really didn't like girls and they really did mean the things they were saying," Ava said pointedly. "Maybe you should take that into consideration next time you hear one of your frat brothers spouting some hate speech, huh?"

Jason reddened. "Duly noted. This has made all of us look at a lot of things much differently."

"Good. Maybe that's a good thing."

CHAPTER THIRTY-EIGHT

Something's Missing

"WHAT DO YOU MEAN THERE'S NOTHING ON ANY OF THOSE BOD-ies to link them to Charlie or Ethan?!" Mills yelled at Ava.

"Exactly what I said. We have Ethan on Mr. Dawson's death, which his attorney will argue was accidental, and we have Charlie on Gretchen's cut throat, which she is recovering from—also accidental."

"No, what about that damned quarter on Nicole's eyelid? Charlie's thumbprint was on that," Mills stated, jabbing her finger toward the door.

"Any attorney worth his salt will argue that a quarter is common currency and is handled by hundreds of people every week, if not more. That print could have gotten there at any time—even when Nicole and Charlie were admittedly sneaking around seeing each other weeks and weeks before. There's no way to prove that quarter didn't come from her pocket."

"She was naked."

"But the killer had to have undressed her, thereby giving him access to her pockets, which could have reasonably had change in them. Some of that change might have been quarters." Ava held up her hands. "It's not pretty, but that's how it is."

"What about the blood from the doorknob at the farmhouse?"

"We sent it to the lab for conclusive tests, and it came back inconclusive. We already know it wasn't Charlie, and there wasn't enough blood to get a conclusive match to Ethan."

"That's horseshit, and you know it." Mills slammed her foot into the side of her desk hard enough to scoot the monstrosity a foot across the tiled floor.

"I don't make the rules, Sheriff, I just have to play by them like everybody else. I'm going to talk to Charlie again now."

Mills snarled and threw her hands in the air as she stormed out of the room.

Charlie grinned at Ava. "Back again? Good news or bad?"

"I just came by to let you know that I will tear your lives apart. I will deconstruct them centimeter by centimeter until I find something that ties you to these murders, Charlie. You and Ethan both. That's a promise." She sat back in her chair. "It's my life's mission, if you will," she said, turning his own words at the slaughterhouse on him.

He laughed as if truly amused. "That's clever. You're very clever, Agent." He leaned forward. "Good luck because I had nothing to do with them, and neither did Ethan." He sat back and spread his hands, feigning an innocent look. "We are innocent of everything except terrible accidents for which we are greatly remorseful, and from which we will likely never fully recover."

"Ethan is screwed. He killed your adoptive father, and there's no getting out of it."

"Sure, but mommy-dearest only required some stitches, so I'm not the murderer you keep claiming I am. And if I know my mother, she will forgive me for my folly. I had my troubles growing up, and she helped me through those." He put a hand over his heart and smiled. "She loves her son, and her son loves her."

Ava left without another word. He was sick and twisted, and she knew there was no getting anything out of him but more veiled taunts.

CHAPTER THIRTY-NINE

Access Granted

CHARLIE'S PICKUP HAD BEEN IN EVIDENCE COLLECTION FOR WEEKS, but Ava and Ashton were standing at the door for the keys the day the team was finished with it.

"I don't know what you hope to find that we didn't, but here you go," the man said, dropping the keys in Ava's hand and taking the signed papers from her.

"Did you check the GPS system?" Ashton asked.

"No, we saw it there, but we just figured it wouldn't have anything of any interest, so we left it alone." He scoffed and shook his head. "What do you think? Of course we did. It's in the reports. Makes for fun reading. Try it sometime." He walked away.

"Somebody who was never socialized at all," Ava said.

"I want a crack at that GPS. I can break into it and pull up everything that's ever been deleted," Ashton said.

"How long will it take you?"

"Just a few hours at most."

"Can you download those trips onto your computer?" Ava asked as she looked at the GPS screen in Charlie's truck.

"Already in the process. From the looks, this one is back in the woods where it's going to be difficult to access. It's not going to be somewhere just any vehicle can drive to, I think."

"Should we borrow an ATV from Mills?"

He thought for a moment and then shook his head. "I think the SUV we had the other day will do the trick. It's all-wheel drive and high enough off the ground, but it's going to be a rough ride probably. That's far back on the mountain."

"We don't know what will be there," Ava said. "Let's have Mills send some people with us. They know the area better than we do."

"Agreed."

Ninety minutes later, Ava stopped and sent up silent thanks that the drive was over. The team stopped behind her in a Land Rover.

"I don't think he brought his new shiny pickup here," she said to Ashton.

"No. Probably the Escape."

"What are we looking for?" Deputy Latham asked.

"Anything that looks out of place. We think he dumped evidence up here," Ava said.

Latham made a quick, approving "Hrm." He and the team lined up off the side of the rutted road and started shuffling through the recent deadfall of leaves. Ava and Ashton helped. The other side of the road was a steep embankment that was impossible to search. It was nearly straight down.

Twenty minutes into the search, Latham yelled. "Got something."

Ava and Ashton joined him. The team had already photographed the site and begun digging.

"I hope to hell it's not another body. I don't think I could handle another one so soon," Latham said.

Marsh took a knee. "It's a metal box." He pulled it out of the dirt and dusted it off.

"Give it to me," Ava said. "Don't open it, don't touch anything."

Marsh held it out as if it might be poison.

Ashton put on gloves and took it from her. "Go spread the plastic in the back of the car."

Ava ran to the car and prepped the makeshift worktable. Everyone showed up with Ashton. He placed the box on the plastic and opened it carefully.

He pulled out the items one at a time and laid them on the plastic.

A woman's gold ring. A lock of hair. A finger. An ear. A keychain that seemed to be fashioned of braided hair, and a piece of tattooed skin pinned to a piece of folded leather.

Marty and Greenlee walked away muttering and shaking their heads.

"You know what all that is, right? I mean, I don't have to explain any of it, do I?" Latham asked, pointing to the horrors on the plastic.

"I think we pretty much know, deputy," Ashton said. He pointed to the ring. "That belonged to Charity Beaumont. The lock of hair is probably from Laura Halvorsen because it has a chunk of scalp attached, and her body at the slaughterhouse had a chunk missing. The finger, if tested, would come back a match to Elise Abbot, and as we all know, her body was missing the middle finger. Ashley Garland was missing her right ear, and Tina Leeyung's neck had been badly damaged, and her photos show her with that tattoo, so that would be hers."

"That only leaves the keyring, and I'm going to venture it belonged to Luna Bradford," Ava said.

"It was braided horsehair from a horse she loved as a kid," Latham said. "Everyone knew the story in town."

Ashton went to work on the pieces. There were fingerprints and DNA. "I'm not going to do this here. I want it done in the lab, correctly, and with zero possibility of a screw-up or contamination," he said. He placed everything back into the box, closed it, and placed the box in a plastic evidence bag, which he sealed.

Finally, they had something amounting to a break in the case. It had taken long enough.

CHAPTER FORTY

Pinning the Devil

"Y ou just can't get enough of me, can you, Agent? Better be careful, or people will start to gossip about us," Charlie said.

"Let them. They'll be talking about a metal box that I found buried on the mountain when they talk about us."

His eyes bulged for a second.

"Oh, what was that? Did I just see that armor crack? Did the monster finally peek out from a crack in the plaster? I think he did, and he looked scared. He should be because his fingerprints and DNA are going to be all over the items in that metal box. "You never thought it would be found, so you didn't bother cleaning any of it, did you?"

He sighed and shook his head indulgently. "I could have just found all that stuff lying around on the side of the road, in an abandoned building. Hell, I could have bought it in a flea market, or a curiosity shop. You know those oddity shops like on TV? Maybe I got it there." He gave her a one-sided grin that would have been charming if it hadn't been attached to a real-life monster.

"But we both know that's not true, Charlie."

He shrugged. "I'm not telling you anything. A woman a lot like you started ruining my life before I was even born."

"I'm nothing like your mother. Nothing." She leaned forward. "By the way, I have someone looking into her death, also. We might be adding another name to the list of your charges soon."

"I'll save you the trouble, Agent. I did it. Well, she really did it, but I helped her on out of this world. Out of my life. I was tired of the abuse and the constant string of men coming and going. At fourteen, I was old hat at loading her needles for her. Then one day, I just didn't have to do that anymore."

"And you wonder why your daddy signed away his rights so easily?" she asked, scoffing. "Where you're going, it doesn't matter anymore. All your mommy and daddy issues won't be important anymore."

AUTHOR'S NOTE

Dear Reader,

I am thrilled to share with you the ninth installment in the Ava James FBI Mystery series, *Behind the Mask!* I hope you enjoyed exploring the mysterious streets of Pine Bend alongside Ava. I gotta tell you, writing this book was an absolute blast. I mean, who doesn't love delving into a small tight-knit community with its own fair share of juicy secrets, especially with the spine-tingling vibes of Hallows' Eve adding that extra layer of thrill?

If you're looking for more fall/Halloween thrills and mystery, I invite you to experience the latest installment in my Dean Steele Mystery Thriller Series, *No Escape.* The story takes place in the quiet town of Harper, where four years ago, three teens were murdered against the backdrop of Halloween. Their body parts were found in the most bewildering way. The mystery didn't end there – far from it. The body count kept climbing, with no clues in sight. Now, it's up to Dean to learn who the true Hallows Eve killer is before he builds another scarecrow out of his victims.

I would also like to take a moment to ask for your help in keeping the Ava James' series alive. As an indie author, your reviews and support are vital in keeping the series going. If you could take a moment to leave a review for Behind the Mask, I would be enormously grateful. Your feedback allows me to continue to grow and improve as an author, and it ensures that Ava and the team can keep solving mysteries and catching criminals.

Thank you for your support and for joining me on this journey. Ava and the team are counting on you, and I can't wait to see where our adventures take us next.

Yours,
A.J. Rivers

P.S. If for some reason you didn't like this book or found typos or other errors, please let me know personally. I do my best to read and respond to every email at mailto:aj@riversthrillers.com

P.P.S. If you would like to stay up-to-date with me and my latest releases I invite you to visit my Linktree page at *www.linktr.ee/a.j.rivers* to subscribe to my newsletter and receive a free copy of my book, Edge of the Woods. You can also follow me on my social media accounts for behind-the-scenes glimpses and sneak peeks of my upcoming projects, or even sign up for text notifications. I can't wait to connect with you!

ALSO BY
A.J. RIVERS

Emma Griffin FBI Mysteries

Season One
Book One—*The Girl in Cabin 13**
Book Two—*The Girl Who Vanished**
Book Three—*The Girl in the Manor**
Book Four—*The Girl Next Door**
Book Five—*The Girl and the Deadly Express**
Book Six—*The Girl and the Hunt**
Book Seven—*The Girl and the Deadly End**

Season Two
Book Eight—*The Girl in Dangerous Waters**
Book Nine—*The Girl and Secret Society**
Book Ten—*The Girl and the Field of Bones**
Book Eleven—*The Girl and the Black Christmas**
Book Twelve—*The Girl and the Cursed Lake**
Book Thirteen—*The Girl and The Unlucky 13**
Book Fourteen—*The Girl and the Dragon's Island**

Season Three
Book Fifteen—*The Girl in the Woods**
Book Sixteen —*The Girl and the Midnight Murder**
Book Seventeen— *The Girl and the Silent Night**
Book Eighteen — *The Girl and the Last Sleepover**
Book Nineteen — *The Girl and the 7 Deadly Sins**
Book Twenty — *The Girl in Apartment 9**
Book Twenty-One — *The Girl and the Twisted End**

Emma Griffin FBI Mysteries Retro - Limited Series
(Read as standalone or before Emma Griffin book 22)

ALSO BY

A.J. RIVERS & THOMAS YORK

<u>Bella Walker FBI Mystery Series</u>

Book One—The Girl in Paradise*
Book Two—Murder on the Sea

Other Standalone Novels
Gone Woman
* Also available in audio

Made in United States
North Haven, CT
25 September 2023

41948531R00148